YOU & I
Rewritten

A NOVEL

CHIP PONS

To the man who stood beside me on that ledge, took my hand in his & leapt so fearlessly into the unknown with every fiber of his beautiful heart—

My life is infinitely better because you love me.

AUTHOR'S NOTE

"Grief never ends, but it changes. It is a passage, not a place to stay. Grief is not a sign or weakness nor a lack of faith, it is the price of love."

Dear Reader,

While *You & I, Rewritten* is a work of fiction, there are moments that come from a deeply personal place. It features content that may be difficult and potentially triggering for some. Parts of this story are mine—inspired from the darkest moment of my life. If after reading this, you see that this is part of *your* story as well, my heart is forever with you and know that you are *never* alone.

Content warnings: alcoholism, death of a parent, panic attacks, parental abandonment, grief, PTSD, physical abuse, military sexual trauma.

CHAPTER ONE

"Klair, I swear on all things holy, if you make me late, I'm going to—"

I find myself being held against my will on the very busy, very public corner of 47th and 6th as my petite yet indomitable best friend rather forcefully yanks me around like a disgruntled mannequin in the name of *better lighting*.

"Yeah, yeah...you'll willingly throw away your oldest friendship and vow to never speak to me again," she says, unimpressed, not even remotely concerned there could be a very real possibility I'm telling the truth. Even though she's been an East Coast girl for most of her life, the twang of her Texan childhood roots still makes an appearance from time to time. *Especially when she drinks tequila.*

"No offense, *William*," she hisses, knowing full well just how much I *adore* the use of my full name. *Not.* "But the wrath your mother would unleash on me if I didn't send her a picture of you on your first day at your fancy new job is far more intimidating than *anything* you could threaten me with. Now hold still."

She ignores the not-so-subtle gesture I make with my hand

and resumes snapping away with her phone, leaving me standing as awkwardly as ever on the front steps of Austin Publishing House like a grumpy preteen on their first day of middle school.

Just breathe. The all-too-familiar spike of anxiety courses through my veins as I start to internally spiral over the magnitude of today. Moving back home is not always looked upon as a positive change in one's life, but when Klair shared the advertisement for the junior editor position here in New York City, I leapt at the opportunity for professional change—whole-heartedly and with more careless vigor than I ever thought I was capable of. Risks aren't my thing, even ones that mean coming home and being smothered by loved ones, so the significance of this moment is definitely not lost on me.

"Okay, for this one, can you try to look a little more excited? Oh, oh...maybe do a little jump or something?"

"*Anndddd* that's where I draw the line. I'm out of here." I mentally take back what I said before. She may be my oldest friend, but she's also the *biggest* pain in my ass. You know those girls that are so stunning you just randomly feel compelled to dislike them? That's Klair Thompson. I would too if her heart wasn't equally, if not more, beautiful. *Damn her.* Not much has changed about Klair since we were kids—she's still all long legs with even longer brown and effortlessly wavy hair and a smattering of freckles across the bridge of her nose. Brimming beneath those big brown eyes of hers is a glint of mischief—one that has gotten us in *and* out of every shade of trouble imaginable.

I pause at the entrance to Austin Publishing House—my new home—and stand in awe of the significance of this moment. At the age of twenty-seven, the path leading me to today hasn't always been easy or linear, but I try to live each day with a humility and appreciation that comes from a firm belief that nothing is guaranteed in this life and in the blink of an eye, everything can, and most undoubtedly will, change. So while this new change and risk terrifies me, I am ready to leap into the proverbial unknown and throw myself headfirst into whatever comes next.

Rise. Heal. Overcome.

The line plays in my head over and over and over again as Klair reviews the dozens of photos she's just taken. Honestly, it's been the phrase most consistent with courage and new beginnings my entire life, as one of those sayings I've just always muttered without questioning it. But today, as I embark on what Klair and I are labeling *My Next Great Adventure*, I can't shake the feeling that this next chapter is going to be the one that changes everything.

"Hey, ugh, Will?" Klair says while dramatically waving her hands in front of my face. "If you don't stop wasting our time out here, we're going to be late."

Klair's self-labeled comedic timing interrupts my deeper-than-normal introspection as we head arm-in-arm through the heavy double doors. There's just something I love about new beginnings. The chance to wipe your slate clean, completely starting anew in an environment where people know only what you want them to know.

Perfect.

After a quick meeting with human resources and being toured around the expansive office building, I finally get a moment to exhale at my new desk—which I have to admit made me far more excited than it should for being the tiniest cubicle in the history of cubicles. I fire up my new computer, lay out my agenda and Taylor Swift wall calendar, because *duh*, and lean back in my surprisingly comfortable office chair. *This* is adulting.

Klair, editor extraordinaire, local fashion icon, and the person I trust most in this world, leans over our shared desk wall and hands me a small, wrapped brown box.

"What's this? I say, as she places the box in my hands.

"First days can be overwhelming," she says, flashing me a warm smile. "But I wanted you to feel welcomed, appreciated, and a part of this phenomenal team right from the start."

"Klair Thompson...you did *not* need to do this."

As I undo the perfectly fastened bow and lift the lid, I see that she's filled it with all the essentials a new employee in our field could possibly need: a notepad and pens, a personalized mug filled with those fancy coffee pods for the break room, and an adorable succulent to bring some life to my windowless desk. It's such a sweet and unexpected gesture from someone who has already done so much for me over the years that I'm overcome with emotion.

I don't even hesitate before stepping forward and giving her a hug, which she happily returns. "Thank you, Klair," I whisper. "I can't tell you enough how happy I am to have you back in my life like this."

"Likewise, mister...but hey, HR just called, and it seems there was some sort of mix up? You need to pack up your things and head on back to Chicago," she says, wiggling her fingers in my face.

Again, such top-notch humor. *Barf.* "Well, I instantly regret anything nice I have ever said to you...Has anyone ever told you how obnoxious you are?"

"If by obnoxious you mean hilarious, then yes...daily."

I can't help but laugh at the fact that nothing has changed over the years. Growing up, Klair and I spent every waking moment together. From braces and the most awkward of phases to first crushes and heartbreaks, we've seen each other through all of life's ups and downs. But I could always count on Klair to find the humor in it all. No matter what we had going on, there she was, finding a way to make me laugh harder than anyone on the planet.

The rest of the morning is a blur. Klair wastes no time in spilling the office gossip, dragging me from cubicle to cubicle and introducing me to everyone in sight, as well as pointing out which break room is stocked with the best snacks. *I feel seen.*

"Come on, we've got an impromptu staff meeting and we may or may not be already late," Klair says, a whirlwind of efficiency as she starts grabbing her coffee, notepad, and several pens. Before I have time to allow my anxiety about punctuality spiral out of control or even ask what we're about to walk into, she's grabbing me by the arm, ushering me down the hall toward the large conference room. Thank God I have Klair with me as my guide while getting my bearings because even though I had an office tour earlier this morning, if I had to navigate back to this conference room alone, I'd be lost for ages and, paired with my tendencies toward punctuality, I would be slowly reeling into psychosis.

Pushing through the heavy, frosted-glass doors, the other members of the team, all who I met earlier this morning and have since failed to retain a single one of their names, are settling into their seats.

"Ah, there you two are," says a voice I instantly recognize from my multiple rounds of interviews. Mitch Austin, founder and owner of, well, *everything*, stands from his seat at the head of the long, marble conference table.

"I'll keep this quick because I know we all have a lot on our plates," he says through a genuine smile and excited eyes to the rest of the team. Mitch is one of those middle-aged men who finds himself luckily hanging onto his youthful appearance with ease—just a light graying at the temples and deep expression lines around his eyes. His tall frame still shows the signs of an active lifestyle not yet restricted by his age.

"But I'd be remiss if I didn't take this opportunity to introduce you all to our newest editor, William Cowen."

My palms instantly begin to sweat as I feel every eye in the conference room turn toward me as I stand frozen in the doorway. *Definitely wasn't expecting this.* I smile at a woman I believe to be named Jane and she gives me a *'Buckle Up'* smirk that sets the tone for what I just walked into.

"He comes to us from Chicago and brings a fresh perspective and a deep understanding of our market, so do your best to make him feel right at home here," Mitch says as I begin fidgeting with the button on my suit jacket. "And if memory serves, he's a big taco guy, so I'm sure he'd appreciate all your local lunch recommendations," he adds, giving me a wink, and I'm torn whether I should feel mortified or honored that he remembered me devouring eight tacos during our initial lunch meeting. *Probably both.*

Clearing my throat, I step forward, wiping my now disgustingly sweaty palms on my new suit pants, and face my new coworkers.

"Hi everyone, like Mr. Austin said, my name is Will Cowen and I am so excited to be a part of this team." I give them the brightest and most eager smile I have as I wait for some verbal or nonverbal feedback, but instead, I'm met with the most awkward silence. *Nothing? Not even from smirky Jane over there?* I glance at Klair but can't get a read on her facial expression, so obviously I should just continue. *Right?*

"I got my start in a much smaller publishing house, but I'm ready to hit the ground running and I promise I'll get up to speed in no time. Throw whatever you've got at me." *Confident, helpful, charming? Atta boy.* Well, that went as well as it could have, but my parents always told me that there is nothing more important than a first impression.

Several people step forward, one after the other enthusiastically shaking my hand while offering semi-forced smiles and words of welcome. I know I'm new, but it's apparent that the team's baseline mood is tense, and I can't help but wonder why.

"Anything to add, Graham?" I can hear Mitch ask across the room. The team before me parts slightly and the man Mitch must have been speaking to comes directly into my line of sight.

He's stunning and instantly, I'm intrigued.

So, this is the notorious Graham Austin. My eyes haven't left him, it's like they can't, and even as I take a step back, easing into safety and calm after reclaiming my spot next to Klair, I find myself fixated on the man before me. He's young—much younger than I would have expected for the managing editor of Austin Publishing House—and his demeanor is unbothered as he leans casually against the wall. But from his perfectly manicured scruff to his simple, tailored appearance, there isn't anything casual about this man. He screams purpose and control. I make a mental note of his eyes—although, I can't pinpoint their color from where I'm standing, the intensity of his stare is disarming. It's obvious to me that Graham Austin is perhaps the most physically perfect man I've ever laid my eyes on, but what's more attractive is the professional aptitude he exudes.

"Welcome to the team, Will," he says, disinterested and all business as he stands, straightening the lapels of his crisp navy suit, and turns back to the rest of the team. "However, if no one has anything else work-related, let's wrap up so we're not wasting anyone's time."

With that, he gathers his things and exits the conference room, an unspoken signal to the rest of the team that it's time to get back to work.

I lean against the doorway, doing my best to keep my gaze upward and the smile plastered on my face as everyone exits, even though I'd be perfectly fine crawling into a deep, dark hole and never coming out.

"What. The. *Hell*. Just. Happened," I angry-whisper to Klair once we've made it back to our desks. I'd walked back in a daze, feeling conflicted because yikes, that did *not* go well and my anxiety doesn't tolerate weird social interactions like that, and how in the world is someone like Graham Austin real. That scruff. Those eyes...Should I be *this* turned on in the workplace? *Down, boy.*

Without saying a word, Klair comes over and gives me a quick hug. She places her hands on my shoulders and looks me right in the eyes.

"Listen, you cannot take *that* personally. As your best friend in the entire world and now your cubicle buddy, I failed you by not giving you a heads up, and for that, I'm sorry. Forgive me?"

She gives me the cutest and most dramatic puppy dog eyes that under the worst of circumstances, I'd probably have a hard time not giving into.

"Knock it off...Obviously I forgive you." I can't help but laugh as I swat her hands off of me. "I just wasn't prepared for whatever *that* was. Like that wasn't just in my head, right? He totally dismissed me?"

"Yes and no. With Graham, you'll learn that he's entirely business-oriented. Period. He comes in, does his job—exceptionally well, I might add—and goes home. His only focus is growing this company and being the next generation of leadership in publishing."

On one hand, I can wrap my head around that. Knowing

now who he is, he clearly has a legacy that dictates his every move. So, without wanting to come across as just the son who inherits it all, I can only assume he wants to prove to everyone just how competent and worthy of it all he truly is. But on the other hand, there was a noticeably different vibe in that conference room than when I met some of the team earlier. They are reacting to Graham's level of intensity, and from the freshest set of eyes in the office, is that really the most successful work environment?

Knowing my gears are churning on overdrive, Klair continues to soothe my nerves.

"I promise you, Will, that wasn't about you. This is how he always is. But between you and me, because very few people have witnessed it, that man is truly one of the kindest and most loyal souls I've ever met. He's been there for me in ways that have blown my mind."

With that, she turns her attention back to her work, and I try to do the same. The rest of the day goes off without a hitch, but I keep having this unhealthy feeling that the interaction I had with Graham earlier was in fact about me...or at least partially about me.

I dive back into work, knowing in my heart that at this moment there isn't anything to be done about this new delicious thorn in my anxiety's side. Flipping through the stack of manuscripts Klair handed me this morning, I'm more determined than ever to show my team just how appreciative and ready I am to be here.

It's not lost on me that I have a perfect view of Graham's office from my desk. Every so often, I sneak a glance in his direction only to find him pacing on the phone behind his partially frosted glass doors. There's no denying he takes his job seriously and from what Klair's told me, the man's got one hell of a work ethic. I'm all for professional competence—it's all I aspire to be, but now I'm just curious as to what makes this prickly man tick. He's young, attractive, and clearly succeeding professionally. He can't be *this* intense all the time. Right?

I've lost track of how many hours it's been since I have left my desk, but by the embarrassing sounds coming from my stomach, I know I've missed lunch and then some, a nasty habit I picked up as I was just getting my foot in the publishing door and desperate to impress my boss.

"Klair, wanna get out of here and—" I start and then stop as I take in her empty desk. *The bitch left me!* Klair is notorious for her Irish exits, so much so that it's almost no longer surprising when she just randomly disappears. *Almost.*

I gather my things, turn off my computer and grab my phone to send her a snarky text as I walk down the long, deserted hallway toward the elevator bank.

> I'm so glad your fun little disappearing act phase didn't go away. Jokes on you, girl... I was going to treat you to drinks as a thank you for helping me survive my first day!

I hit send and jam my phone in my pocket before pressing the elevator button. When it finally pings open, I step in, and just as the doors are about to close, the manuscript I've taken with me comes free of its binding, causing someone's life's work to fan across the filthy elevator floor. Rolling my eyes at this day that just keeps getting better and better, I bend down to start gathering them back together when a perfectly manicured, veiny hand pushes a few pages in my direction.

Please be anyone else but him.

I lift my gaze to Graham's perfect face, which is now radiating with intrigued concern. Probably for my clear mental and physical incompetence. Just kill me now already.

"Here you go." After handing me the pages, Graham stands, slinging his bag back onto his shoulder and turning to face the now-closed elevator doors. This wasn't some clichéd movie meet-cute where our hands delicately brushed while looking deep into one another's eyes. No, this was all common courtesy, filled with the same uncomfortable silence of every elevator ride in the history of elevators. *If this guy didn't think I was a loser before, he most certainly does now.*

"Thanks," I say...at least I think I do? My voice might have gotten lost within the awkwardness now lingering between us.

As the doors spring open and we both habitually take a step forward to exit the painful confines of the elevator, I feel compelled to break the silence. Per usual.

"Graham, I just want to reiterate how excited I am to be on this team." He's turned to face me full on, and standing here in the deserted parking garage and illuminated by the worst overhead lighting known to man, it feels like the first time I really get to take him in. Graham's features are dark but inviting. His naturally sun-kissed skin and bright, hazel eyes compliment his full but manicured scruff and effortlessly styled hair that's the color of smoked ash. He's alarmingly tall with broad shoulders and long legs, the sharp suit he's wearing does nothing to hide the impressive physique standing before me.

And those lips...don't even get me started on those perfect lips that I know are going to send my mind into a delicious tail-spin. *Reel it in.*

"I've only spent a few hours with this team, but I can already tell that it's a great one to be a part of." I decide to push my luck further while I still have his attention. "I'm sure you're busy or have a million other plans, but I haven't eaten all day and I could really use a drink. Want to join me? Klair showed me this really great place that's just a few blocks away."

He looks me square in the eye. I swear, everything Graham does appears to be fueled by purpose. But for the first time, his expression softens, ever so slightly...almost as if he's mentally decided to relax and physically release the tension of having to be *on* all day.

"I appreciate the offer, truly." His tone is genuine and light, a welcome change, but I can assume what's coming next. "Unfortunately, I have plans with my father this evening."

We've reached the point in our walk where it's time to part, but suddenly, I don't want this moment, despite it being utterly painful, to end. He turns back in my direction and for the first time since meeting this organized and capable professional, he flashes me the most dazzling smile I've ever seen. The *make you question every infatuation and attraction you've ever had* kind.

The kind of smile that screams trouble.

"See you tomorrow, Will." I've been stunned silent and left unwilling to ruin this movie-worthy moment with anything other than a slow wave.

Graham Austin runs a hand through his styled hair, laughs as he gets in his car—a sound that I'm now determined to hear again and again and again—and drives off, leaving me alone with the nagging thought that I just experienced one of those life-changing moments you always hear about.

"Oh okay, so you *are* alive?" Klair is sitting on the couch in sweats when I get home, her hair in a massive bun on the top of her head. I set my bag down on the kitchen table and shrug out of my coat, kicking my converse off toward the direction of the front door. "Where the heck did you disappear out of thin air to, without a care in the world of how your best friend was going to make it home after his first day?"

She rolls her eyes at me as I plop myself down next to her, invading her space and sprawling out as far as humanly possible.

"Jesus, Will...I don't think you could be *more* dramatic if you tried," she says as she forcefully pushes me off of her. "I had a few errands to run that I just wanted to knock out before coming home. Sue me." She ceremoniously waves her hands to the coffee table, where I'm just now noticing several boxes of pizza and bottles of red wine. "Besides, I couldn't let your first day on the job go uncelebrated."

Klair opens the box and serves us each a slice as I uncork the wine and pour us a glass of my favorite pinot. *She knows me so well.*

"Ugh, thank you so much." My mouth is salivating at the cheesy deliciousness before me. "I am STARVING."

We raise our glasses and they clink.

"To first days!" she says, smiling.

"To getting to work with your bestie," I add, bringing my glass to my lips and taking a much-needed pull of the sweet and oaky wine.

"I'll drink to that," Klair adds, joining me in my sip.

After enthusiastically devouring the pizza and helping ourselves to some heavy-handed pours of wine, Klair and I sat back in total contentment. Trying to distract myself with a reality television binge, my mind is still in overdrive after the two very different but intriguing encounters I had with Graham earlier. My first impression of him during our staff meeting, beyond being an absolute stud—*and those lips*—was that he appeared cold and truly unbothered about how he came across to those around him.

But then we met in the elevator and his entire demeanor

seemed...softer? More open? I can't quite put my finger on it. What I do know is that despite my full day of administrative tasks, meet and greets, and an overall immersion, I haven't been able to get Graham Austin out of my mind.

"So, what's the deal with Graham?" I ask, turning to Klair. "Because earlier, you said how he's one of the *kindest souls you've ever met*, and I'm sorry, but that's not the vibe I got today. What am I missing?"

"I've been waiting for you to ask," Klair says, turning off the TV. "What do you want to know?"

Everything, duh. "Well, for starters, what did you mean before when you mentioned he was there for you? What happened?"

I watch her inhale a large breath, closing her eyes before releasing it, and suddenly, I feel like our evening is about to take a turn toward something more serious. I straighten my back and turn fully toward her, showing her that she has my undivided attention.

"A few months back, I was casually dating this guy," she begins, looking down at her hand. I'm wracking my brain to remember who it could have been, but to my knowledge, Klair has been single for quite some time. Clearly knowing how my brain works, she adds, "I never mentioned him because it really ended before it started. But despite it being brief, it got serious *really* fast.

"Ian was charming—like, *incredibly* charming—and when I met him, I couldn't believe how quickly I began falling for the guy. He was sweet and attentive and made me feel like the most special woman in the world...at first." Her tone is sharp which raises every best friend red flag I have. "It wasn't physical or anything like that, but almost as quickly as he had come into my life, he changed. Or I should say, he showed me who he really was."

Reaching over, I grab her hands. "Klair, I'm so sorry...why didn't you tell me? I had no idea you had to put up with something like this."

She looks up at me, her kind eyes are filled with a sadness that usually isn't there. "I thought about calling you a million times about it, but honestly, I was embarrassed. I let this man's treatment of me really get the best of me. I went from feeling like I was on top of the world to...nothing." Her voice is a whisper. "But what could you have done, right? You were halfway across the country, and I just felt like this would have freaked you out."

"You're damn right it would have freaked me out...but I would have been there for you, love." I lean over, wrapping her in my arms.

"I know, I just didn't think it was best to involve you in something like this," she says, her head now on my shoulder. "I didn't want to be the reason you came running back home." *Typical Klair, always protecting me, even at her own expense.*

I pull back, looking her in the eye. "No matter what is going on in your life, good or bad, I will always be there for you like you've been there for me. Our friendship is unconditional."

"Trust me, I know that." She's smiling again. "Honestly, this was just a stupid blip, but I know when things are serious, I can and will always come to you."

"Good. So, if you don't mind me asking, how does Graham fit into all of this?" My curiosity is piqued. Was it someone he knew? Someone they worked with?

"Oh, Well, Graham must have overheard a rather tense conversation between Ian and me." Her cheeks flush. Like me, Klair has always tried to separate her personal and professional lives, so I can imagine this only made the situation worse.

"Ian showed up at the office to pick me up for dinner as I was wrapping up a few projects. He didn't like the fact that I wasn't ready and when Ian got mad, he got *really* mad, causing him to say some incredibly hurtful things about my body, my career...our sex life...and never once apologizing for them. There I was letting some guy talk to me like trash...how pathetic does that make me look?" Before I can interject, she adds. "I know, I know...it just was a situation I never thought I'd be in. I started justifying it. Or at least entertaining the idea that maybe some of the things he was saying about me were true." A tear rolls down her cheek and I take her hands in mine again.

"Klair, you are the most beautiful, kind, and accomplished person I know." She looks down as I continue. "Out of anyone in my life, it is *you* who has always inspired me to be a better version of myself because you have and always will be the prime example of grace, selflessness, and dedication. Nothing and *no one* can ever take that away from you."

"I appreciate you saying that, and looking back, I *know* these things. I think I just got caught up in a situation that was incredibly toxic and confusing." Her ability to look at deeply emotional situations this logically is inspiring. I've always admired Klair's strength and the grace she displays when life gets hard. But this is different...this situation clearly got to her. *I still want to beat the shit out of this Ian character.*

"So, Graham walked into our section, hearing all the awful things Ian was saying to me—publicly, I might add—and I was humiliated. I had only been at the company for a little over a year and the last thing I wanted was my very blunt and direct colleague, who happens to be the boss's son, to think I'm the girl that brings boyfriend drama into the office." I can totally see how Klair would worry about that with someone like Graham, but also the workplace in general.

"I started packing up my things to leave and Ian seemed more and more irritated with the entire situation. It was like every little thing about the moment set him off, and for him to be so brazenly disrespectful, I just wanted to get out of there." It's hard for me to picture Klair getting flustered like this. In all the years I've known her, she's always been the one to handle all our ups and downs with ease, which tells me everything I need to know about the severity of this situation.

"We bumped into Graham on our way to the elevator and I'm telling you, I've *never* seen him look as angry as he did in that moment. He was standing there looking larger than life, his eyes wild, never taking them off Ian. He said, 'Klair, cancel your evening's plans...we just got a massive project dumped on us and it's all hands on deck. Tell your boyfriend you'll have to reschedule.'"

"What did Ian say to that?" Based on my first impression of Graham, I can only imagine the sharpness in his tone and the intensity of his gaze. Just thinking about it has me feeling all sorts of intimidated.

"I mean, what was he going to say to Graham, he towered over Ian." Klair laughs. "Honestly, I don't even remember. I just remember him huffing off into the elevator and that was the last time I ever saw him."

"Did you talk to Graham about it?"

"Kind of?" The memory causes her to smile. "He ordered Chinese food and we sat in silence in the conference room together until he asked, 'What can I do?' And then I just started crying hysterically. Like ugly, snot-everywhere crying, and poor Graham, he looked like he didn't know what to do. But he ended up coming over and just giving me the tightest hug and he didn't let go."

Even though my heart hurts for what Klair went through, the image of Graham hugging my best friend, being there for her when I couldn't, makes me want to smile so hard.

"I don't know how long he held me in that conference room, but when he finally let me go, all he said was 'You know you deserve better.' His definitive statement made me wake the hell up. For weeks, I'd become this version of myself that I didn't know anymore, and he was so right. I *did* deserve better than that. I pulled out my phone and ended things with Ian right then and there...and I never once looked back. For weeks, he checked on me every single day after that and those little check-ins meant everything to me."

"Wow," is all I can say as Klair reaches to refill each of our wine glasses. Graham intervened in a moment when others might not have and it clearly made all the difference for Klair, an act I will forever be grateful for.

"Yeah, so I get it...he's a little harsh and blunt in the office," she states kindly as she gets up from the couch. "But like I said before, he's so much more than that when you take the time to get to know him."

"Hey, Klair?" I say as she's heading to start getting ready for bed. "I'm sorry I wasn't here for you during all of this, but I'm so glad to know you weren't alone."

She smiles and blows me a kiss before heading into her room, leaving me alone with my thoughts of this protective and warm version of Graham.

A version I hope to see more of.

CHAPTER TWO

I'VE BEEN AWAKE FOR SEVERAL HOURS WHEN MY ALARM finally goes off.

A considerable amount of time was spent begging my over-active mind to let me sleep. But it had other plans—I tossed and turned all night as thoughts of Klair's previous relationship and this new role and Graham's look of confusing disapproval had me spiraling down an anxious and inescapable rabbit hole.

Ripping the warmth of the covers off like you would a band aid, I swing my legs over the edge of my bed, stretching my body and rubbing what little sleep I had out of my eyes. After slowly padding over to the bathroom, bumping into nearly everything in sight, I take stock at the disheveled mess staring back at me in the mirror. My unruly and thick sometimes-brown, sometimes-strawberry-blonde hair is sticking up in the most epic yet unintentional mohawk that I am always tempted to leave—Klair says it's a hard pass—and the dark bags under my greenish, grayish eyes could pack a commercial 747 to the brim. *Sexy.*

I give the state of my body a once over. My shoulders are flecked with freckles that only get more prominent in the sun and unfortunately, I never quite grew into my lanky arms and legs. I've always been lean but I'm officially at that stage in my late twenties where caffeine, stress and thoughts and prayers aren't enough to entirely ward off the consequences of late-night fast-food binges and the dessert I can never seem to say no to. As I climb into the downpour of the scalding hot shower, I make a mental note that it wouldn't kill me to step into the gym every now and again, so I should probably look into getting a local membership. *Maybe tomorrow.* I rush through the remainder of my morning routine, throwing on a pair of slim navy chinos and a pale blue oxford, grab my loafers and race out of my room before my new roomie has the chance to complain about me making her late.

Klair and I have quickly settled into a routine that works for both of us. We alternate prepping dinner and setting the coffee for the next morning, loading the dishwasher and making sure our wine collection is always stocked. For as long as we've known one another, this is the first time we've ever lived together and thankfully, it's been nothing short of amazing. If you ever get the chance to live with your best friend, do it.

But one of my favorite things about this new living situation is our shared fifteen-minute walk to work each morning where we talk about the important things in life: reality television, our interpretations of the latest Taylor Swift Easter eggs, and our dating lives. *Or lack thereof.*

"I think I've been on a tragic date with every single guy in the city...and honestly? Each one gets worse and worse," Klair groans as we make our way into the office. Austin Publishing House is in the heart of Manhattan and despite our obnoxiously early wake up call, the city is brimming full of life as its inhabitants head in every direction to start their days.

"Wait, but what about the architect from the other night?" I ask Klair as we cross a crowded intersection.

She loops her arm through mine to avoid getting separated

among the growing number of pedestrians. "I don't know. He was nice but..."

"Excuse me, you came home smiling from ear to ear, talking about how sexy and charming he was! What do you mean you *don't know?*"

Klair rolls her eyes at me. "We'll see...don't start planning the wedding yet. But what about you, my sweet friend? Anyone catching your eye?" She changes the subject but despite her best efforts, can't hide the smile plastered across her face.

I've only been back in the city for a few days now and truthfully, the thought of dating or even putting myself out there hasn't even crossed my mind. Change has always been hard for me—too much of it at once tends to put me in a permanent state of nerves. *No thanks.* Between the move and starting this new job, I think that's about as much change as I can handle at once.

But then Graham's smile from the other night in the parking garage comes crashing into my thoughts. His strong gaze. The sound of his voice during our staff meeting. His tall, lean body —*Woah,* That doesn't count. Obviously, he's impossibly gorgeous and wildly successful in our career field so it's only natural I would be drawn to that sort of...whatever that is. However, I've also seen him be so cold and seemingly detached from basic human empathy in the office. In such a short amount of time, I've already seen the toll his *direct* approach to leadership has on the rest of the team—it's too much, and I don't think he even realizes. That's *definitely* not the energy I need or want in my life. *Right?*

"I think the *only thing* the two of us need to be paying attention to is making sure we aren't late again...come on," I say, tugging Klair along faster as we approach the steps to our building.

"Fair point...You can't afford to have a repeat of your first day," she says, sticking her tongue out in my direction as we step through the wide double doors of APH.

I rush to catch the closing elevator, throwing my arm between the heavy metal doors. "Um, excuse me? Whose fault was that?"

"I think we *both* could have handled that differently." Klair and I laugh as we ride the elevator to the twenty-first floor, heading into another busy day in the office and when the doors reopen, dropping us off on our floor, I check my phone to see the time.

Ten minutes to spare, thank goodness.

Fun fact: I learned rather quickly that working in a well-known publishing house is dangerous for someone who is perpetually clumsy and completely out of control of his own body's movements at times—someone like me, because you never know who you are going to run into. Quite literally, in fact —as I have just run headfirst into one of my favorite authors of all time moments after rounding the corner from the elevator bank, nearly knocking her to the ground in the process.

"You...you're Alexis Wingate," I say in a much higher pitched tone than normal. Humiliation washes over me when I realize who I'm awkwardly holding on to.

"And you're going to have to carry me to my next meeting if you don't let go," she says through a deep, red-lipped smile as she glances down at my hands that are firmly on either side of her arms. I rather cartoonishly drop my hands to my sides, my cheeks burning bright red as I take an overly dramatic step backward and she smooths out her chic-cut, blonde hair. Alexis is one of those exceptional talents who can bounce back and forth between writing heart-pounding and diabolical thrillers and then turn around and write tear-inducing and totally swoon-worthy romcoms—all while remaining incredibly *real* and deeply connected to her fans.

22

A.k.a. me, the super fan who's keeping her from what I'm sure is a very important meeting. "I'm so sorry, Alexis...I, eh... wasn't paying attention. I'm a *huge* fan. Like, I've read everything of yours. Um...I'm also Will. Will Cowen. Not that you needed to know that..." I should stop talking now. Is it hot in here? Just me? I'm acutely aware of the fact that Klair is standing just behind me with what I can only imagine is a far-too satisfied look on her face as she watches her starstruck friend completely bomb.

She quickly waves off my apology. "Don't even worry about it, Will...I must have needed that shock to my system." I could die of embarrassment. "But between you and I, I'm secretly hoping my editor also wasn't paying attention to the latest draft I sent him. Because *wow*..." It's cute to see an icon like Alexis Wingate be this humble but there is no reality where anything she's written isn't perfection.

"Um...please tell me we aren't talking about *The Lady of the House*? Because I would *literally* sell my soul and swear-off men for all of time to read your next book." Good one, Will—that was a sentence you just said out loud to a literary legend.

She laughs at my awkwardness as she rummages through her oversized handbag. "Here, don't tell Graham you got this from me," she says, pressing a mockup of her book against my chest and I fight every urge to not jump up and down out of excitement. It doesn't matter how long I've worked in this industry. When I get the chance to read something new from one of my favorite authors—especially before anyone else does—I revert right back to the younger version of myself who just discovered his obsessive love for reading.

"Alexis?" an impatient voice calls out from down the hall causing all three of our heads to simultaneously swivel. It's no surprise that Graham, who's clearly been waiting, is the one working with someone of her caliber. Standing in the doorway of his office, his stare is filled with annoyance, agitation and just a smidge of assholery. As much as I would love to continue fangirling over Alexis and her impeccable writing, style and overall icon status some more, inconveniencing the Ice King isn't how I want my day to start.

"That's my cue, Will Cowen. Be a doll and let me know what you think of chapter seventeen. It's a little...*twisted*. Even for me," she says, raising an eyebrow as she turns to meet Graham. I watch in embarrassing awe as the two of them continue down the hall toward his office.

Klair loops her arm through mine but before she has the chance to point out every which way I just completely embarrassed myself, I beat her to it. "Just don't...I'm extremely cognizant of the train wreck that was."

We continue down the hall arm-in-arm. "Will, I'm offended! I would never bring up how you just physically accosted a New York Times Best Selling author in the workplace and then went on and on about how obsessed you are with her."

"Mmhmm." I'm going to need a neck brace after the eye-roll I just gave her and as we both settle into our desks for the morning, I do my best to put the awkwardness of all of *that* out of my mind—especially the displeased expression permanently etched on Graham's face.

Thankfully, my morning mellowed out significantly after that, eh, professional run-in with Alexis and I was able to finalize some remaining onboarding documents and set up my email inboxes and desktop in a way that just makes sense. After dragging Klair to the break room for another cup of coffee, we're about to step into my first official meeting with our smaller editorial team when she turns to me, a half-panicked, half-apologetic look flashing across her face.

"Please don't hate me," she says, placing her hand on my shoulder and momentarily stopping me in the doorway. "We *may* laugh about this later...but probably not."

What? I don't have time to badger her about the meaning of her vague and ominous statement because she's already pulling me by the arm into the conference room where Audra and Jane, both members of our marketing team, are already waiting. Mark, who seemingly handles everything graphic design related, comes in shortly behind us and takes the empty seat next to Jane. So far, everyone I've met has offered nothing but the warmest of welcomes and have been instrumental when it's come to understanding the size and scope of APH. More importantly, they seem to genuinely welcome and appreciate my fresh perspective as they've briefly filled me in on the projects they're all respectively leading.

Well, everyone except for Graham—who's seated at the head of the table typing away on his phone.

"Alright everyone, we're going to be doing things a little differently this morning," Klair says and I can see a flicker of confusion ripple across everyone's faces. "To officially welcome Will to the team, Mitch asked me to put together a little ice-breaker activity."

She procures a random stack of envelopes I somehow managed to miss earlier and shuffles them in her hands, flashing a playful grin in my direction. "Get ready for the first-ever APH Team Building Extravaganza," she says. Judging by the not-so-muffled groans coming from around the table, I can tell she might just be the only one who's excited.

"These envelopes contain a combination of randomly generated riddles, clues and partner challenges that I swear I haven't peeked at. We'll work in groups of two to get through as many of them as we can in a one-hour window."

Oh, joy...mandatory fun. As much as I would prefer to do any and all team building activities at a happy hour with a cocktail in each hand, I do my best to play the role of supportive friend by resisting the urge to audibly object with everyone else around the table. Even Graham, who's finally looked up from his phone, gives a subtle roll of his eyes.

"Mark, you'll partner with Jane," she says, slowly slinking around the conference table and handing him an envelope. I preemptively turn and smile at Audra, excited at the opportunity to get to know her a little better in a one-on-one setting.

"Audra, you and I will partner up. And the final pairing will be..." *Shit...wait. No!*

"...Will and Graham." I stare daggers at Klair as she extends the envelope in my direction and our names come out of her red-lipped mouth. Even though my back is slightly turned toward Graham, I can only imagine the annoyed gaze plastered across his smug face. Klair was right—we definitely *won't* be laughing about this later.

My palms are instantly slick with sweat as I grip the arms of my chair and without any warning, my leg begins to shake under the table. Before I can even wrap my head around what's happening and the extent of Klair's premeditated best friend betrayal—*dramatic, I know,* the conference room empties out as Jane, Mark, Audra and Klair saunter off, blissfully unaware of my inner turmoil as I'm left awkwardly alone with Graham Austin.

I know I need to turn around to face him...but like, do I *really* have to? Can't we just sit here in soul-crushing silence, and he can go back to angry-scrolling on his phone for the next hour? He probably wouldn't even notice if I crawled across the office floor and snuck out of the room.

I turn toward the window...I could maybe climb out of that?

The sound of Graham clearing his throat snaps me back to reality, canceling all my totally realistic escape plans and forcing me to sit just a little straighter in my chair. I mentally shout a long stream of obscenities at Klair for doing this to me as I slowly turn toward my waiting partner.

He's leaning back in his seat, his hands neatly folded on the edge of the glass tabletop. My gaze instantly goes toward his pointer finger which he is slowly and meticulously tapping against his black, leather notepad either subconsciously or out of annoyance. *Definitely the latter.*

"Um...hi," I say once we finally make eye contact.

Instead of initially responding, Graham stands, pocketing his ever-buzzing phone and crossing his long arms. I hate that my not-so-subtle eyes wander over the man standing before me. Despite his obvious disinterest and standoffish manner, there's no denying he wears the hell out of a suit.

"Shall we?" he asks, his tone oozing with impatience. My list of obscenities directed at Klair grows longer as I rip open the envelope she gave me. Inside, there appears to be a checklist of random items found in an office that we are meant to find.

"It looks like our challenge is an office scavenger hunt. We find the items listed and snap a picture...sounds easy enough." I do my best to appear calm, cool, and collected—three things I doubt I'll ever be capable of being in the presence of Graham. If we are forced to *bond* like this, I'm at least going to be as friendly and professional as humanly possible. "The first item we need to find is an orange sticky note."

He opens his notepad and flips back a few pages. "Here," he says, flinging an orange sticky note in my direction. I watch as it slowly twirls between us and lands on the table in front of me. *Really?* I silently raise my phone and snap a picture of the sad piece of paper that is inscribed with Graham's impeccable penmanship, a to-do list. *How fitting.*

"Next?"

I glance down at the list. "A personalized coffee mug?"

Graham grabs his notepad and heads toward the conference room door. "Follow me." I struggle to keep up with his hurried pace and for only being slightly taller than me, his stride sure is fast. He rounds the corner and leads me directly to his own office, opening the door—that almost slams into me as I follow him—stepping behind his desk and opening one of the drawers. It's the first time I've been in his office but before I can even look around, he retrieves a mug and turns it upside down so the few random objects—a couple of pens, some loose change and what appears to be a pin in the shape of a stack of books—come pouring out and scatter loudly on the surface of his pristine desk.

I can't help but take the rushed intensity of his movements personally and I feel my throat close. Allegedly, the whole point of this exercise was to make me feel like a welcomed member of this team yet all Graham has managed to do is show me just how bothered he is being in my presence.

He slides the coffee mug across the table between us and when I pick it up, I see *Austin Publishing House* written in gold script across the navy mug. I can guarantee this isn't what was meant by "personalized" but I'm not going to argue with his logic considering almost every inch of this building has his family name adorned across it.

Taking my phone out to document our second item, I look up to find Graham back to speed-texting which momentarily silences the ever-present *ping* of whatever matter keeps pulling his attention.

I swallow hard, furious at myself for letting his lack of professional decorum or at a bare minimum, common courtesy, cause my anxiety to spike like this and when I glance over at his furrowed brow and laser-like focus, I don't know how much longer I can keep up this façade. I pull out the list I had jammed into my pocket and quietly unfold it.

"Alright, the next item we have to find is a coworker wearing a blue shirt," I say, praying the hurt and embarrassment is not as obvious in my tone as I fear it is.

He briefly looks up from what he's typing, cocking an eyebrow at me in the process. Raising his phone, Graham snaps a photo of me. "Done."

Remembering the light blue oxford I threw on this morning, I let out a breath I hadn't realized I'd been holding. "Graham, I don't think that's..." I stop myself when I realize he's back to texting. "You know what? It doesn't matter." I glance down at the several items remaining on our checklist and all I want is for this torturous exercise to be over with.

"Well, that was the last thing on the list..." I lie, quickly turning to leave his office. "I hope you have a good rest of your day, Graham." I couldn't tell you if he acknowledged my exit or not and frankly, I don't care. Based on this entire interaction, I'm pretty sure I could set myself on fire right now and he wouldn't even notice.

Everything about this man has left me dazed and confused and while I don't know if I have the mental willpower required to fully understand all that is Graham Austin, all I can think about as I walk down the hall, disappointment flooding my nervous system, is that taking this job just might be one of the biggest mistakes of my life.

CHAPTER THREE

There is no denying that I am standing on the edge of a full-blown Will Cowen spiral.

My recent interaction—correction: *interactions*, plural—with Graham have played on a torturous loop in my mind and as much as I want to vent to Klair, I've chosen not to tell her about the whole ice breaker from hell fiasco. The last thing I want to do is make her feel responsible for how badly the scenario she concocted for Graham and I backfired. Because let's face it—the *only* one responsible for whatever that mess was is Graham.

Quitting isn't a realistic option, but I'd be lying if I said I hadn't thought about calling up my old boss in Chicago and seeing if my position had already been filled. I don't think I'd ever forgive myself if *a boy* was the reason I walked away from an amazing opportunity. Do I need Graham to like me? Absolutely not. I can't see us shooting the shit at the proverbial water cooler anytime soon but it for sure would make working together far more tolerable if I didn't think the man was physically inconvenienced by my presence.

So, in typical Cowen family fashion, I spend the first hour

or so the following morning creating a pros and cons list about the current state of my life—which may seem trivial, but right now? I can't trust the tangled mess that is my brain and I need to feel some semblance of control if I'm going to avoid a total meltdown.

Pro: For the first time ever, I get to work alongside Klair. Outside of job progression, that's pretty much the biggest and only perk about taking this job that I was excited about.

Con: Graham Austin appears to hate me.

Pro: APH is leading the way when it comes to sharing diverse stories, promoting Own Voices and is *exactly* where I want to be working.

Con: Graham Austin *definitely* hates me.

Pro: That parking lot smile. *Ugh.*

Klair leans over our shared wall, interrupting my professional existential crisis but as always, it's a welcome and much needed distraction. She's been poring over a manuscript since the moment we sat down this morning.

"Quick question: do you think the whole *friends-to-lovers* trope is becoming overplayed? I feel like I've seen eight come across my desk in the last month."

I love talking about romance with Klair. She and I agree on most things, and while I'm a total lost cause for brooding love interests and impossible storylines, Klair needs her romance to be anchored by logic. And while we may differ on the tiny details, a happily ever after is a *must* for both of us. "You know me...give me as many *Will they, Won't they* moments as possible! Why do you ask?" I put my pro-con list away for now because I can guarantee this conversation will be far more interesting and let's be honest, a great distraction for my mental health.

"I'm just really stuck on the believability of the relationship of these main characters, you know?" She hands me the manuscript she was just reading and points to a highlighted section. As I read and reread the section she's indicated, I see it's a very stereotypical childhood-crush-turned-adult-best-friend—one who's forced to hide their true feelings.

"I wouldn't say this is a case of it being *overplayed*," I say, fanning the pages and skimming their contents. "Maybe you could adjust the timeline slightly? Force our main characters to come *back* into one another's orbits earlier and make their relationship feel a little more natural? Just a thought..."

"Oh, I like that...I'll make that note and see if that changes how I feel about it. See? This is why I adore you," she says, her gears clearly turning as she begins scribbling in the margins.

"You *know* I'm always here to help...especially when it comes to romance tropes."

Before I can turn my attention back to my computer, Klair and I are suddenly joined at our workstation by a visibly irritated Graham.

"Klair, have you finalized the edits I gave you yesterday?" If his tone wasn't so sharp, I'd be able to appreciate the fact that he's dressed in a tailored, light gray suit that makes his hazel eyes pop in stark contrast to his crisp white dress shirt.

"I'm actually wrapping them up now and will have them to you shortly," she responds, barely lifting her gaze. Her tone is light despite the obvious irritation he's exhibiting. *What is with this guy?*

"Oh hi, Graham. We were just talking about romance tropes. What's your favorite? Enemies to lovers?" I ask, perhaps placing too much emphasis on the word *enemies*.

He turns his gaze toward mine, those piercing eyes of his give me a once over and it takes every ounce of self-confidence to not cower away.

"I don't have one," he says, his tone matching the indifference of his gaze as he returns his attention back toward Klair. "Can you just get those edits to me as soon as you're done?"

After delivering his marching orders, Graham leaves as abruptly as he appeared and heads toward the break room. *Don't do it, Will. Don't do it...*

"Hey, Graham...do you have a second?" I call after him, gathering whatever courage and calm I can muster as I follow him down the hall and into our office breakroom.

"Will, I don't think tha..." I hear Klair whisper behind me, but it's too late. *Something* is up with this man. After our first interaction, I was bothered by the way he casually dismissed me during our staff meeting. It was unlike anything I've ever experienced in my professional career—especially on someone's first day. When we spoke later, his demeanor seemed completely different so I gave him a pass and chalked it up to a potential bad day. Especially after everything that Klair shared with me about him being there for her when she didn't even ask for it.

But then the humiliating ice breaker activity happened, and I have just been fuming ever since. No, I am most certainly addressing this. *Right the fuck now.*

He's standing at the sink with his back—*his wide, muscular back*—to me, meticulously hand washing a solid black mug in our communal sink. "Have I done something to offend you, Graham?" I ask, crossing my arms in the doorway.

Nothing.

His attention is turned toward washing his mug, but there is absolutely no chance he didn't hear me. He just continues scrubbing. At this rate, he's going to strip the mug of all color.

"Because I don't know if we've gotten off on the wrong foot, or if you just aren't a people person but..."

He stills. The sound of the streaming tap water overwhelms the space between us as he slowly reaches for a dish rag and begins towel-drying the mug in his large hands.

33

"What gives you the impression I'm not a people person?" he asks, his tone just as cold as before but now laced with a hint of something I can't quite put my finger on. *Intrigue?*

It looks like I struck a nerve. *Good.* Graham's back is still toward me— I sidestep to my right ever so slightly to be at least adjacent to his line of sight.

"Oh, I don't know, maybe the fact that three times now within my first week working here, you've either quickly dismissed me or seemed painfully bothered by me speaking in your presence or whatever the hell that team building exercise was, and..."

Placing his mug down gently on the counter, he turns to face me. "I don't think that's..."

"No, no..." I interject, taking a step toward him. "That's *exactly* how you've made me *feel*—unwelcome."

His eyes snap to mine at the bluntness and honesty of my words. For the first time since meeting Graham Austin, I see concern flash behind the calm and unbothered demeanor I'd been introduced to.

I take another step toward him, invading the space he seemingly works so hard to put between himself and the rest of the world. "You do realize people around here are responding to whatever it is you're putting off, right?"

Shock. Surprise. *Amusement?* Graham's face goes through a wide array of emotions. He opens his mouth to say something but then quickly closes it, a smile tugging at the corners of his mouth. *Ugh, that mouth.*

I pat him on the arm as I turn to leave, both as a sign of potential friendship and as a warning. "Which is such a shame because I came here *specifically* to work for and with people like you..." I pause in the entryway, noticing his gaze now following my every move. Locking my eyes with his, I pray he takes my words to heart. "But no one wants or deserves to work in a toxic environment.

"I certainly don't," I say, turning my back to him as I exit the break room not giving a damn about whatever professional consequences may come from addressing him like this.

CHAPTER FOUR

"Yup, I've got your contact information jotted down right here and will get back to you if there's any update…Okay… Mhmm…Bye." I hang up the phone a little too aggressively because when I do, Klair lifts her head up from the manuscript she's reading and appears annoyed.

"I'm sorry," I groan. "I've been pitched romcom after romcom and I think my brain might actually be bleeding. Is it possible to die from too much fake romance?" I throw myself dramatically over our shared table and melt onto all of Klair's belongings. "Klaaaaaair…pay attention to me. Your best friend is dying!"

She slams the pages she's been trying to focus on down on the table and bolts up from her chair. Clearly, we *both* woke up and wanted to cause a scene in the office today. "Oh my GOD… will you *please* shut that obnoxious little mouth of yours? *You* are killing *me*," she says while shaking her head and laughing. She walks over to her desk and grabs a large, thick envelope that she unexpectedly and rather forcefully throws at me.

"Here," she says like an overly-annoyed parent dealing with a frustrating toddler. "This was delivered for you this morning."

Partially confused, I begin opening the mailer when she adds, "Take it and let the adults get back to work." She blows me a kiss so I know she's joking as she returns her attention to her work.

I remove a thick manuscript bound with a deep navy cover page in thick card stock from the envelope, the title *I Should Have Told You Then* written in plain, gold script centered on the front. Inside, I find a notecard.

Dear Will,

I was given your contact information through a mutual acquaintance in a rather serendipitous manner so I apologize for reaching out to you like this out of the blue. My name is Lana Taylor and in your hands is the one and only copy of my novel, *I Should Have Told You Then*.

I can only imagine how many letters like this you receive and understand that my writing may not be for everyone, but if you have time, I would love to talk to you about it. Thank you for your consideration and I hope to hear from you soon!

Respectfully,
Lana Taylor

She's listed her contact information below in the neatest, most precise penmanship. I turn the card over and over in my hands. Mutual acquaintance? She could have listed who, right? *That's odd.* I glance back up at Klair, clearly immersed in whatever story she's reading, and wonder if she has any idea who Lana could be referencing. I grab the manuscript and turn to the first page, deciding I can inquire with Klair later about this mystery acquaintance and what she knows.

From Lana's very first sentence, I'm instantly captivated. Her voice cuts through the pages, demanding every ounce of my attention while transporting me to moments in my own life.

Everything I love about the written word and an author's ability to grab their reader is all right here. Sure, there are technical errors and a greenness that is expected of an inexperienced author, but from the very first page, there is something unteachable about Lana's writing that most authors would kill for—a voice of truth mixed with the brutal honesty of loss.

It's clear that Lana is no stranger to pain. I have no idea who she is or what she's been through, but there is a rawness to her writing that tells me she knows what it feels like to be hurt by a loved one, that she is no stranger to the complexities of grief.

Reading her words crack open my chest, threatening to open my own wounds that I've deluded myself into thinking have been healed for years. It's then that I know I'm going to work with her. I have to. Stories like this—more importantly, authors like Lana—are what made me fall in love with writing in the first place. To be able to move someone so deeply by weaving together a specific set of words is something I find so impressive and beautiful. *And daunting.*

I sit, devouring her words and the intricacies of her story-lines, and for the first time since joining APH, I feel inspired. I fly through her pages, filling the margins with notes and edits only I can decipher, and I begin planning my pitch to Graham and the rest of the team because books like this *need* to be out in the world. I feel it in my gut: Like me, readers will find themselves tangled in the web she's woven, drowning in the cascading words of her prose and only coming up for air when she allows them to.

Klair still has her head in whatever it is she's reading, but I know she'll want to see this. "*Psssst.*" She ignores me. "Hey Klair...*pssssssssst.*" I can feel the weight of her eye roll as she looks up at me, even more annoyed than earlier. Is it bad that I secretly enjoy getting under her skin?

"Yes, my child?" Her attempt at hiding any frustration is feeble. "What could you possibly need now?"

"Well that package you handed me earlier? It's a manuscript." I get up, bringing Lana's book with me and head over to her desk.

"I figured...seeing as this is, you know...a publishing house after all." The sarcasm rolls of her tongue as she sits upright, marking the page she was on and crossing her arms.

"HA HA." I mock at her. "No, it's like a *really* good manuscript. Like one of the best ones I've read in a while. Here, look." I flip through the pages, looking for the specific passage I had in mind and hand it to her.

She takes the pages from me, scanning to the section I've highlighted with her lips pursed and starts reading.

"The hardest part wasn't acknowledging that she never chose me," Klair reads aloud. *"The hardest part was accepting that this moment—the one that I'd been dreading my entire life—was definitively and heartbreakingly never about me."*

Klair reads on, her hand over her mouth and I watch as she experiences the same range of emotions I did while reading Lana's work.

"Will," her eyes are filled with tears. "This really is special. It's such an authentic and unique voice. But, and I only ask this because I care, are you going to be able to work on this?"

"Of course I am," I say, dismissing her concern. "This," I say, waving the manuscript in my hand. "This is why I wanted to get into publishing in the first place—to connect with and amplify authors like Lana who speak so passionately about the human experience and the pain we cause one another."

"I couldn't agree more," she says, putting her hand on my arm. "I've just scratched the surface and can already tell how deeply emotional this one is, so I just want to make sure you're not voluntarily taking on something that will be too much for you, that's all."

Her concern is genuine, which is one of the reasons I love her so dearly. Maybe she's right—*she usually is*—I do have a soft spot for familial trauma.

"You *know* I'm an emotional junkie, girl...my bleeding heart lives for stuff like this!" I walk back to my desk and put Lana's manuscript in my bag. "Besides, it'll be the perfect balance for all this lighthearted, make-you-smile romance," I add, pointing to my now towering pile of recent submissions.

Klair shakes her head, turning her attention back to her work. "That may be so, but just make sure that *your* emotions are prioritized during all of this, okay?"

"Scout's honor."

The rest of the day goes by in a blur and as Klair and I pack up to head home for the night, the promise of Lana's novel has ignited more inspiration than I've felt in a really long time. If I'm being honest, it's the first time I've ever connected this intimately and immediately with the words of a new author. I just pray this moment of happenstance transforms into something beautiful.

For both of us.

CHAPTER FIVE

"Okay, can we go over this one more time?"

Klair and I have been sitting in our living room for the last two hours, sharing a bottle of red and running over my pitch of Lana's book.

I've spent the last few days poring over every word in her manuscript. *Obsessing over it, really.* At this point, I feel like I know it inside and out.

"Absolutely not," Klair says, bolting upright, nearly sloshing red wine all over our couch. "As much as I love you—which is a lot—and as much as I love Lana's book—again...a lot—no more." She gets up to stand in front of me, her hands on my shoulders. "You got this. You're stressing yourself out for no reason. Damn, you're stressing *me* out and this isn't even my pitch."

I know she's right. I'm totally in my head about this one. From a business standpoint, this book is a slam dunk, it practically sells itself, and from a reader's perspective, Lana's book will speak to a broad audience...something the publishing house will appreciate.

"This is my first pitch in this role, Klair...I'm allowed to be a little nervous." My admission hangs in the air. There is nothing

I *hate more* than coming across as unqualified for a position, but I know that with Klair, her support is unwavering.

"Of course you are, and as someone who has known you a *really* long time, trust me when I say that you got this. Graham, and the rest of the team for that matter, are going to love this book regardless of how your pitch goes...it's a money maker." I scowl at her. "But...I've heard your pitch—way too many times—and your passion is contagious. Have some faith in yourself."

Easier said than done. I spend the rest of the evening doing everything in my power to *not* think about the coming workday, but when I'm not thinking about the pitch, I'm thinking about Graham's mouth...which makes me start thinking of the pitch again. *Kill me, now.* Before moving back to New York, I never felt pressure like this. Is this new-job jitters? Or something more?

Eventually, I'm able to shut off my mind and succumb to a much-needed night's rest. As much as I'm certain my dreams will be filled with some chaotic combination of public speaking and Graham's gaze and sad books, I wake up refreshed and as ready as I'll ever be. After showering and going back and forth on the perfect outfit—*let's be honest, I went with Klair's recommendation*—I head out into the kitchen, seeing that my fabulous roommate has prepared a cup of coffee for me. *I don't deserve this girl.* Triple checking that I have everything I need for this morning's meeting, I head out the door, more energized than ever to get this pitch over with and get the blessing to move forward on this project.

"Ughhh, what is that for?" Klair objects after I sneak up behind her, wrapping her in a massive bear hug. "Too tight! You're going to wrinkle my outfit." She laughs as she swats at my arms.

"I just adore you and am so lucky to have you in my life." It's true—I couldn't imagine my life without her. "I don't know if I tell you that enough, but I really do appreciate everything you've done, and continue to do, for me."

She rolls her eyes at me. "It's because we're family, William. I would do anything for you, just like I know you would do anything for me." Extending her finger, she touches my nose and whispers, "Boop," before laughing maniacally because she knows I hate and secretly love when she does that...especially in public.

"Don't you have some big pitch to get ready for? Go on... shoo." She gets back to work as I head to my desk smiling. Our staff meeting isn't for another twenty minutes, ample time to grab another cup of coffee and make sure all of my materials are printed and presentable for the team.

As I head to our office's shared snack area to brew my coffee, I look up to see Graham pacing in his office on a phone call, clearly animated in the discussion he's having. He's wearing his usual business attire: dark navy suit, crisp white oxford shirt slightly open at the neck, and a pair of impeccably polished brown dress shoes. *Drool.*

Outside of the obvious physical attraction I have to the man, it has been amazing to get a small glimpse of his work ethic. It is so apparent to me how much he cares about the success of this company, but more importantly, he seems to genuinely do everything within his control to ensure the success of our authors...especially the smaller ones, a quality that I think is so rare in our industry. *Or at least overlooked.* When everything is numbers-driven and reliant on sales, performance, and marketability, it's easy to forget that at the core of what we do are real people. Something Graham has made sure to remind us of on more than one occasion in my short time on this team. *That's why he's going to love this book, dummy.*

I enter the conference room early, ready to fight like hell for Lana's book if need be, and start to mentally go over the notes Klair gave me last night. *Let your passion shine through. Let your passion shine through. Let your passion...*

"Good morning, Will." Graham's cool tone snaps me out of my new mantra, igniting a whole new set of nerves that I don't really want to be dealing with right now.

"Good morning," I all but sing.

Bleh, too eager.

Why does this man turn me into a blubbering idiot? I swear I'm competent and it would be *so* nice if I felt like Graham was getting to see that. Am I reaching for the stars here?

The rest of the team files in, quickly taking their usual seats upon realizing that Graham is already at the head of the table tapping his pen against his notebook, the physical embodiment of agitation.

"Alright, let's get started." Graham has his meticulous to-do list in front of him. "Audra, where are we with the covers for the new YA series?" Before Audra can answer, Klair comes not-so-gracefully into the office, a box of delicious-looking goodies from the bakery around the corner in her hands.

"So sorry, everyone," she whispers, clearly embarrassed for showing up late to yet another meeting. "I was dealing with a shellfish emergency on the phone with the caterer for our New Voices in Writing Gala." Looking toward Graham as she takes her seat next to me, she adds, "I brought treats to make up for my tiny tardiness."

"Is there anything you need from me for the event?" Graham doesn't appear to be bothered by her interruption. *Thank goodness.*

"Oh no," she says, waving off his offer to jump in. "I've got it handled...but I appreciate the offer." Graham and Klair have one of the best working relationships in the office. Let's be honest, *everyone* has a great working relationship with Klair. But somehow, she's the only one who gets this version of him, and knowing a little more about their history, it totally makes sense.

"Well, let me know if and when you need anything from me." Looking around the table, he adds, "...or from the rest of the team since this is an event for all of us. Anyway, where was I...Audra?"

Graham proceeds to tick off items on his list as the team provides their updates. He grills Mark for statuses on several upcoming releases, taking extensive notes as Mark rambles on. He goes over the budget with Jane briefly before circling back to Audra with a few adjusted timelines he needs them to pass along to their authors.

Besides the so-called "shellfish emergency," Graham listens intently as Klair goes over the upcoming event she's been leading the planning efforts on. He clearly trusts her professional judgment and overall vision because he rarely interjects and when he does, it's him offering his assistance to take things off of her plate.

"Before we wrap up, any new business?" He looks around the table at each of us, lingering when his gaze meets mine.

Ow! Klair kicks me under the table. *Oh...New business means me.*

Clearing my throat, I sit up straight in my chair. *Let your passion shine through.*

"I actually have something, Graham." He'd already anticipated the meeting was concluding but reopens his notebook with a cocked eyebrow. I take that as my sign to continue.

"Recently, a manuscript came across my desk that I really think we should consider. It's titled *I Should Have Told You Then* and written by a fresh, new voice, Lana Taylor."

The entire team is giving me their full attention, but all I care about is the expression on Graham's face. *He's beyond difficult to read.*

"She's written a shocking and reverent portrayal of grief, regret, and familial trauma," I continue. Graham looks down, now disinterested.

Breathe.

"And while there's still a lot of work to be done, which I'm willingly and enthusiastically signing on for, I can confidently say I've never quite read anything like this. Breaking free from stereotypical rom-coms and political thrillers, this book fills every gap missing from our current roster: humanity, resolution, and second chances. It'll sell itself."

His eyes dart back to mine, looking at me intently with the slightest smirk on that face of his. My insides melt.

"I'm definitely intrigued," he says while jotting something down in his notebook. "In the interest of time, can you get me a few revised chapters by the end of the week?" Turning his attention to Klair, he adds, "Let's make sure Ms. Taylor receives an invite to the gala. Can you work with Will to make sure he's prepped?"

"You know it," Klair says, her words exuding excitement.

Did I just pull this off? I look at Klair and she gives me a thumbs up. *Yes!*

We all begin to exit the conference room with Graham's various marching orders. Klair starts bombarding me with details about the gala—dates and times and dress codes—but all I can think about is that my pitch made Graham smile. And how the sight of said smile, regardless of how slight it was, makes me feel like I'm going to collapse on the spot in a pool of happiness.

"Will, can you hang back for a second?" Graham's voice interrupts my lingering thoughts of his smile and rips me right back to reality. Klair hovers in the doorway, her eyebrows raised in concern but I give her a *I got this* wink as I turn to face Graham once more.

"Of course—what's up?" I do my best to lean casually against the conference table despite having no clue as to what kind of conversation this is going to be. His demeanor has shifted from the very poised man who was just leading our staff meeting to someone now looking down and weirdly fidgeting with the binding of his black notepad.

Graham slowly raises his gaze and I'm met with a heart-breaking softness I could and would willingly get lost in. "I think it's safe to say we got off on the wrong foot and I'd like to change that. I know I haven't given you the warmest of welcomes..." *Excuse me, what?* I definitely wasn't expecting *that.* "...especially during our little scavenger hunt. I was dealing with a personal matter but that's no excuse."

He takes a step forward, extending his hand which I instinctually take. "Hi Will, I'm Graham and I'm very much looking forward to having you on our team." His hand is warm, soft but with a more than subtle strength behind his grip.

"Oh—um, okay—hi, Graham...I'm...eh, happy to be here?" If his smile didn't match the genuine tone of his words, this mock-reintroduction may have been the most cringe-worthy moment of my professional career. Despite all of our previous interactions, there is something undeniable about a smiling Graham Austin.

His grin widens as he looks down, subtly signaling me to the fact that I am still slowly shaking his hand, which I quickly let go of, shoving my now sweaty palm into my pant's pocket. Despite the break in contact, my fingertips are tingling from the heat of his strong grasp.

"That being said, I'm happy to help in any way with Ms. Taylor's book," he says, taking yet another step forward and placing his hand on my shoulder. My head swivels, locking in on his grip on my arm. *Um...this is intimate.* "It sounds spectacular so just let me know what you need."

What do I need?

What I need is to desperately put some distance between us right now. This new version of Graham is tantalizing and I fear I just might do or say something I'll regret.

"Um—I appreciate the ugh, clean slate?" I awkwardly stammer out, slightly more tongue tied as he gives my shoulder a gentle squeeze before dropping his hand. *Get it together.* If I was partially intrigued by Graham's professional intensity before, I most certainly am now.

Needing to think clearly and get some much-needed Graham-free air, I take an over exaggerated step backward. "Everything seems pretty straight forward but I will let you know if and when I need anything." Having reached my limit of public displays of flustered awkwardness, I quickly make my escape.

Pausing in the doorway, I glance back toward Graham who hasn't moved an inch.

"I'm *really* happy to be here," I reiterate and am once again met by the smile that will surely be trouble.

Because it's true and for some reason, I genuinely want him to know it.

———

I arrive thirty minutes early for my first meeting with Lana Taylor.

The coffee shop she selected is just a short, fifteen-minute walk from the office. I choose a secluded corner with a view of the front door that will make it easy for her to spot me when she arrives.

I'm on my second vanilla latte, ignoring the extra jolt of

caffeine that's causing my leg to shake slightly. *Nerves?* Maybe. I just really want this to go well. When I reached out to Lana following my pitch to Graham and the rest of the team, I couldn't get a read on her level of interest, despite her being the one to reach out to me directly. Her tone was cautious, even icy, but I guess that's somewhat hard to gauge over the phone.

Over the last couple of days, I've been completely absorbed by Lana's manuscript. Reading and rereading the copy she sent over, which is now covered in scribbled comments and sticky notes, it's been easy to be completely absorbed by her words. Their ability to fill every page with a rawness and truth in an engaging way has got me more excited than I've been in a really long time. It's like this book was destined to come across my desk.

There's work to be done, sure, but after today, I'm hoping that Lana and I can roll up our sleeves and dig in. Throughout my career, *that* has always been my favorite part of this job. Helping an author transform their first draft into something bigger, more magical. It's that moment where you get to sit back and watch the sense of pride wash over someone else, and *that* moment is one I can never get enough of.

Nothing is official yet; this meeting is less of a formality and more of a chance for me to really peek behind the curtain and see if Lana is someone our team would end up working with. It's also an opportunity for her to decide if I'm the right editor to work with. Based on our brief email exchanges, my gut is telling me that this is going to be a very easy working relationship for both of us, but choosing the person to edit your work is deeply personal and I want her to see just how serious I am about her writing.

"Will Cowen?" a quiet voice interrupts my thoughts.

Glancing up at who I'm assuming is Lana, I quickly set my coffee down and stand up, extending my hand in her direction.

"Good morning...you must be Lana," I say as she places her hand in mine, shaking it firmly. Her dark hair is chopped slightly above her shoulders, complementing the sharp but kind features of her face. Dressed in loose fitting, stylish neutrals, she stands tall with a strong and poised posture—the epitome of someone dressed to handle business in a way that isn't overstated or too much.

"It's so nice to finally meet you." She's much younger than I was anticipating. In my head, I'd been picturing someone closer to my parent's age rather than mine, but this realization only makes me that much more excited to work with her. "Can I get you anything? Coffee? Tea?"

"A tea would be great," she says, taking a seat.

As I turn to grab her drink, I can feel her inquisitive gaze on me. Clearly, I'm not the only one doing the sizing up.

Sitting back down after placing her drink in front of her, I pull out my copy of Lana's manuscript and put it on the table between us.

"Straight to business?" she laughs.

"No time like the present, right?" I say, tapping the cover of the thick document. "If you don't mind me asking, how did you come across my name? This isn't normally how the whole process works."

She looks at me, uncertainty filling her dark eyes before breaking eye contact and looking down. "Long story short? It's one of those friends of a friend of a friend scenarios where I was at a party and casually mentioned I was writing something and your name was passed along. After debating whether to contact you..." she says, waving her hand in my direction, "here we are."

"Lucky me, then," I say, genuinely smiling at her. "Do you mind if I ask you something?" She nods as I lean in closer.

"You've touched on some very heavy subjects, which I can

only assume are written from some sort of personal experience
—are you prepared for that to be out in the world?"

I can see Lana's gears turning and it's immediately clear
she's someone who chooses the words she strings together with
great care.

"For me, a first-generation Japanese American whose
mother couldn't see beyond her own cultural upbringing and a
father—well, a father I've learned to stop asking questions
about...I think it's foolish to think the pain of a writer's past
doesn't inadvertently find itself woven within the heart of their
work."

She shifts her gaze toward the window as the vulnerability
of her words lingers between us—one that tugs at my heart in a
way that is far too relatable and confirms my initial gut feeling
about her *despite* the unusual nature of our paths crossing.

"That's all I needed to hear. I don't know if you've sent this
to anyone else or not...frankly, I don't care. I want to be the one
to work with you on this."

"Really?"

"Absolutely. If you choose to do so, I'd be honored to work
with you."

"Why?" she asks, her voice soft.

"Because you have a profoundly unique voice, Lana. One
that many authors would kill for. It's the reason why I wanted to
meet with you today...to tell you that in person. If you decide to
work with me, great. I can promise you that I will throw everything I have into making sure this book is your best work possible. And if not? I wanted you to hear from me that what you've
written matters, and it deserves to be shared."

She's staring at me through narrowed eyes and I'm certainly
not going to be the one to break eye contact. But after what feels
like the longest staring contest in the world, her lips pull up into
a faint smile. "Where do we start?"

Genuine relief crashes over me. I wanted this. I really, *really* wanted this.

"Well, for starters," I say, pushing her manuscript toward her, "you can begin with these minor edits."

Lana fans the pages in front of her, her eyes widening at the amount of notes and comments I'd left in the margins. "Minor edits?" she says, putting her head in her hands. "What the hell did I just sign up for?"

I laugh, reaching across the café table and patting her arm. "Oh, *this* is nothing. Just you wait."

We both start laughing as we dive into a conversation about the first couple of chapters of her book, our working relationship already starting on a high note.

Klair bombards me the second I get back to the office.

"Well?" she asks, taking a seat on my desk.

"I think it went really well. Like *really* well." Lana and I both left seemingly on the same page that we would move forward working with one another. There's a lot of paperwork to fill out on my end, but in the meantime, I gave Lana some direction to begin the editing process, which she promised to get a jumpstart on.

"That's amazing, Will. See? I told you it would."

"As always, Ms. Thompson...you were right," I say, laughing and leaning my head against her arm.

"Don't you forget it," she teases, reaching to mess up my hair.

"I would rethink that if I were you," I say, quickly pulling my head out of her reach. "Get back to work before Graham comes out here and sees you being a nuisance."

"HA HA...But the only thing Graham would see is you

looking at him with heart eyes." She gets up from my desk, sticking her tongue out at me. *This girl.*

"*Klair!* Can you *not* do that? Thanks," I say, shaking my head at her insinuation. But, I mean, she's not wrong. That man is *fine.* I fire up my computer, open a new email and begin drafting a message to Lana.

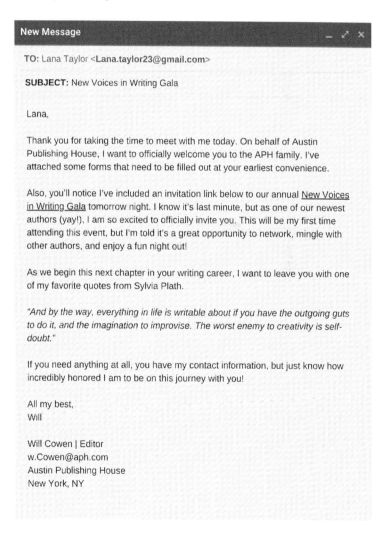

New Message

TO: Lana Taylor <**Lana.taylor23@gmail.com**>

SUBJECT: New Voices in Writing Gala

Lana,

Thank you for taking the time to meet with me today. On behalf of Austin Publishing House, I want to officially welcome you to the APH family. I've attached some forms that need to be filled out at your earliest convenience.

Also, you'll notice I've included an invitation link below to our annual New Voices in Writing Gala tomorrow night. I know it's last minute, but as one of our newest authors (yay!), I am so excited to officially invite you. This will be my first time attending this event, but I'm told it's a great opportunity to network, mingle with other authors, and enjoy a fun night out!

As we begin this next chapter in your writing career, I want to leave you with one of my favorite quotes from Sylvia Plath.

"And by the way, everything in life is writable about if you have the outgoing guts to do it, and the imagination to improvise. The worst enemy to creativity is self-doubt."

If you need anything at all, you have my contact information, but just know how incredibly honored I am to be on this journey with you!

All my best,
Will

Will Cowen | Editor
w.Cowen@aph.com
Austin Publishing House
New York, NY

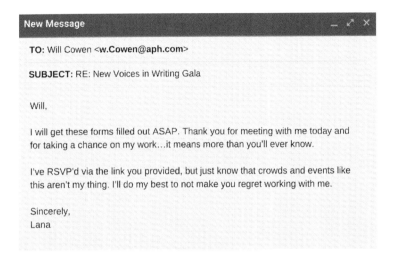

TO: Will Cowen <**w.Cowen@aph.com**>

SUBJECT: RE: New Voices in Writing Gala

Will,

I will get these forms filled out ASAP. Thank you for meeting with me today and for taking a chance on my work…it means more than you'll ever know.

I've RSVP'd via the link you provided, but just know that crowds and events like this aren't my thing. I'll do my best to not make you regret working with me.

Sincerely,
Lana

Her quick reply makes me smile—I knew I liked her for a reason—and as excited as I've been since her manuscript came across my desk, this is the first time that this whole situation has felt real. Seeing my team's excitement and interest in Lana's work and then finally meeting her in person solidified this whole thing. I just pray that my gut about her and about this book is right.

CHAPTER SIX

I'VE JUST SENT MY SEVENTH UNANSWERED TEXT TO LANA, which causes me to throw my phone clear across the room.

Tonight is the publishing house's annual New Voices in Writing Gala, one that introduces our newly signed authors to the world of publishing and allows them the opportunity to be wined, dined, and celebrated before their lives are turned upside down, especially if we all do our jobs right.

It also allows us editors to show off the fruits of our labor, and tonight was supposed to be the night I got to proudly show off my prized-acquire.

Sure, her inexperience bleeds through the pages she's sent me, but what she has is a deeply personal story that I believe will have the potential to punch any reader straight in the heart. Everything else is workable.

I place my hands on either side of my bathroom sink and lock eyes with my reflection.

"Will Cowen, this is not the time for nerves."

These pep talks started off as a way to cope with my worsening anxiety when I was younger, but lately, I've relied on them more and more as a reminder that I can do whatever "hard thing" life throws my way.

"She will be there, everyone will fawn over her, and tonight will be perfect. Get. It. Together."

Unzipping the garment bag Klair hung on the back of my door, I can't help but smile at the beautifully tailored deep-blue suit she picked out for me. One of the many, many perks of living with Klair is access to her extensive fashion knowledge. I can always count on her to make sure I'm dressed for any occasion, albeit I do have to reign her in sometimes. But not today. Today, she knocked it out of the park.

I step out of my bedroom just in time to watch Klair, decked out in an emerald slip dress and looking every bit the fashionable influencer that she is, ceremoniously pop a bottle of champagne and pour two glasses with a flourish. Her long brown hair is styled in loose curls that frame her face perfectly. Everything about Klair is over the top, from her choice in home décor to her glamorous style, but because she is so genuinely sweet, it never comes across as too much.

"Oh ok...wow! You look amazing." She hands me a rather large pour of our favorite bubbly and gives me a twirl so I can really take in every inch of her beautiful dress.

"I want to raise a toast to you, my *oldest* and dearest friend." I ignore the extra emphasis she places on my age and lift my glass to meet hers. "We've been through a lot together, you and I. But I just want to say how thankful I am to have you back in my life like this."

"We're doing one of these?" I have to keep it light or she'll have me sobbing in seconds. Not many people can sway my emotions as easily as Klair can these days.

"Shut up and let me finish. Your friendship means the world to me, Will, and I am so excited to be heading into this next chapter of our lives together just like the old days. So cheers to the leaps of faith we've taken to get to where we are today and to the ones we're about to."

Well, that did it. Klair is the only person in my entire life who truly knows me, inside and out. She knows my past—my real past—and she's never once shown me anything but kindness. She's my most fierce protector and I will never be able to repay her for that.

"I think you're trying to kill me," I say, attempting to clear the lump forming in my throat. "I don't know what I did to ever deserve a friend like you, but I hope you know that I am forever grateful we chose one another as family."

We each take a long sip from our champagne flutes, the delicious bubbly snapping me out of my emotional mood the second it touches my tongue. "Come on, let's get out of here."

Our building's expansive lobby has been completely transformed in the space of a few hours.

I'm left utterly speechless as Klair and I enter. Gorgeous drapery has been hung in every direction, creating the most intimate enclosure complete with twinkling lights, with candles on practically each surface—*this MUST be a fire hazard, no?*— and soft, live music. This entire vibe has Klair written all over it.

"Oh baby girl, you outdid yourse—" My compliment trails off as I turn to see Klair whisked into an enthusiastic embrace by random members of our team, clearly having the same reaction I am—utterly and completely shook. She mouths "Sorry" in my direction but is clearly loving everyone's reaction to her genius.

I help myself to another glass of champagne from an impeccably dressed server, mingle with my team and make introductions when necessary, and resist every urge to check my phone every five seconds. *Come on, Lana…where are you?*

The crowd parts ever so slightly, giving me the perfect view of Graham and his father, Mitch—the picture-perfect duo—charming everyone in their presence. For an older gentleman, Mitch is quite handsome and has built an enviable career with that contagious charm, a trait clearly passed on to his delicious son.

No. Not tonight...no matter how mouthwatering Graham looks in that oh-so-tight-in-all-the-right-places suit, tonight is work!

Literally shaking the beginnings of a tantalizing daydream involving a shirtless Graham and a copy room from my head, I scan the bar hoping to make eye contact with Klair. She's in her element and as much as I could use an ally right now, or even a drinking partner in crime, she deserves all the praise and attention she's receiving after pulling this event off. Downing my drink, I force myself back into the throngs of book lovers to mingle, praying that Lana gets here soon so I don't look like the most incompetent editor in the history of editing.

"She's not coming."

I can see Klair trying to find the words to make this situation better, if they even exist, but instead she just sits with me as I make another glass of champagne disappear. *Classy.*

"I know this whole thing came out of the blue, but this was supposed to be our big night, Klair..." I can feel my voice getting louder and I'm sure I'm making a scene, but right now, at this very moment, I truly don't care.

I went to bat selling the hell out of Lana's manuscript.. Everyone, and I mean *everyone*, has been buzzing about this one, and selfishly, I couldn't have been happier that it was mine.

"Listen, why don't we put down the champagne for the

YOU & I, REWRITTEN

evening..." Klair's voice is on the edge of concern. I must be close to embarrassing myself. "Let's get out of here. We can grab some burgers on our way home, watch some mindless reality television show, and put all of this out of our minds until tomorrow."

I know she's right—there's absolutely nothing I can do now to make the situation any better. Lana's phone appears to be off and the last thing I need is to be seen at a work function somewhere between publicly intoxicated and belligerent. This is just something I'll have to address later.

"Burgers and trash television with you sound heavenly right now. I'm in." But before I can move from my claimed spot at the bar, the one and only person at the entire event I desperately did *not* want seeing me like this plops himself into the empty seat right next to Klair.

"You really created something magical tonight," Graham says to Klair, a mix of relief and appreciation filling his voice. He turns to me and adds, "Good to see you, Will. I hope you're enjoying your first event as part of the team." I can't tell if he's being genuinely kind or if he's taken in the sight of the six, or is it seven, empty champagne glasses in front of me. "These things tend to be rather boring."

"What, you're not a fan of everyone orbiting around you with endless compliments and bright ideas? That doesn't seem fun to you, Teddy Graham?" *I said that out loud...Great.*

They both stare at me. Klair has a look of horror plastered across her face while Graham gives me the slightest smirk.

"Ah," he says, leaning closer and turning to Klair. I get a whiff of his cologne as he does and pick up notes of tobacco and vanilla, historically a very dangerous combo for me, but I've never smelled anything quite like *this*. "I see Mr. Cowen has been enjoying the complimentary open bar you so generously arranged for us this evening." Now turning that gorgeous mug in my direction, he adds, "It's usually a sign to call it night when you think mocking colleagues is the right move."

My heart is suddenly in my throat, threatening to choke me to death, and honestly? I'd welcome it if it got me out of this moment. I think he can see the pure panic radiating from every inch of my body, so he places a soft hand on my arm and gives me the same smile that nearly stopped my heart the other day.

"I'm just messing with you, Will."

I exhale, letting out the breath that's been trapped in my throat this whole time. *Oh thank God.* Klair's eyes flit from Graham's rather large hand which is still firmly placed on my forearm up to mine and suddenly, I realize no one is speaking.

"Well...I should probably check in with the event planner to make sure that everything is good to go for tear down," Klair says as she stands up and starts to walk away. *No, No, NO!* I mentally shout at her. "I'll check in on you boys in a moment."

And with that, she disappears back into the hustle and bustle of the event, which weirdly has gotten its second wind since I last looked, leaving Graham and me in the continued awkward silence.

As if he can read my thoughts, Graham reaches over, grabs a few customized bottles of water from behind the bar, stands, and says, "Follow me."

Which, of course, I do.

He leads me away from the hum of the event and around the corner to a makeshift seating area made up of rearranged lobby furniture. Every movement of his is fluid. He exudes an awareness of the space he takes up in this world and just moves through life so sure of every step he takes. For someone who literally slams into every wall and is the human embodiment of physical chaos, it's refreshing to see..

Before he sits, he slowly removes his satin suit jacket and

neatly folds it over the arm of the sofa, revealing an even more powerfully toned body than I could have ever imagined.

"Sit," he says, pointing to the open seat next to him, which I do immediately. Maybe a little too forcefully, because the combination of my awkward movements and the two of us being over six feet tall causes my thigh to brush up against his. The closeness causes a tingling wave of electricity to radiate across my body that is almost impossible to ignore. "Is everything ok?" he asks quietly but full of concern, as if he's nervous to hear my answer.

I don't know what the right thing to do here is: Do I downplay it all and tell him that everything is fine? Do I answer honestly and explain what I'm truly feeling? Or do I tell him all I want to do is rip him out of that tux.

"Well, let's see...aside from the crippling fear that I look like a complete failure to my team because my one author didn't show up tonight?" I say with as much dramatic sarcasm as I can muster. Leaning closer, I look him dead in the eye. "Or maybe I'm just relieved it didn't take you too much longer to figure out a clever and convenient way to get me alone."

There is no taking a statement like that back, drunk or not. Despite the alcohol coursing through my veins, everything about this moment snaps into crystal clear focus. I want him. I want Graham Austin in every way imaginable and when I see his perfectly stoic face crack into the slightest smile at my clunky forwardness, I could combust right then and there.

I'm well aware that I'm accidently invading the space between us and potentially leaping head-first over some professional lines, but tonight, I'm giving myself a pass on overthinking. For once, I don't want to obsess over consequences or insecurities. Graham is without a doubt the sexiest man I've ever seen and if I have anything to say about it, those delicious lips will be on mine any moment now.

"Your author didn't show...so what? I can't tell you how many times I've been stood up by an author who slipped down the creative rabbit hole. And honestly? I'm glad she didn't show up." I scoff at this feeble attempt at making me feel better. He's not the one who looked like an idiot tonight. "It probably means she's lost in some story idea based on feedback you've given her. At the end of the day, she's providing you updates and chapters, right?" I nod, not breaking eye contact. "There you go...that's all that matters. Who cares if she didn't show up to some lame dinner party. There will be plenty of time for that once the book is published."

Not convinced that his words made me feel any better, he continues, "Will, believe me when I say this isn't on you. No one is upset. No one views you any differently. Things happen." Not realizing how badly I needed to hear these words from someone I admire professionally, I lean back and physically feel my shoulders relax. He's right...of course he's right. Lana is a grown woman, and I can't control the actions of others. For the first time this evening, my anxiety wanes and I'm able to exhale.

"Thank you, Graham." I angle my body so I'm looking at him more directly. "I don't know why I get like this sometimes... where the little things become overwhelming, and the big things become insurmountable."

That confession was a lot deeper than I intended to go with a man I had confidently assumed would be making out with me by now. He doesn't appear to be bothered by the sudden turn our conversation has taken. Per usual, Graham is looking at me with his full focus, giving the gravity of our conversation the attention it deserves.

"I really am passionate about this job and sometimes, I can't separate my emotions when I have important things going on. I guess that's not the best thing to admit to someone you work with and um, *kinda* for, huh?"

"I'm going to stop you right there, Will." He literally puts his hand up in my face and drunk-me is tempted to high-five it. I don't. "There is absolutely nothing wrong with recognizing how we each react to stress and anxiety. Trust me when I say I've been there, done that. There is no shame in being in-tune with our emotional and mental health needs." He sits up straighter and soft, attentive Graham is suddenly replaced with serious, I-mean-business Graham. "But if anyone in this organization, regardless of who they are, makes you feel otherwise, I need you to tell me immediately. I have a zero-tolerance policy when it comes to these kinds of issues, and I know my father feels the same way."

I've never questioned Graham's dedication to this company before, but tonight, here in this cluttered corner of our building's lobby, I'm getting a glimpse at just how strong and selfless of a leader this man is.

"Because at the end of the day, the work can wait. There is *nothing* more important than our people." As if I couldn't be swooning any harder over this man, he adds, "Which now includes you, Will."

Dead. Deceased. Graham has single-handedly taken my anxiety about a potential professional mishap, understood it, given it value, and then thrown it out the literal window. All while looking like this? I think he might be a unicorn?

Despite the weirdness and tension and *whatever* the hell all of that was from our initial meeting, I stare in awe of the man who's been in my life for barely any time at all. Somehow, he's managed to make me feel *seen* and *understood* in this moment hidden away from the music and our colleagues and the pressure of it all.

"Oh God, I deserve this hangover. I really do," I say to an already showered and glamorous Klair as I move slowly from my bedroom to the kitchen. "Coffee. Now," I growl, my head throbbing with every step. *Note to self: complimentary champagne doesn't mean you have to drink it ALL.* She's already two-steps ahead of me, with two piping hot mugs already poured on the counter. "You're a goddess, Klair...don't you *ever* forget that."

She laughs as I take a deep sip, willing the caffeine to bring me back to life.

"And you're going to make us late if you don't start getting ready *now.*"

Sighing as loud as humanly possible, I stomp back to my room, wincing in pain with every movement of my body. *Never. Drinking. Again.* I mentally chant this lie repeatedly as I cut my morning routine to just under twenty minutes. Despite dragging my feet all morning and the fact that my head feels like it's *literally* going to explode, we still get to work early.

I keep thinking about last night and how foolish I probably appeared to Graham. Even though he met the entire situation with kindness and used it as a moment for professional mentorship, I still feel like I failed. Looking at his office, I notice he hasn't made it into work yet, so I decide to use the next couple of free minutes to leave him a little note of appreciation for last night. After debating what to write for what feels like an eternity, I settle for simple. Can't go wrong with straight and to the point, right?

Teddy Graham—is that a thing? I'll stop. Maybe.

Thank you for last night...
I really appreciated it!
-W

Before placing the note on Graham's desk, my eyes wander over the framed art and personal photographs, books, and memorabilia displayed in his office. For being so Type-A, he's sure got a lot of stuff. I spy a photograph of a very handsome Graham at his college graduation standing side-by-side with Mitch, whose face radiates pride and love for his son. There are ticket stubs to the premier of Wonder Woman—a closeted comic book nerd? *Sexy*—and a signed Los Angeles Lakers basketball. *Who is this guy?* I head over to Graham's desk, admiring the neat lines of his handwriting on his calendar when the sound of the opening door startles me. *Shit...shit...SHIT!*

"What are you doing?" Graham's inquisitive voice pierces through the silent office, causing me to drop my note. I look up to see him standing against his now closed door, arms crossed and an amused look on his face. At least he doesn't *seem* mad?

"I...I was just...I'm so sorry." I bend down to pick up my dropped note—*THUMP*, smacking my head on the edge of Graham's desk in the process. My ears are suddenly ringing and my vision's blurred and for the briefest of moments, two very concerned-looking Grahams are heading directly toward me.

"Ughhh, oh my god. I'm fine...This is fine." I grab my head, trying not to shout at the top of my lungs, but before I can die of embarrassment, Graham's immediately by my side, his strong hands on my arms guiding me to his desk chair.

Beyond a bruised ego and a little dizziness, I seem to be okay.

"And what do we have here?" Picking up my note from the floor while keeping one hand firmly on my shoulder, a smile forms across that handsome face of his after reading it.

"Is this going to be our thing now?" he asks, sliding the note into the pocket of his dress pants.

"I should probably get back to my desk..." I stammer out, standing to make my escape as quickly as possible.

Graham keeps his hand on my shoulder, clearly sensing, and probably feeling, the unsteadiness of my movements. There it is again...that same spark of electricity I felt last night. The heat radiating from his touch only amplifies the pull I feel toward him and sends a very untimely dose of desire throughout my entire body. I'd be lying if I said I didn't want more.

Searching Graham's expression for some sort of guidance on what is going on, I can't tell if what I am seeing is concern, kindness, or pity. Could it possibly be lust? The seconds slow as I stare deep into his eyes and I find myself wanting to know everything there is to know about what makes this man who now has me sweating, tick.

"Thank you, again...for last night, and I guess for right now?" I mumble as I turn to leave, giving Graham one last glance over before stepping out his office.

I watch as his full lips part and I hear him take a deep inhale. "It was my pleasure." I might still be disoriented from the desk's assault on my head, but I swear his gaze has now shifted from my eyes to my lips—the subtle move leaving me more dazed than any head injury could render me. Forcing myself to abandon whatever staring contest this has now become, I exit his office and head back down the hall toward my desk. I'm physically unable to ignore the prickling sensation that he's following my every movement. *What. The. Hell.*

I'm going to save time by accepting that the next several hours will be spent overanalyzing every second of that interaction. So, while my brain takes a sharp nose-dive into flirty Graham territory, I'm blissfully unaware that Klair is standing right behind me. When she finally announces her presence, I all but jump out of my skin. I just might *actually* have a concussion.

"Alright, who's got you sitting over here drooling?"

I can feel myself turning red from her public audacity and the truth behind her words. "Okay, I was initially joking, my sweet little cubicle bestie, but now I think I need a real answer... Is it a boy? Was it last night at the event? Oh my gosh, is it Josh from H.R.?" I can practically hear her wheels turning.

Totally embarrassed by one, her assumption that I would *ever* be into Josh and two, her inquisition into my nonexistent dating life, I know that she's not going to let this go until I give her all the details.

"Can you *please* keep it down," I hiss, looking around to see who else might be paying attention to her oh-so-professional outburst. "I am *definitely* not into Josh."

I lay it all out there. The elevator ride and the moment in the parking garage where I had invited him to dinner, how he seemed interested at first, but then shot me down. About him pulling me aside last night at the Gala and the kindness he showed me. About the electricity I feel every time we touch. And then the stare. Klair is hanging on my every word and the more I divulge, the bigger her smile gets.

"Wait...our Graham?" Klair asks after all but picking her jaw up off the office floor. "Graham Austin? The same work-obsessed Graham who silences an entire meeting with a single questioning eyebrow raise?"

"The very same."

"You do realize how rare this is, right?" she asks, leaning back in her chair. "In my four years of working with him, I've barely seen Graham have *any* sort of interaction that isn't work-related. Like I wouldn't be surprised if that man slept in his office. And forget dating. I've never seen him show a single ounce of interest in anyone. Like, ever."

As she goes on, I can't contain the smile forming at the thought of Graham potentially being interested in me. I know that I'm a catch and even consider myself semi-attractive, but compared to Graham, I feel completely plain. And that's just visually...I don't even want to start comparing myself to him professionally.

Still, I can't stop myself from getting caught up in the visual of the two of us together in that quiet corner last night, so seemingly comfortable with one another. I can still feel his strong and sure grip on my arm, and I know that if I'm being honest with myself, I definitely want to feel it again. But does he? Klair seems to think so. He certainly has an effect on me. For someone who has always been naturally uncoordinated and in constant battle with his long limbs, I feel myself turning into an even bigger klutz around him—which is less than ideal. At our team huddle earlier, he mentioned that he would be accompanying his father out of town for a few days and while the thought of *not* seeing Graham leaves me feeling off—we'll address that much later because, *yikes*—it'll be nice to clear my head, develop a plan and figure out a way to calm the hell down whenever he's around.

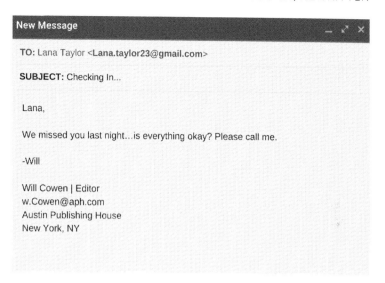

CHAPTER SEVEN

GRAHAM HAS ONLY BEEN GONE FOR LESS THAN TWO WORK days but his absence is felt in every moment of my day in the office. The more I immerse myself with this team, the more I realize just how big of a role Graham plays in all of it. From overseeing the branding and marketing to crafting perfectly timed schedules, launches, and press releases, Graham is single-handedly doing the work of multiple departments. Perfectly, I might add. And the more I see this, the more inspired and intrigued I am to get to know the *real* him.

For the life of me, I can't get his deep burning gaze out of my mind. I'm not ashamed enough to admit that I've been fantasizing about how intoxicating it felt to have his strong and sure hands on me. Klair literally just kicked me during our last meeting regarding who knows what while shaking her head, as if she was privy to the endless loop playing in my head of a shirtless Graham. I can almost hear her sneer *Get it together, William.*

I force my attention back to *anything* pertaining to books and publishing or even forming coherent, safe-for-work sentences, and pray that the final hours of my day fly by. It's

Klair's birthday after all, and despite these confusing feelings I have about Graham not being here, I am so excited to spoil her in person for the first time in years. Because when it comes to Klair, I've learned to expect nothing but the unexpected.

"Will, if you don't take this shot right now, I will never, *ever* forgive you," Klair shouts over the deafening bass, shoving another dangerous vodka shooter in my face. We've made our way into the heart of New York City nightlife and Klair is in her element. Dressed with the intention to turn every head in the club, and succeeding, she beams in her party attire, a tight and sequined gold plunge dress, complete with the obligatory "Birthday Bitch" sash and matching tiara. *Subtle.*

I've always said if I was straight, I'd marry Klair on the spot. Beyond her obvious beauty, she has the kindest, most selfless heart and truly makes everyone feel better about themselves. I can't help but laugh as she wraps her arms around my neck and smashes our faces together, looking me right in the eye.

"Look, I know you're missing our *fearless* leader." Her words are only slightly slurred thanks to the unknown amount of shots she's been sneaking behind my back. "But please have fun tonight. I want you to...AHH! Oh my god, you came."

Klair, who is making my ears bleed with her deafening screams, sprints—well, tries to...she is wearing sky-high heels after all—and launches into the open arms of a tall, devilishly handsome stranger. Waving me over, she turns and is suddenly more radiant than before. Despite the dim lighting, I can see how wide her smile is, looking up at who I can only assume is Dean, the guy she claims she's just casually dating.

Casual, huh? She's a goner.

I remind myself to grill her about the seriousness of this new development as I reach out to shake Dean's hand but instead, he pulls me in for a hug. Like, not a bro-hug; an actual I'm-a-straight-man-who's-comfortable-with-my-sexuality hug.

"I have been begging Klair to finally introduce us, man." Dean's excitement is endearing and I can tell he's being genuine. He lets me go, flashing the most adorable, crooked smile. He's about my height and by the fit of his very stylish outfit—*Klair must have gotten to him*—it's clear that this guy enjoys staying active. But as eager as Dean appears to be meeting me, he seems desperate to get Klair on the dance floor. The two of them disappear into the sea of bodies with her turning back to give me a wink. Instead of returning to my spot at the bar, I down my drink and join them.

Klair and Dean, already settled into their rhythm by the time I make my way to them, excitedly welcome me to their spot on the dance floor. Dean hands me another shot he's mysteriously acquired, flashing that grin one more time, and the spell Klair is clearly under makes sense.

"Cheers!" he shouts as we clink our glasses together. "To our stunning birthday girl."

And suddenly, I'm no longer with them because Klair, who is the human embodiment of a heart-eye emoji—or the smirking devil one, let's be honest—grabs Dean by the neck and kisses him with everything she's got.

The burn of the shots catches up to me so I turn to make my way back to the bar to grab a water when I feel a pair of rather large hands grab my waist. It's been a while since I've been out like this, but instead of recoiling from the stranger's touch, I let the music guide my body, now in sync with my new dance partner.

He doesn't say anything as he pulls my toned body against his and I'm fine with that. I don't even turn around to see whose body I'm grinding into, but when I feel his hot breath on my neck and the grip on my hips tightens, I feel the deep pull of arousal course through my veins. I position us so I can still keep an eye on Klair, who at this point has been lifted off the ground and has herself wrapped around Dean. *Ok girl...I see you.* Clearly, the two of them are *just* fine.

Not knowing who I'm dancing with only intensifies my confidence. At the end of the day, it is not about whoever this strange man is, but instead, it's about feeling powerful and desirable. I close my eyes and let go of my loosened inhibitions, allowing the music to vibrate to my core. I push back against my stranger, feeling his arousal with every movement. I could get used to feeling this powerful and attuned to my body.

As the drum of the beat accentuates our every movement, I can't help but wish that it was Graham I was pushing up against. That it was Graham's perfect lips brushing against my neck. The thought of Graham alone sends me spiraling into the depths of lust and I never want to leave. But even in the simmer of this moment, nothing compares to how I feel around Graham. There is something so magnetic about being around him, as if at any moment I'm going to physically combust. I can almost feel the intensity of his stare.

No, wait, I can literally feel those piercing hazel eyes on me. But he's not supposed to be home until tomorrow?

I look up and Graham and I lock eyes, my own personal voyeur standing in the shadows, arms crossed and brow furrowed. There is no mistaking those broad shoulders and I swallow hard as I take in his bulging biceps for the first time thanks to his fitted, short-sleeved polo shirt. More prominent in the stage lighting, his immaculately trimmed stubble accentuates a bone structure that would make the ancient Greeks quake with jealousy.

Emboldened by the liquor and driven by an overwhelming desire for this man, I leave my interim dance partner without a single word and weave my way toward Graham through the growing, panting crowd.

Finally making it to the wall where Graham had just stood, calling to me like the most delicious siren there ever was, he is now nowhere to be found, seemingly disappearing into thin air from one second to the next. Heading toward the exit, more determined than ever to see the man who has been monopolizing so much space in my mind, I pass the long line of eager bodies ready to unwind, round the corner, and slam directly into the solid mass of a man leaning against the side of the club.

"I hadn't realized I was in the presence of such a captivating dancer." Graham's voice is playful but I can sense a tinge of something bitter. Jealousy?

I hate how much I like that.

His large hands are placed squarely on my chest as I raise my gaze to meet his.

Please don't look drunk. Please don't look drunk. I repeat the words in my head, noticing the delay in my movements. *Why does he have this effect on me?*

"You should have come out and joined us, Mr. Austin." I playfully poke his arm...his very solid and toned arm that I am now noticing has a tattoo peeking out from his tight sleeve. He looks incredibly good in a form-fitting maroon polo tucked into dark gray slacks, paired with a simple pair of loafers. Polished and effortless. *Klair would approve.*

Distracted by everything about this man, I don't even notice Graham has shifted our position ever so slightly until my back is pressed securely against the wall. My breath catches at the realization that we are just inches apart at this point. Inches that could so easily be removed if I were to just step a little closer to him, but his firm grip is holding me steady.

Am I that drunk that he feels the need to support me right now? Oh my god...I'm sloppy.

"Clearly you were having fun...who am I to interrupt?" Graham is most definitely teasing me. Before I can respond, he adds, "Besides, I've never been one to share."

I swallow hard at his admission. *That means he wants me all to himself, right?* Instantly, my heart rate begins to quicken and I can't stop stealing glances at that tattoo that is just begging to make an appearance.

"Aren't you supposed to be in Baltimore until Monday?" I ask, not necessarily trying to deflect or change the subject, but definitely needing to give my poor heart a break. "Did you wrap up early?"

Graham visibly tenses at the mention of Baltimore and lowers his gaze to the ground as he takes a step back. "I was needed back in the office." His tone is vastly different from before and disappointment washes over me as he creates more distance between the two of us.

Clearly, something went down on the road that bothered him. Or maybe drama back in the office?

"Well, I'm glad you're back," I say, trying to ease the tension. Besides, it's the truth. Being around him is exhilarating, and after spending the week obsessing over his brilliant mind, having him in front of me again is like Christmas.

Ever so slowly, Graham looks me in the eye with that stop-you-in-your-tracks smile. "Is that so?" he asks as he cocks his head to the side, his eyes zeroing in on mine.

All of my efforts to calm my heart have completely gone out the window as I feel him closing the space between us again, his movements like that of a hungry predator stalking its prey. This man is utterly intoxicating, even more potent than the shots Klair forced upon me earlier. From the warm and spicy scent of his cologne to the clear strength behind his hold, I am in trouble with Graham.

His face gets closer to mine, seemingly in slow motion, and

I'm afraid to move in case I ruin the moment. At the feel of his waist pressed against mine, I can't help but struggle against his hold on me.

"Graham," I all but moan, trying to get more of him to touch more of me. Normally, I'd be humiliated that some man is causing these sounds to come out of my mouth, but with him, I want him to know the effect he's having on me.

All of a sudden, he's pressing me into the wall, the full weight of him against my body. I don't know when or how he managed to get both of my wrists in the vice-like grip of his hands, but I will never, *ever* complain about it. I can feel his cock throb against mine, clear now to both of us this is what we want. *Of course he's massive.*

I keep waiting for the kiss to come, to crash over me like it has in my dreams and mid-meeting fantasies, but it never does. Our breathing is matched as he slowly grinds into me, exhaling desire and inhaling one another. Out of the most delicious sexual frustration, I open my eyes to find Graham gazing so intently at me, ever so slightly biting his lower lip.

I should be the one doing that.

Graham, looking conflicted on what to say or do next, leans forward and slowly plants a lingering kiss to my cheek. His stubble burns every nerve ending as he releases my hands and whispers in my ear, "Don't be late Monday, Will," causing me to melt at the feeling of his lips on my ear.

As he turns and walks away, I'm left throbbing, panting, and with my damn mind blown into fragments of pure lust for this man. Taking a moment to collect myself and ensure any visible signs that my, *er*, arousal is no longer on display, I head back into the sea of horny and tangled bodies in search of Klair and any excuse to not go running after the man who just turned my world upside down.

My entire weekend was spent overanalyzing what Klair proudly nicknamed "The Wall Treatment" on our way home from the club. At least there isn't any confusion as to whether or not Graham is into me. At least physically, I could sense how his body reacted to mine and I could feel just how badly he wanted me. As I try to sort through a weekend's worth of emails and map out my to-do list for the day ahead, my mind is consumed by the delicious ache of his dick against mine and the way his scruff felt against my skin.

We haven't even kissed yet. I'm hopeless.

I forcefully push these distracting thoughts from my brain, which happen to be getting dirtier by the second, and attempt to get some work done.

By the time lunch rolls around, I'm wondering why I haven't had my usual Graham sighting by now. Usually, I see him fast-walking between meetings or popping over to his team's desks to deliver due-outs in his cool but direct manner. Under normal circumstances, I would find myself antsy, waiting to see his handsome face, but now, I feel completely undone as if he's ignited something inside of me that can only be extinguished by his presence. *Or his lips.*

My mind begins to wander to all the places I'd like those lips to travel when Graham makes a hurried entrance through the writer's section and all but slams his office door. Despite looking as put together as ever, I can tell something is off. Not knowing if I should check on him or if that would be weird, I gather my things and head to meet Klair at our favorite bistro around the block instead, which serves the most mouth-watering autumn squash soup. At the thought of food, I realize I've worked straight through my usual breakfast and am instantly starving.

CHAPTER EIGHT

FEELING MUCH MORE MYSELF AFTER AN UNNECESSARILY large lunch and catch-up with Klair, I head back to my desk, ready to take on the rest of the afternoon. I'd been right in the middle of going over several marketing and social media plans before lunch and I am eager to pick up where I left off. The ping of my email inbox pulls my attention from the document in my hand and I notice it's an email from Lana, who all but fell off the face of the earth after the gala.

This'll be good.

It has taken all of my professional willpower to refrain from sending her an angry message loaded with jabs about common courtesy and honoring the commitments that we make, and as I open her message, I exhale away any temporary irritation I feel.

TO: Will Cowen <w.Cowen@aph.com>

SUBJECT: PLEASE forgive me

Will,

First and foremost, I am so sorry for my unprofessional behavior. I can only imagine what you must think of me, and honestly, I deserve it. The idea of attending that gala, despite it being a once in a lifetime honor, overwhelmed the hell out of me. Mingling, being somewhat the center of attention, and having to talk about my ideas truly skyrocketed my anxiety and instead of communicating that with you - someone who has only shown me kindness and support - I froze and went silent. There is no excuse that will justify my behavior, but I hope you know that it had nothing to do with you and I truly am sorry.

After speaking with Graham last week, I can assure you that this will never happen again. I will do the work, communicate with you better, and I promise you I won't just disappear again. You deserve better than that; this novel deserves better than that. If you give me another chance, I promise you I will show you how much working together means to me.

Respectfully,
Lana

There is an instant wave of burning heat radiating over every inch of my body. She *spoke with Graham? What the hell? When?* I slam my laptop shut, way harder than intended, and push away from my desk, causing Klair to jump in her seat, a confused look on her face at my outburst.

I try to stabilize my now irregular breaths, each one searing my lungs as if the air I'm inputting into my body is laced with razors. I am enraged. *Graham doesn't think I can do my job. Graham doesn't think I can handle this. That's the only explanation as to why he would intervene.*

Anger isn't an emotion I'm used to feeling, but right now, in this moment, I feel betrayed, like the one person I've been working my ass off to impress, both personally and professionally, has had a good laugh behind my back and has taken matters into his own hands.

Anxiety, doubt, and utter self-loathing, the emotions and negative thoughts I try so hard to keep buried, come bursting through the surface with unparalleled force. My usual self-talk and regulated breathing is powerless to how I'm feeling right now and I know the only thing that will release some of the tension and frustration I'm feeling is to talk to Graham and figure out his reasoning.

"Will, what's going on? Are you okay?"

I ignore the clear worry in Klair's voice as I beeline toward Graham's office door, forcing it open, and slamming it shut behind me. Hard.

His head snaps up from whatever it is he's working on and I see the start of a smile splash across his face, but that all changes the second I open my mouth.

"Is there a reason you went behind my back and spoke to my author without me?" My tone is pure ice. "I just want to know why you felt compelled to leave me out of something this important?" I stand there, my body tense from the betrayal I feel, arms crossed to show just how closed off to him I am.

He silently closes the book he was reading and sets down his coffee. I narrow my eyes as he rises from his chair and steps around his desk, buttoning his navy suit jacket in the process. He closes the distance between us, each thoughtful step seemingly slower than the last to really accentuate the heaviness of my anxiety in this moment. He doesn't stop until he is right in front of me, so close that I can smell his spicy cologne and the faint remnants of caffeine.

"I'm going to stop you right there," he says, staring me down. His expression is soft, concerned even, but his eyes could burn a hole right through my heart. *Shit.* "I am not one to devalue the feelings of others, especially you of all people, Will. But I think now is an important moment to remind you of professional decorum in the workplace." He is every bit the dismissive and blunt man I met on my first day. I attempt to swallow the lump that is lodged in my throat. I know I've just crossed so many professional lines and made a spectacle in the office. I can all but feel the stares of our team on the other side of the door eagerly trying to figure out what's going on inside of Graham's office.

"Because at the end of the day, the success and failures of our team fall on *me*," he says as he jabs a finger sharply into his own chest. He takes another step closer, his dominating presence overwhelming. "Yes, I ended up speaking to Lana after our conversation at the event. Her not showing up after the time and effort *my* team has given her writing was a bad look and I wanted to remind her that *you*, as her editor, deserved better, and if we were going to continue a working relationship, she needed to treat you with the respect that comes with your expertise."

His words are a punch straight in the gut. *Of course* Graham involved himself and it literally had nothing to do with me because he's right, this is his team and his family's business. Hell, he was on some level defending me. Tears threaten to betray me in a moment when I need to appear strong.

I have to get out of here.

"Your feelings are valid, Will." He steps around me, brushing my shoulder gently as he passes to open the door, sending that all too familiar electric spark across my skin, leaving me rooted in place. "But going forward, I'd urge you to remember that I don't need to run the way we do business by *you*. Is there anything else you so urgently need to get off your chest? Or can we all get back to work?" His cold tone is my dismissal.

He's standing in his now open doorway, our team clearly trying their best to appear busy and not at all vested in the alpha male throw down that just occurred in Graham's office.

Move, Will. MOVE. You look like such a pathetic idiot right now. He knows it, the entire office now knows it...you know it.

I don't want to face him. I don't think my heart could handle another Graham Austin stare-down right now, so I quickly turn and exit his office without raising my gaze to meet him. As I head down the hallway toward my desk, I see Klair out of the corner of my eye, my jacket and phone already in an outstretched hand. Klair, whose eyes are brimming with sympathy and concern, doesn't wait for me to say anything when I get to her—I don't think I could right now without completely breaking down in tears.

"Go," she says gingerly rubbing my arm. "I'll cover you for the rest of the day if anything pertinent pops up. Go home, relax, and I'll be there soon."

It's in moments like this that I'm most appreciative for the relationship I have with Klair.

Succumbing to the nagging voice in the back of my mind telling me to *turn around*, I risk another glance in Graham's direction. His tall and muscular body appears slumped as he leans into his office's door frame. Our eyes meet for the briefest of moments, his face scrunched with confusion, and I watch as he releases a fractured breath, turning away from me and closing his door behind him...closing his door on me. *Closing the door on the hope of us.*

"Well, there's another thing I've ruined," I mutter to myself as I exit the heavy double doors of our office, dragging the weight of my shame with me.

"God, Klair...I fucked up so bad." I'm in full panic mode and poor Klair is doing everything in her power to help me come down from this as we sit together on the couch, her arms around me. "I barged into his office like some dramatic asshole, demanding answers and speaking to him so cruelly. Not only did I humiliate myself professionally, I treated the guy I am *so* into like trash." I drop my head into my hands, feeling Klair rub my back.

"I have to admit I was a little shocked this afternoon." Klair's voice is tiptoeing the line of worry and bluntness. "I've never seen that side of you before." I'm instantly humiliated, which I know wasn't her intention, but hearing the surprise in Klair's voice shows just how out of line I was earlier.

I lean my head against hers. "I can't come up with a valid excuse for my behavior. There is none." The tears I've been holding back all evening now begin to fall. "Sometimes, I just can't rein in my emotions. Seeing that email from Lana made me feel so incapable." My confession releases the grip it has had on my heart for a while and now I'm full-blown sobbing into Klair's shoulder. "It made me feel like he didn't think I was good enough."

Klair, who's clearly struggling to shift against the weight of my body, turns to face me. "Will, you look at me right now." She takes my face in her hands and wipes my tears with her thumbs. "I'm not going to sit here and tell you how you're feeling is wrong because on some level, you believe those things to be true, which absolutely breaks my heart." Her voice cracks and she pulls me into a hug. "But there is not a single soul in your life who thinks you're not good enough. I hope you know by now that Graham is for sure included in that statement."

I'd like to be able to say *Of course I know that, silly*, but I never know where I stand with that man. One moment he's thrusting against me out of nowhere at the bar and the next he's staring daggers into my soul. Do I think he is sexually attracted to me? Maybe. Do I think he likes me? Absolutely not at this moment. He *most definitely* loathes me.

"Ehhh, I'm not so sure about that." *Not anymore at least.* Untangling myself from Klair, I give her a kiss on the top of her head. "I can't thank you enough for tonight. You have no idea how much just sitting here with me means. I'm going to take a shower and try to calm down."

"I love you forever, Will Cowen." she says as I head to my room. "Nothing will ever change that."

"I know, and I love you more, Klair Thompson," I shout over my shoulder before closing my bedroom door.

Right now, the only thing that sounds good is letting the scalding water of my shower release some of the tension I feel across every inch of my body. I light my favorite candles, put Taylor Swift on shuffle and head into my bathroom, stripping along the way. Stepping into the heat of the cascading water is an almost instant relief from the pounding headache I've had all afternoon. Massaging my favorite mint shampoo into my hair, the thought of Graham comes crashing into my momentary peace...the sound of his voice, his smile, those big hands and how they felt on me.

Arousal burns through my veins, outweighing any other thought right now, and I feel myself harden as I let my hands trail over the peaks of my chest, the defined sections of my stomach. I grip my cock at the thought of Graham grinding against me, his thick bulge pressed against mine. I moan remembering just how good it felt having him against me, feeling his desire match my own. As I start to slide my hand along my length, I picture what could have been if Graham hadn't walked away that night. I see him grabbing my hips and pulling me closer to him.

Fuck, this feels so good.

In this fantasy, I watch him turn me around so fast and push me up against the wall, spreading my legs and biting my neck as I push back against him. *God, I need this to happen. NOW.* I begin moving faster, the promise of release getting oh so close the more I think about Graham. His toned body. The way he says my name. Everything about him intoxicates me and despite what happened today, I want this man so fucking bad it's killing me—I need him.

I feel myself reaching the point of no return, knowing my body and how desperate it is for release. I continue stroking my now throbbing cock, the anticipation building higher and higher...*thump, thump, thump.*

"Will," Klair shouts behind my bathroom door, causing me to completely freeze, dick in hand. "Can you please come out here?" I sigh looking down at my now limp member.

Sorry old friend, moment's passed...isn't living with a girl so fun?

I finish, not in the way I wanted to, in the shower, towel off, and quickly throw on some sweats.

"What is *sooo* important that you interrupted..." my voice trails off as I stare that answer right in the eye.

"Hi, Will." Graham's voice is much kinder than it had been earlier, but my nerves are instantly shot seeing him here in our apartment. "Do you have a second?" He's soaking wet and completely disheveled, a look I've yet to see on him, but he's as beautiful as ever.

Klair stares down Graham, glances at me, and then back to our dripping visitor, her knowing eyes narrowing. "Well...Dean and I are going to grab a bite to eat so you guys take all the time you need." Turning to me, she says, "But if you need anything, my handsome bestie...give me a call and I will come back immediately to deal with this one. Even if his name's on the building, I'll still kick his ass."

Graham clears his throat. "I heard that," he says with a smirk.

"Good, you were meant to." Klair sticks her tongue out at him and throws a towel in his direction, grabs her jacket and purse, and heads out the door, leaving the two of us alone.

*It's like he just stepped out of that shower with me...*I blush and pray he doesn't notice.

He laughs, looking out after her as he runs his hand through his hair. I'm learning now that this may be a nervous tick, a sign that he's slightly out of his element. I watch as he attempts to towel dry himself off. Turning his attention back to me, his eyes appear tired and red. *Has he been crying?*

"Will, I'm sorry for just showing up like this." He sounds unsure, which is so unlike the Graham I know during business hours. "But I just had to see you...to make sure that you were okay." Before even giving me a chance to respond, he's directly in front of me with his hands on my arms, searching my face. "Are you okay?"

I shrug, which he interprets as my body telling him to not touch me, so I grab his hand and pull him toward the couch. "Sit with me for a second?" *I have no idea what to say to him. Hell, I don't even know what to say to myself!* Sitting there next to Graham, who clearly has been worried about me, I find myself relaxing for the first time since the entire ordeal earlier today. I reach over and squeeze his hand, a gesture that feels slightly too intimate for this moment but he doesn't seem to mind. I run my thumb over the prominent veins on the top of his hand, memorizing each and every line and the way it feels in mine.

Lifting my gaze to his, I stare into those beautiful eyes, scared to open up to the man who makes me feel this deeply already. "Graham, I owe you the biggest apology. I was beyond out of line and for that, I'm truly, truly sorry." I've never been one to shy away from apologizing. It's something I feel is so important in every relationship, regardless of the nature, but owning up to Graham, showing him that I know I messed up...I just hope he knows it's genuine. *He has to.*

"I don't even care about that, Will. All I care about is that you're okay." His confession makes my heart contract. *Does he care about me?* "I'd like to think that I've gotten to know you over these last few weeks and it was clear to me something was off." He squeezes my hand, smiling at me in the most reassuring way imaginable.

"No, you're right." Vulnerability is not my strength. I know this and for the last ten, fifteen-ish years, I've gotten by just fine pretending that everything in my life is perfect. Sure, I can open up to Klair, but that's only because she's been in my life longer than anyone else. *And because she's been there through it all.*

But Graham deserves more from me. As a teammate and as...whatever else he might become.

"I was trying to explain this to Klair earlier, but there are these times in my life when it's incredibly difficult for me to separate logic from emotion. My brain and my heart battle each other sometimes. As much as I hate that it happens, my emotions overpower any sort of logic in those moments. And well...you were on the receiving end of what that looks like. My insecurities skyrocket, my self-doubt explodes, and I'm left questioning anything and everything."

There's something so new in his expression, as if he's been trying to figure me out all this time and the final piece just clicked into place. It's disarming and overwhelming, but I never want him to stop looking at me like this. He reaches over, ever so slowly, and puts a warm hand on the side of my face.

"Please tell me you know that there's nothing wrong with that?" he all but whispers. I lean into the warmth of his hand and close my eyes, afraid if I keep gazing into the intensity of his stare, I'll break apart again. "I've always believed our emotions and our passion are a sign of strength. If we're sharing our truths right now...It's no surprise that I may come across as detached or emotionless. In the office, I know I'm direct...but that doesn't mean I wouldn't *want* to connect more socially with everyone." He looks down, dropping his hand from my face. *No, please put it back.* "But you, you so clearly aren't afraid to show the world your warmth and that you have this big, kind heart. Never apologize for that."

Hearing Graham open up about his own struggles with emotional connection makes me want him even more. *Is that even possible at this point?* It takes every ounce of self-restraint to not lunge at this man.

He looks back up at me, his eyes filled with all the compassion in the world and says, "While I was only trying to do my job, I hope you know that it was never my intention to hurt you, Will. Or make you feel the way you did." His sincerity touches me in a way I wasn't expecting. If I was drawn to competent and commanding Graham before, this side of him is something else entirely. Something I've never experienced. "Because the way you looked at me..." His voice cracks. "I never, *ever* want to make you look at me like that again. I don't think I could handle it."

His admission leaves me speechless. *Tell him how you feel. Tell him what his words mean to you. Tell him SOMETHING.*

"Graham...I..." I'm struggling to find words worthy of his, but I reach back over, taking his warm hand in mine again. "I just hope you know how sorry I am and that nothing like that will ever happen again in the office. I'll give you my word." Graham smiles, giving my hand another squeeze before he releases it and stands.

"Thank you for saying that, Will. I forgive you just as I hope you forgive me." I nod my head. "It's late and we've both got an early morning tomorrow, but I will say this," he says from the doorway, his hand on the knob. He turns to face me, his eyes glance from my eyes to my lips and I can feel the anticipation radiating off his body, the spark of electricity filling the space between us. "I *am* here for you. In the office or...otherwise. So if you start to feel this way again, please know that you can always talk to me."

"Thank you, Graham." His kindness toward me in a moment when I probably didn't deserve it after the way I treated him today, especially so publicly, threatens to bring back the tears. "That means more than you know."

With the gentlest of smiles and a small wave, Graham turns, racing back into the rain just when he'd begun to dry off, leaving me equal parts nervous about the coming workday and excited to see him again.

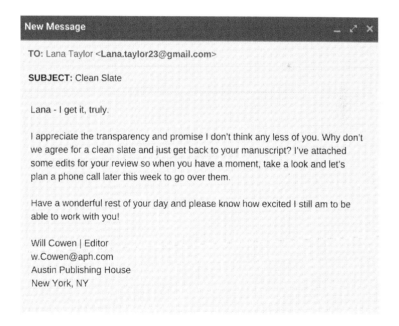

New Message

TO: Lana Taylor <Lana.taylor23@gmail.com>

SUBJECT: Clean Slate

Lana - I get it, truly.

I appreciate the transparency and promise I don't think any less of you. Why don't we agree for a clean slate and just get back to your manuscript? I've attached some edits for your review so when you have a moment, take a look and let's plan a phone call later this week to go over them.

Have a wonderful rest of your day and please know how excited I still am to be able to work with you!

Will Cowen | Editor
w.Cowen@aph.com
Austin Publishing House
New York, NY

CHAPTER NINE

HANGING MY JACKET UP THE FOLLOWING MORNING, THE slightest flash of yellow catches my eye on the framed picture of my college friends and me at winter formal.

I NEEDED LAST NIGHT...
MEET ME LATER?
NONA'S ON MAIN ST. 7
P.M. – G

P.S. THIS WAS A GOOD
LOOK ON YOU.

Unable to hide the grin that only a note from Graham could put on my face, I grab the piece of paper, put it in my desk drawer, and pour myself into my work so that I can rush out of here on time tonight. If I get everything done this afternoon, I'll have enough time to run home, rinse off, and change before meeting him for dinner.

I peek over the cubicle wall at Klair. "Psst. Guess who asked me to dinner?" I whisper which causes her to snap her head up from her computer, giving me the best friend forever attention an occasion like this deserves.

"Stop. Did he text you?" she asks. Come to think of it, Graham and I haven't exchanged phone numbers yet, so he couldn't possibly message me even if he wanted to.

"No, but there was a note from him on my desk. He must have left it here when we were out of the office." It genuinely makes me smile picturing Graham Austin sitting in his office writing his little note and waiting for just the right moment to deliver it.

"That is probably the sweetest, most adorable thing I've ever heard. Who even still does that?" Klair says while visibly melting. "Where did he ask you to meet him?"

"That new Italian place downtown, Nona's."

To no one's surprise, Klair, the most connected woman I know, has not only been and gives me a killer recommendation for an appetizer and wine selection, but she is close, personal friends with the owner and chef.

Taking the sticky note with me, I excitedly make my way toward Graham's office. I can see he's on the phone, clearly listening intently to whoever he's speaking to but when I peek my head in the doorway, he waves me in anyway.

"Si, si—pero necesito estos contratos firmados," he says with a natural bravado that stops me in my tracks. "Just make sure to get those contracts signed and sent over as soon as you can."

Holy. Bilingual. Hotness. I had no idea Graham spoke Spanish, let alone this fluently.

"¿Y el autor está de acuerdo?" I am literally speechless but at the same time, not at all surprised. "The author agrees, right?

And there aren't any issues?" Is there anything this man can't do?

Graham looks up from the notes he's been taking, his stare burning straight through me. It's not lost on me that I'm publicly hanging on every syllable of his perfectly accentuated words despite being utterly lost in translation. His voice is different when he speaks Spanish. It's richer and somehow, more alluring? *It's sexy as hell.* "Perfecto—gracias. Thank you, Mariana. Adios," he says, hanging up his phone and crossing his arms.

"Well hello Mr. Cowen...what can I do for you?" Graham knows *exactly* what he's doing and based on the smug grin plastered across his face, he knows it's working. Per usual, he's dressed impeccably. He's perfected the balance between buttoned-up business attire with his pressed plaid oxford that's open at the collar and fashionably casual with his deep navy suit pants that are cropped at the ankle showcasing his cognac loafers.

"Um—hola? I wasn't aware that you spoke Spanish."

He laughs as he steps around his desk before casually leaning against it. "It's not my party trick, Will," he says through a smile. "I'm sure you've noticed that my father is extremely Caucasian but my mother was actually born and raised in Spain so I grew up bilingual. Occasionally, like today, it comes in handy in the office as I'm trying to sign this up-and-coming author based in Spain."

"That's...um, convenient?" More like arousing.

He raises his eyebrows at me questioningly. "So, was there a point to this *very welcome* visit or did you just come to gawk over the fact that I can roll my *R's*?" I'd like him to roll his...

Oh, duh. I wave the sticky note I've been holding. "I actually just wanted to give you an in-person R.S.V.P for tonight. I'm really looking forward to it."

Graham runs a hand through his hair and I find myself

itching to know what it would feel like if I were the one doing that. "I'm glad—so am I."

The rest of the day goes by in an equal parts anxious and incredibly excited blur. After I send off one final email, pack up my things, and say a quick goodbye to Klair, who wishes me luck with a wink, I race home with just enough time to get cleaned up, changed, and out the door in time to beat Graham to the restaurant.

All my life, I've prided myself on being respectful of others' time. So, when I walk into the restaurant almost ten minutes early and see Graham already being seated, I smile to myself knowing that he must be the same way. Which, come to think of it, isn't surprising at all with his weekly staff meeting always starting at eleven a.m. on the dot.

He hasn't seen me yet which gives me a quick moment to take him all in as the waitress hands him a menu. Wearing a fitted, plaid blazer, a stark white button down, and dark denim jeans, Graham looks every bit the successful businessman, but my smile widens as I look down to see he's wearing a classic pair of Chuck's with this outfit and I all but pass out.

God, he's sexy.

"Will," he says, catching my attention.

How long was I staring and objectifying him like an idiot? *Get it together.* As I make my way to the table, I'm glad I opted for a dressier outfit and feel pleased that my sweater, collared shirt, and jean combo are in the same complementary color scheme as Graham's.

"I'm so glad you could make it," he says while standing up. He seems unsure of how to greet me so I just go in for the hug like I always do. I mean, he practically grinded me into oblivion against the club wall, so I think an innocent hug in public isn't crossing the line.

Wrapping my arms around his toned body, I inhale the uniquely spicy smell that makes my eyes roll to the back of my head. I make a mental note to see if I can find something similar to spray around my apartment because I never want to be without that smell.

"Thanks for the invite," I say after I've let him go and am taking my seat. "It was the best surprise to come back to the office to." I feel like I should make some attempt to hide my excitement, but honestly, it would be impossible.

We stare at each other for a moment and as soon as he opens his mouth to say something, our waitress comes over with a bottle of wine in her hand. "Good evening, gentlemen. My name is Carly, and I'll be your server this evening." She uncorks the bottle and pours generous servings into each of our wine glasses, placing the bottle on the table and setting a rectangular card down next to it. "I'm going to give you a few moments to look over the menu and I'll be back shortly to take your order."

Graham looks at the bottle and then to the note with a cocked brow. When I reach for the note, he quickly scoops it up and sticks out his tongue like a cocky schoolboy on the playground.

"You snooze, you lose, Cowen. You've got to be faster than that." His face breaks into a knowing smile after he reads the note, and he slides it over to me once he's finished. "It's for you."

*Let Mr. Wall Treatment know that
if he hurts you, I'm coming after
him...have fun!*

Xoxo, Klair

I nearly spit out my wine. If Graham's smile didn't make my entire body burn the way it did, Klair would have gotten an earful for using her connections to embarrass me like this.

I can feel my face reddening. Should I try to address it? Just laugh it off and pretend like I have no idea who this mystery Klair person is? *You all work together, idiot.*

"Mr. Wall Treatment, huh? I like it." Graham is sitting taller in his chair and, if possible, his chest seems to be even more pronounced, his new nickname clearly doing something to his ego.

Honestly, as soon as I read the note, my stomach dropped in fear of his reaction. You never know how a gay man will handle something like this considering it involves someone he works with closely. I believe he's out? Graham doesn't seem like the type of man to hide who he is, but it is definitely not my place to go around sharing intimate details of someone's life like that... even if it directly involves me.

For a moment, I feel remorse for breaking the most sacred and respected rule in the gay man's handbook: never out anyone. Even if he was in our apartment last night, Klair doesn't fully know the extent of our...friendship? Relationship? *Ugh.*

"I like that you've been talking to your friends about me," Graham says after a long sip from his glass. I watch in slow motion as his tongue licks a lingering drop of red wine from his bottom lip and all previous fears and shame are quickly forgotten. "So, do dates with you always come with complimentary wine or is this a special occasion?" he says through a dazzling smile.

"Oh, am I on a date?" I tease, resting my chin on my hand. "Where is he?"

"Someone's a jokester." His facial expression transforms into the most devious smirk I've ever seen. *God, that should be illegal.* Leaning in closer causes his leg to press firmly against mine, sending a spike of pure adrenaline through my veins. "This *most certainly* is a date, and at the risk of being forward, you're a little *too* overdressed for my liking." He leans back in his chair and cocks an eyebrow, smirking even more as he grabs his menu.

Well shit...I'm hard.

Our server returns with impeccable timing, placing our waters and some ciabatta bread on the table—which I nervously begin munching on, granting me the slightest moment of clarity or else I'd be even more *dicknotized* by Graham than I already am. We each place our orders—the pesto tortellini for him and the carbonara for me—and Graham adds the bruschetta for the table. Klair's recommendation and my personal favorite.

"So, if you're done squirming in your chair after that last remark, is now an appropriate time to start bombarding you with stereotypical first-date questions?" *Jaw. Dropped.*

Gulp. "Do your worst."

"Alright, let's start with some easy ones...You're originally from this area, right? What was it like growing up here?" he asks, resting his chin on his fists.

"It was great, truly. The art, the food, and the sights...there's nothing like it! Even after all these years, I feel like I'm still discovering new places and things to do. What about you?"

"Hey now, I'm the one asking the questions tonight," he jokes. "But you get one...we moved here from Los Angeles when I was a sophomore in high school, and there's nowhere in the world that has the amount of magic New York City does."

"I couldn't agree more." I take another sip of my wine, willing whatever this liquid courage everyone's always talking about to kick in so I don't mess this up.

"Moving on...siblings?"

"Nope, I'm an only child, but at this point, I consider Klair family...does that count?"

He laughs, a deep and velvety sound that I could listen to all day. "You two are that close, huh? How long have you known one another?"

"I mean, you did see her note, right? Klair has everyone convinced she's this sweet and delicate little flower, but she will *throw down* for the people she loves," I explain, laughing as shenanigans from our childhood start popping into my head. "Klair has been in my life for as long as I can remember, honestly. I'm pretty sure she had dinner with our family more nights than not."

Graham listens intently as I begin sharing—*more like over-sharing*—stories from our childhood. From family vacations and summer camp adventures to pulling pranks on boys in middle school and high school dances. He hangs on my every word, laughing and smiling as I reveal more and more about my child-hood. The waiter brings our food and despite the aroma of the beautiful spread placed before us, the conversation continues to flow between bites—savory and cheesy melt-in-your-mouth bites that *almost* cause unflattering moans to escape my lips. I swear if I wasn't on a first date right now, I'd be seductively licking my plate clean and asking for another order *to-go*.

"And you two haven't..." he asks through an inquisitive grin and raised eyebrow.

"Oh, god no," I say, nearly choking on my pasta. "Klair is gorgeous, but when I say she's like a sister to me...I mean it."

"Got it. Alright, let's see...what about your favorite shows and what kind of music you listen to?"

I take another sip of my wine just in case my taste in music and television makes him regret dining with me. "One Tree Hill is the best show in the history of television, and I'm the self-appointed President of the Taylor Swift Fan Club."

"Hmm, I don't think I've ever watched that show, but here's the more important follow up question then..." I peek at him through my fingers, suddenly intrigued. "What's your favorite Taylor era?"

Oh. My. God. Total and utter shock consumes me. Did I perhaps snag a...*Swiftie?*

"I knew I liked you for a reason," I say, trying to pick up my dropped jaw. "But this will definitely be a conversation for date two because I could talk all things Ms. Swift all night."

"Okay, okay...fair enough. How about if you could have any superpower, what would it be and why?"

"Yikes, I have *no* idea...maybe something cliché like flying or invulnerability?"

"Come on, Cowen...don't be so basic," Graham taunts.

"Basic, huh? Sounds like you have the *perfect* answer for that one lined up so I'm calling a redo on the *one question* I'm allowed to have because I already knew you were from LA." I mimic his position, leaning forward and resting my chin on my knuckles. *Such a power move.*

Graham laughs once more and I've already decided it's my favorite sound ever. "If I could have *any* superpower, it would for sure be the power of persuasion."

"Um, I'm pretty sure you already have that one down," I confess.

"Is that so?"

"Oh yeah...I'm pretty sure you could tell me to read the phone book and I'd ask how many times," I say, emboldened by the wine. It's true and I'm not even embarrassed about it. Already, Graham has this hold over me that I know is going to be dangerous...but only in the best possible way.

He flashes a smile while shaking his head at me. "I am literally failing to come up with a witty response to that," he says through laughter. "But I guess we'll have to find you a phone-book. *Immediately.*"

"I guess you will," I say, leaning even closer to him, stretching out my leg and letting it brush against his. My heart melts when I see him smile at the physical contact. "What else do you have for me?"

"I'm glad you're not sick of my questioning yet," he says, bumping his toned leg against mine. "Since we work in publishing...what kind of books do you enjoy reading?"

"Honestly, I feel like my taste in books is all over the place depending on the mood I'm in...but I'm a big thriller and romance guy. And if you can combine the two?" I fan my face dramatically, causing another laugh to escape Graham's lips. "Give me *all* the steam."

"I think I can help with that..." And with those seven little words, I don't know how much more I can take of this before I leap across the table and straddle him on the spot. After our plates have been cleared and our waitress returns with Graham's credit card—he insisted on paying—we're both leaning anxiously toward one another.

"I'd like to ask *one more* question."

"Shoot."

"Can you *please* say something else in Spanish?" I ask, doing my best to appear charming rather than undeniably thirsty.

Graham smirks, clearing weighing over my surprise bonus

question. "¿Cómo se siente ser tan guapo sin intentar?" he says, softly placing emphasis on every single word.

"Ooh! Guapo...I'm fairly positive I know that one," I say, feeling all the blood rush to my cheeks. *He thinks I'm handsome...maybe?* "But the rest?"

"I asked how it feels to be so handsome without even trying. Come on...let's get out of here." He stands and extends his hand toward me which I happily take as he proceeds to lead us out of the crowded restaurant.

I don't know if it's the wine or the intoxicating company but I am just very thankful his back is turned toward me because my ears burn bright red at his sweet compliment.

"I had a really, *really* nice time tonight," Graham says, shoving his hands in his pockets and leaning against the doorframe. We're standing on our front patio after he offered to walk me home and all I keep thinking is how tonight was truly magical. I felt like it was the first time Graham felt comfortable being fully himself around me and I loved every second of it.

He's lingering. We've been in this back and forth dance of "almost" moments and it suddenly feels like it's all been leading to right now, standing here with him on my porch after a night like tonight. Taking a step closer to him, I desperately want to eliminate as much distance as possible without seeming desperate.

But fuck. I need to have those lips on me. Come on, Graham, kiss me already.

"I did, too. Everything about the evening was..." I pause, trying to find the right word, "...perfect." We're now standing chest-to-chest, just inches apart. My arms are at my sides, but I allow my fingertips to brush the length of his solid thigh, itching to feel more and loving the grin it puts on his face.

This is fucking torture.

"I'll say." Graham's voice is almost lost to the pounding in my ears. The deafening silence of the stillness now forming between us is so overwhelming, I begin to tremble. I need his lips on mine. I watch as his eyes take in this moment, every glance to my lips makes me feel like combusting right here and honestly, it could be a real possibility.

"Oh hell..." I all but growl at Graham, grabbing the lapels of his jacket and pulling him toward me, hard. I hear him chuckle but that quickly stops as I crash my lips onto his, feeling the contradiction of his rough stubble compared to his impossibly soft lips.

Our bodies press together, inhaling heavily as our lips finally touched. *I can't breathe...I can't...ugh.* Graham's hands are on my hips, pulling me closer to him as I deepen our kiss, my tongue sliding into his inviting mouth. Our breathing quickens as I bring my hand to the back of his neck, grabbing a fistful of hair and pulling him close, the bulge in Graham's pants now impossible to ignore any longer.

I mean, good, because I'm over here harder than I've ever been in my life.

Breaking our kiss, Graham throws his head back, exposing his neck and impressive jaw line, the most satisfying moan escaping his lips. I take this opportunity to plant kisses along his neck, bringing my hand to that impressive bulge and feeling it strain against the fabric of his dress pants. I give it a squeeze. *This is mine.*

Pulling Graham's mouth back to mine, claiming his pillow-soft lips and allowing the sweetness of his skin combined with the spiciness of his cologne to invade every one of my senses, I whisper between kisses, "I'm going to need you...to come... inside...right now."

He pulls back just far enough to catch a glimpse of my face, raising an eyebrow at me. "Is that so?" His voice is soft in my ear, but his arms tighten around me.

"100 percent yes," I say to him as I start shifting our weight toward the door. He squeezes me tighter but then places his hands on either side of my face. I stare into the eyes of the man who literally just took my breath away and left me throbbing at the same time, who made the rest of the world slip away into oblivion. The same man who looks at me like no one ever has before, so intently and sweetly. He plants the softest kiss on my lips, lingering with a tenderness that makes time itself stop to catch its breath.

"That," he says, his lips still pressed to mine, "...that was mind-blowing." He nuzzles into my neck, wrapping his strong arms around me, as I say a silent prayer that he never lets go. If I had to live in a single moment for the rest of my life, it would without a doubt be this one.

CHAPTER TEN

"THESE PHOTOS ARE GORGEOUS." GRAHAM, NOW IN MY room, is standing in front of the gallery wall I put together. "Did you take all of these?" I shut and lock the door—*you never know with Klair*—and turn to face him, feeling the intense need for him spike again.

"Do you really want to talk about photography right now?" I cock my head at him, my voice may be soft but my intent couldn't be any louder. I cross the room, never breaking eye contact with him, until I am once again standing directly in front of Graham, his scent enveloping me. "Because I don't want to talk about photography right now." I slide my hands up his chest, pushing my groin into his. *Oh, someone's ready!* I grab the lapels of his jacket, pulling him closer to me. "Right now, what I really want is you." Bringing his lips to mine, I add between kisses, "...all of you."

Graham's arms are around me, his grip impossible to escape. *Not that I would ever dare.* My need for this man is overwhelming, to the point where I can't think straight, but right now...right now isn't the time for thinking. Right now, the only thing I need is to get Graham out of these clothes. *Immediately.*

He reaches up and grabs the back of my neck to turn my head, running a trail of kisses from my neck, up my jaw and to my ear. "Anything you want, it's yours," he whispers, his words unlocking something I've been trying so desperately to tame. I slide my hands into the waistband of his dress pants, pulling him toward my bed when he starts to shrug out of his suit jacket.

"Let me," I whisper into his ear. Feeling him slump against me, his breathing picking up, I remove his suit jacket, letting my hands glide across the strength of his shoulders, and fling it to the chair across the room. Reaching for the buttons of his shirt, I plant gentle kisses on his lips, his stubble, as I slowly undo each one, feeling the warmth of his skin burning beneath my touch.

His hands move from their firm grip on my waist and traps my wrists in them. "Will, this is *fucking* torture," he mutters between gritted teeth, his tone rich with need and desire.

It's my turn to show off my best devilish smirk. *Good.*

Crashing my lips to his and invading his mouth with my wanting tongue, I make quick work of the remaining buttons of his shirt. Sliding the open garment over his muscled shoulders until it falls to the ground, my movements are now driven by my intoxicating desire to see him naked.

Graham's hands are on the hem of my sweater and lifting upward, quickly ripping it over my head. He goes for my waistband at the same time I go for his, each of us desperate to explore every last inch of unseen skin. We stand there, briefly taking one another in, the sight of Graham naked literally takes every last trace of air from my lungs. His broad shoulders and defined chest and stomach are enough to make me drop to my knees right then and there, but when my eyes continue south and confirm everything I felt through his pants and then some, I could die on the spot.

I push him back toward the bed until his long legs hit the

edge, causing him to sit. He looks up at me through hooded eyes, his gaze laced with want and in the most deliberate of ways, he slowly places soft kisses along my stomach and down my side, trailing his fingertips gently across the most sensitive parts of my skin. His touch sets every nerve ending ablaze.

Pulling me forward onto his lap, he positions my body as close as humanly possible as he wraps me back in those strong arms.

"You...are truly...the sexiest man...I have ever...seen," he whispers between kisses along my neck. The torturous combination of his words and feeling every inch of him pressed against me makes me moan. When he brings his lips to mine once more, I thread my hands in his hair, holding on for dear life as both of us begin to pant. I want him.

He lowers us slowly backward on the bed, my full weight on top of him now and I will never get enough of feeling Graham's skin against mine. He positions me between his legs, reaching around and grabbing my back, pulling me closer to him as he kisses me once more.

"Will..." he breathes, what he wants couldn't be more clear.

"Are you sure?" I ask, leaning over him, in complete awe of the gorgeous man beneath me.

"I've never been *more* sure." Raising off the bed slightly, he plants a reassuring kiss on my lips. "I *need* you," he moans, reaching down and grabbing my cock. "I need you inside of me, *now.*"

Adjusting slightly as I reach over to my nightstand, I grab the small bottle of lube from the drawer and feel the slick liquid coat my fingers. Gliding them over myself to ensure I have enough, I reposition against Graham, feeling him push against me in a way that causes my eyes to roll into the back of my skull. Graham releases the sexiest of sounds as he fully relaxes after several slow, deliberate thrusts.

"Damn, you feel incredible," Biting my lip, I thrust all the way into him, the feeling of him stretching around me is unlike anything I've ever felt. He reaches up and grabs the back of my neck, pulling my mouth back down to his.

"Fuck me...hard," he moans against my lips. *Done.*

Pulling back out slightly, I slam back into him as the speed of my thrusts increases, each one sending shockwaves of pleasure radiating throughout my veins. I know I won't be able to keep up this tempo for too long. The friction our bodies are creating combined with the sight of Graham beneath me looking as mouth-watering as he is will surely send me over the edge in a matter of minutes.

I lean down, kissing along his shoulder and neck. "I will never *not* want this, Graham...I will never be able to get enough of you."

"You won't have to, handsome..." he whispers against my ear and somehow, I know he means it.

Our bodies are in perfect sync as I pump in and out of him. I reach down, stroking him with every thrust and feel him throb in my hand, his grip on my back getting tighter and tighter.

"God, this feels amazing. Don't stop, Will. I'm so...I'm so fucking close," he pants, his pleas obliterating any self-control I have left.

I slam into him deeper and harder, each thrust promising the sweetest release. "Graham...I'm...I'm going to come..." I yell, completely unable to control my physical reactions as I cross the point of no return. I fist the comforter and furiously stroke him as my body begins to shake. With a final thrust, I'm catapulted over the edge, feeling the throb of my release over and over again deep inside of Graham.

"Yes, Will..." he shouts, eyes heavy with pleasure and anticipation meet mine before he slams his head back against the bed

YOU & I, REWRITTEN

as rope after rope of Graham's release paints his muscled stomach.

Still pulsing deep inside of him, I collapse on top of Graham —our bodies slick with sweat and the surreal mess we just made. He kisses my temple, wrapping his arms around me once more as our breathing slows and my eyes struggle to remain open. I know without a shadow of a doubt that I have *never* experienced anything like that before in my life.

"Holy. Fucking. Shit." We're both utterly spent and borderline delirious. "I don't even...I can't...Wow." I bury my head into Graham's neck, embarrassed at how tongue-tied I am at this moment.

"Somehow, I know exactly what you mean, stud," he says and we both start laughing, coming down from the most intoxicating of highs. Sex with Graham is unlike anything I could have ever imagined. There were no awkward or unsure moments, no issues figuring out who was going to go where and when. We just...clicked.

Looking over at him now, he is the epitome of a just-laid man. He's got one muscled arm draped lazily over his eyes, barely hiding the flush of his glistening skin in the dim light of the candles. His lips are swollen and irritated from the friction of our scruff and his normally meticulously styled hair is now wild. *He is stunning.*

I reach over, opening my nightstand cabinet and retrieve my favorite polaroid camera. I quickly straddle him before he can object, pressing the shutter button to capture this moment in time forever. *I could literally stare at this man all day.* The print ejects from the device and I put it on my nightstand, waiting for Graham's beautiful form to appear.

"What are you doing?" he asks as I have the camera still to my eye. *Click.* "Would you knock that off?" Graham bucks his hips under my weight, grabbing my hips now. *Click.* "Oh my God, Will! Quit it."

"Make me," I tease. Finally gaining leverage, he has us rolling over, and Graham's very toned, very naked body is suddenly on top of mine. He's smiling down at me, his gaze filled with amusement and a contentment I could get used to. *Click.*

"Alright, my little shutterbug, that'll be enough of that," he says, trying to steal my camera while laughing. "I think I can confidently assess you are in fact a fan of photography," he whispers, his toned body still on top of mine.

"You would be correct in that assessment." I push off the bed slightly to steal a kiss which he happily returns. "It's something that just makes me happy...I like capturing moments that make me smile."

His hands begin slowly roaming my body, stopping to grip my hardening cock. "Hmm, I have something in mind that'll certainly make you smile," he says, leaning down and sucking on my lower lip. "But...you're going to need both hands free, so why don't we put this thing away..." I moan as he glides his hand over me.

"Yes, sir," I exhale as I all but throw my camera clear across the room, feeling him laugh before his lips claim mine once more.

I could barely sleep last night.

Glancing over at my clock, I see it's a little too early to get out of bed but definitely not worth trying to force myself back to sleep. Graham's warm and deliciously naked body is entangled with mine and as the memories of last night play on a loop, sending my brain into overdrive and consuming my every thought, I can't help but grin in astonishment. Last night was pure magic...the date, the kiss, *his body*...it was like a dream.

He stirs, pulling me tighter against his chest. "Good morning, sexy." His voice is a deep whisper against my ear, sending chills down my spine. Rolling over, his arm still wrapped around me, I'm met by Graham's dazzling smile and the most adorable bed head I've ever seen.

"Hi," I say, giving him a quick kiss against his jaw, a more prominent shadow having appeared magically overnight.

He's even sexier...how is that possible?

I bury my face in the crook of his neck, shielding him from the very real possibility that I have the world's worst morning breath, as he squeezes me tighter, his body shifting slightly against mine. Is that? Yup. *Morning wood.*

"Last night was..." he starts, pressing himself against me, *holy shit*...I most definitely didn't dream how impressive *that* was.

"Agreed," I say, playfully biting his neck as he trails his hands down my back, giving my ass a squeeze. As much as I would love to spend the rest of eternity wrapped in this moment with a naked and horny Graham, we *do* have to start getting ready for the impending workday. "Are you hungry?" I ask, afraid to pop this blissful bubble.

He brings my mouth to his, letting his lips linger as he plants the softest kiss. "Starving."

"Well come on...let's get you something to eat!" I rip off the covers, forcing us to face the day's reality, and jump out of bed... instantly regretting this decision when I see him lying there, fully naked and on display.

"And coffee." I throw a pair of sweatpants at him which he

quickly puts on while laughing—the thin, gray fabric doing *nothing* to hide his drool-worthy bulge.

Once we are both fully clothed and semi-presentable, I open my bedroom door to the sweet aroma of freshly brewed coffee. Klair is sitting at the kitchen island, a large coffee mug in hand and a cocked eyebrow at her best friend quietly emerging from behind closed doors with Graham in tow.

She puts her mug down, crossing her arms as a wicked grin flashes across her face. "So, do we all walk to work together or..."

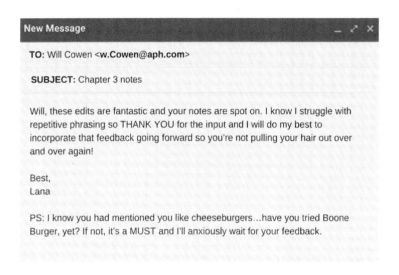

New Message   _ ⤢ ✕

TO: Will Cowen <**w.Cowen@aph.com**>

SUBJECT: Chapter 3 notes

Will, these edits are fantastic and your notes are spot on. I know I struggle with repetitive phrasing so THANK YOU for the input and I will do my best to incorporate that feedback going forward so you're not pulling your hair out over and over again!

Best,
Lana

PS: I know you had mentioned you like cheeseburgers...have you tried Boone Burger, yet? If not, it's a MUST and I'll anxiously wait for your feedback.

CHAPTER ELEVEN

How the hell am I expected to focus on anything other than the fact that I woke up to a deliciously naked Graham Austin this morning? Forget about providing helpful edits or replying to emails, the only thing my mind seems capable of stringing together is an erotic montage of last night's, um, *festivities*.

The burn of Graham's scruff when our lips finally met.

The strength behind his inescapable grip as he pulled me closer.

The tightness of his...

"That good, huh?" Klair nudges me while plopping down on my desk, her question rudely interrupting my *not safe for work* daydream.

"I don't think there are words to describe just *how good* last night was," I admit, knowing there is no confession between us that would ever be over the line. "It was without a doubt the most mind-blowing sex in the history of sex."

"Oh, I heard—"

"Honestly, Klair? There's not a single part of me that's embarrassed. *That's* how good it was!" And it's the truth—from the very moment Graham's lips touched mine, it was like something detonated deep inside of me, a level of physical intimacy and attraction that up until now, had never seen the light of day. I've had plenty of sex—good sex, even. But nothing, and I mean *nothing*, compares to what went down with Graham last night.

There was something so reserved and passionate about his touch. He savored every single second of our night together, slowly exploring every inch of my body with his hands, his mouth—*God, that man's mouth*—in the most torturous of ways.

"I know I have a tendency for theatrics, but—"

"Psh, you think?" Klair interrupts, rolling her eyes at my understatement of the year.

"But…" I continue, ignoring her completely. "I'm slightly overwhelmed by everything I'm feeling about the entire situation."

She puts her arm around my shoulders. "And what exactly is it that you're feeling?"

I don't want to admit it. Because how pathetic would it make me to admit that last night was the first time that I've ever really felt something *more.* That it was the first time I've *wanted* something more from someone else. The things I've craved more than anything in this world—love, stability, passion—all those things seemed well within my reach the second Graham laid his hands on me and if I lost that? I don't know if I would survive that. *Again.*

"I don't know, Klair…everything with Graham just feels intensified," I say quietly as I lean into her. "I just feel like whatever this is with him is important. Like one of those too-good-to-be-true moments that always end in total heartbreak."

"Graham isn't like—oh, speak of the devil!" Klair says, pivoting our conversation perfectly as the subject of our office gossip comes strolling into our section with his hands in the pockets of his sharp charcoal suit pants.

"Good morning, Graham...so good to see you again. And clothed this time."

I fight the urge to pull her sleek ponytail ever-so-gently.

As much as I loved seeing him shrug back into his clothes from the night before, his hair disheveled and looking every bit like a man smiling through a walk of shame, seeing him back in his perfectly pressed workplace armor makes my heart skip a beat.

"Eh—morning, Klair." Oh, all-business Graham is back. His tone is rushed, clearly wanting to get to the point of his morning visit. "Can you reach out to your contact at Howell Literary Agency? There seems to be some contract issues with several of our authors and I need to get to the bottom of it quickly."

"On it." Klair hops off my desk and heads back to hers, clearly hearing the concern in Graham's voice.

"Thanks...Good morning, Will," he says through a slight smile before turning away and heading back toward his desk.

"Um, yeah...good morning, eh, *sir*," I shout after him and instantly hate myself. *Sir? Really?*

I can't be sure because his back is turned but I think Graham is laughing at me as he steps into his office. Nope—he's one hundred percent laughing at me.

Turning to Klair absolutely mortified, I can feel my face turn the deepest shade of red.

"Oh, lovebug," she says in the most maternal and condescending manner possible. "You're definitely going to have to figure out how to pull it together in the office now that you've seen him *totally* naked."

There's absolutely no chance I'll be able to *pull it together*. I think I can confidently assume Graham enjoyed himself last night—more than once. But does that even matter? For lack of a better word, he's essentially my boss so I don't know if that's something either one of us want to get mixed up in. Besides,

Klair has already told me the man is totally married to his work. *Clearly.* If I'm being honest with myself, I can't see him wanting anything more than a one-night fling from me.

"You said it yourself, Klair," I say, doing my best to turn my attention back to the work in front of me. "He's all business."

But there's a very small part of me that is hoping—*praying*—I'm wrong. Because if there is even a chance of *more* with Graham, that's a leap of faith I'm more than willing to take.

Thankfully, the remaining hours of my workday blur seamlessly together. Every thought has been consumed with doubt as to whether some imaginary line has been crossed between Graham and I or if last night was just some tragic one-night-stand. Beyond our horrific *sir* encounter this morning, Graham and I's paths have rarely crossed today—which does wonders for my self-sabotaging anxiety, by the way—and when they did, all I wanted to do was either knot my hands in his hair and kiss him for hours or force him to answer if he likes me...or *likes me,* likes me.

You know, like a child.

Lana has sent over some revisions to a chapter we've been going back and forth on, so I spend the rest of my day reading them for flow and consistency before calling it a night. It's funny —despite the initial hiccups we faced in our working relationship, Lana and I have quickly developed a flow of our own. Maybe it's because I relate to the chapters she's been sending over on such a deeply personal level or it could just be that she just has one of those calming personalities. Either way, I walk away from every conversation with Lana feeling like I've known her for far longer than I actually have. Perhaps she just has an old soul.

"You would *not* believe the day I've had." His tired voice rips my attention from the paragraph I've been reading repeatedly, causing my stomach to do a backflip. Graham strides into our now-abandoned section, his smile widening with each step and as soon as he's within arm's reach, every doubt and insecurity about last night has all but disappeared. *For now.*

Without any sort of trepidation or hesitation to the fact that we are not entirely alone in the office, he kisses my cheek. The burn from his scruff radiates over every inch of my skin and I can't hide the smile it causes. Lingering ever so slightly, hear him exhale, releasing the tension he must have been carrying all day. "Hi, handsome...I hate how little I got to see you today."

"I...I thought maybe you had—" I glance down,

Graham isn't stupid. I'm sure what I'm trying to say is written all over my face. He reaches for my hand, firmly taking it in his. The simplest of gestures, yet one that anchors me through whatever leap we are about to take together. "Do you want to get out of here and grab some dinner?"

Meeting his warm gaze, I rise with my hand still in his. Relief, so intense and welcome that it nearly brings tears to my eyes, rushes over me. I know how ridiculous I am sometimes, especially when I get in my own head, but over the last few years, I've tried so hard to stop punishing myself for the way I feel. Even if I could change the immensity of my heart, I wouldn't.

"I'd love that."

It takes me all of two weeks to trust that what we have isn't too good to be true.

And another for me to admit just how hard I've begun to fall for the man.

And just for good measure, one more for me to realize Graham just might be everything I've been looking for all along.

From day one, he's faced every concern and insecurity of mine head on, giving it value and then just carrying on. For so long, I've learned to mask the complicated parts of who I am.

Not with Graham. He's shown me that *all* of me, especially the messy and anxious parts, are not only worthy of getting to know, but worthy of acceptance. He's made me feel seen and valued.

He's made me feel whole.

Without even realizing it, Graham and I have spent nearly every waking moment of the last three months together. Three of the most as-seen-on-tv, deliriously happy months of my life. And as much as that terrifies me, I've never felt more alive.

As the *very* intense professional he is in the office, I was surprised to learn just how laidback Graham is in his everyday life. He's got this go-with-the-flow personality outside of work that is exhilarating to be around, and I've discovered rather quickly that Graham Austin is up for just about anything.

Like how he enthusiastically threw himself into the oil painting class Klair forced us *both* to attend when Dean had to bail on their romantic date night for a last-minute work thing. Every time I looked over at Graham throughout the class, he was bent over his canvas, meticulously painting the wooden bowl of sunflowers set before us with novice, yet detailed, strokes. Klair and I *would have* been much farther along on our individual masterpieces, but we found the complimentary red wine to be much more our speed.

Or how he quickly agreed to binge all my favorite high school dramas complete with unrealistic storylines, backstabbing best friends and more angst and sexual tension than any eighteen-year-old would know what to do with. I knew I found a keeper when he confidently proclaimed he was *Team Brooke* after watching Lucas choose Peyton for the hundredth time.

But the thing I've come to adore most about him is how he is anything but predictable. From the way he can flawlessly quote every line to every episode of every animated adult cartoon in existence to the way he dances so smoothly in the kitchen while making meals passed down by his *abuelita*, Graham has kept me on my toes with an idiotic smile permanently plastered across my face.

In the smallest of ways and over such a short period of time, our lives have become profoundly intertwined.

"Where's your head at, Mr. Cowen?" he asks, curling up next to me in his king-sized bed. We've just finished yet another meal together courtesy of my new devilishly handsome personal chef—chicken molé burrito bowls complete with homemade guacamole and deliciously spicy queso—and are now each reading in bed, our bodies tangled together under the plush linen comforter.

Setting my book aside and pulling myself even closer to him, I bury my head into the crook of his neck, taking a deep inhale of the rosemary and mint body wash that still lingers on his tanned skin from our shower—the scent that now lulls me to sleep every single night. I slowly trace the intricately drawn tattoo covering his shoulder with my fingertips, a beautiful dream catcher with earth toned feathers, and smile remembering the way his face lit up as he explained its significance. A permanent and heartfelt reminder of a cherished gift from his mother, hung proudly over his childhood bed and meant to inspire a life spent chasing and following the dreams that take our breath away, regardless of how big and scary they are.

"I guess I was just getting lost in the whirlwind of it all," I say, pressing my lips against his jaw.

"Oh yeah? A good whirlwind I hope."

"The best," I admit, sitting up so that I can see his face. "There are moments—very much like this one, where I just am taken aback by how *easy* all of this is."

Graham throws his head back in laughter. "Are you calling *me* easy?"

"You know what I mean," I say, pushing his arm playfully. "I'm saying *this* is easy. You and me." I place my hand over his heart, the warmth of his bare skin burning under my touch.

"Us." he says, leaning forward, gently placing a tender kiss against my lips.

And for the first time in my life, I feel like I'm exactly where I'm meant to be.

CHAPTER TWELVE

"THERE YOU TWO ARE," KLAIR SAYS THEATRICALLY, PER usual. Graham and I just sat down in our office's break room for lunch, an act that has become our new normal during the work week and something I've come to immensely look forward to. Some days we share leftovers, others we have salads or sandwiches. Today, I surprised Graham with southwest wraps and fries from my new favorite cafe across the street.

"Do you boys have plans later?" She plops down in the chair between us as Graham and I exchange questioning glances, unsure of what she has in mind. "Perfect...we're doing game night!" she says before either of us can say anything, throwing her arms around both of our necks.

"That actually sounds like a lot of fun. Is there anything I can bring?" Graham asks, ever the gentleman.

"Nope...just that competitive nature we all know and love," she says, nodding in my direction, stealing a fry from Graham's container and popping it into her mouth. "Dean and I will take care of the rest." I'll never get sick of seeing the ease between the two of them, one of the unexpected benefits of the three of us all working together.

"Oh, it is *so* on, sweet Klair. You might want to give Dean a heads up that when I play, I play to win," I say, leaning back in my chair and flexing my arm muscles, resulting in Graham nearly choking on the wrap he'd just taken a bite of and Klair rolling her eyes at me.

"Have fun with *that*," Klair says to Graham as she heads over to her desk, leaving the two of us back to our regularly scheduled lunch date.

I live for these stolen moments with him, ones where we get a glimpse into what a real future together could look like. Sitting side-by-side, the simplicity of sharing every meal together...the thought makes my heart ache in the best possible way.

"Someone's a little competitive, huh?" Graham says, nudging my thigh under the table.

"Not in an *I'm going to be in a bad mood if we lose* kind of way..." I say trying to appear as innocent as possible. "But let's just say that I may or may not be known to go a *little* overboard."

Graham shakes his head at me, the sweetest smile plastered across his face. "You would think I'd have learned by now to not be surprised by all your hidden talents."

I lean forward so that our knees are touching under the cramped table. "I can think of a few *talents* I'd like to show you..." I say with a wink.

Graham's lips part and I force myself to not lean across the table even further and invade that mouth of his with my own. "Name the time and place, handsome...you can show me whatever you'd like." *Right now? Thanks.*

"Hey, Will? I'm going to need you to at least *try* to roll those salami flowers better," Klair scolds, a sentence I never thought

I'd hear in my lifetime. I look down at my measly attempt at making oily, preserved meat look *artsy* and shrug. From the moment we got home, she's put me to work setting up for our couple's night in. Dean arrived shortly after we did and is rinsing off in Klair's bathroom after sneaking in a workout before the real competition starts.

"First of all, this is literally the first time I've ever done this," I say, holding up my meat flower proudly, though it's looking more like a meatball at this point. "Second of all, not that I'm complaining because you *know* I love a good cheese moment... but don't you think this is *too much* for just the four of us?"

I glance down at the elaborate charcuterie board Klair has laid out. Endless cheeses, meats, and crackers are accompanied by fruit and vegetables, and sweet jams, taking up nearly every inch of our kitchen island. I should have known when she suggested game night it would be a slightly more elevated evening.

Klair bumps me with her hip, taking my place as the designated salami flower folder. "There is no such thing as too much cheese," she says, her laser-like focus now turned toward fixing what I'd been working on.

"That's *for sure* going on your headstone."

"You know what's going on yours? Mediocre at handling meat?" Jaw. Dropped. Getting roasted by Klair is easily one of my favorite pastimes, but this one just might take the cake.

"Holy shit...that's going in the book," I say, struggling to breathe between my laughter as I take out my phone and add this exchange to my ever-growing note of Klair burns.

"What book?" Dean pads into the kitchen, coming behind Klair and wrapping his big arms around her waist as she finishes laying out the rest of the food. The smile on her face when he does tells me everything I need to know about how she feels about him. We haven't spent too much time together since meeting at the bar—the two of them either sneaking away into Klair's room when I'm around or I'm off with Graham—so it'll be nice to spend some quality time with the guy making my best friend swoon.

"Will and I started jotting down all the funny and stupid things we've said to one another over the years." Klair turns to face Dean, her arms reaching up to weave her fingers in the still-damp hair at the base of his neck.

"Consider me intrigued," he says, pulling her body flat against his, his lips moments away from crashing against Klair's when the doorbell rings. *Thank god.*

"I'll get it...I'd hate to interrupt whatever *this* is..." I say, feigning disgust as they feel each other up, when in reality, I'm over the moon Klair has found the same intense level of happiness I have.

Even though I literally *just* saw him at work, I still get the same feelings of excitement every time I see Graham. Tonight is no different as I open the door and see him standing there leaning against the doorway, a covered tray in his hands.

"Hey, you," he says, flashing me a million-dollar smile that stops my heart. Closing the door behind me for a moment alone before the madness begins, I rush toward him, ignoring the fact that his hands are full and press my lips to his. He shifts the container he's holding to one hand, wrapping the other around my waist as he deepens our kiss, his now-familiar scent causing me to fully relax since coming home from work.

"Hi, stranger." I bury my head in the crook of his neck, letting his warmth envelope me. "Is it weird that I missed you? Like *genuinely* missed you?"

"I'm glad I'm not the only one," he whispers against my ear, his smile unmistakable against the side of my head. "Are you ready to dominate game night?"

"Let's show 'em how it's done."

"Oh, *come on*...you've got to be kidding me," I shout, all but slamming my drinking glass down onto the coffee table. Graham has just answered his fourth trivia question in a row correctly and if Klair hadn't suggested we mix up the couples, I would be celebrating right now, but instead, Dean and I are getting our butts handed to us.

Crossing her legs across from us, Klair grabs a new question card with a smug look on her face. "How are you boys doing? Had enough yet?" she asks.

When Graham mouths '*I'm sorry*' from across the living room, I childishly respond by sticking my tongue out at him, causing a deep, throaty laugh to escape his lips.

"Oh, we are just getting warmed up," Dean playfully responds. *Goodness, stop flirting with the enemy.* She blows him a kiss.

"How about you quit stalling and ask the next question?"

Klair shakes her head at my impatience while reading the question on the card. "Oh, my sweet, Will...You're going to love this one. Who scored the first three-point basket in NBA history?"

Shit...shit, shit, shit.

I am not a complete idiot when it comes to sports, but basketball history? I literally have no idea.

"Dude, I *totally* know this one. Do you trust me?" Dean says, nudging my side as he leans in closer.

"It's all yours...it's not like we'll beat these two anyway."

"Alright, pretty girl...the first person to ever score a three-point basket was in 1979 by Chris Ford of the Boston Celtics." He leans back into the couch, crossing his arms and giving Klair and Graham an equally smug stare.

CHIP PONS

Klair's smile grows wider as she places the card in her lap. "That's... weirdly correct!"

Dean and I both jump up from our seats, enthusiastically pumping our fists in the air. We conclude our unnecessary but totally fun celebratory dance with a tight bro-hug and I can't help but laugh at Dean's infectious personality. It's easy to see why Klair likes him so much.

"I hate to ruin this adorable moment," Graham says, grinning ear-to-ear as Dean and I turn our attention toward him, still mid-embrace, "even with that answer...which was very impressive, by the way..."

"Thank you, kind sir," Dean says in a horrific attempt at an English accent while giving Graham a slight bow, resulting in a round of laughter from us all.

"...but unfortunately, Klair and I *still* won by like a hundred points."

The weight of defeat causes both Dean and I to slump back down onto the couch.

"Aw, don't beat yourselves up. Graham and I are just superior in every way," Klair says as she starts clearing our plates, holding the remains of our delicious charcuterie spread.

"Well, we did our best...at least we lost with dignity," I say toward Dean, completely ignoring her.

"We can sleep soundly tonight knowing we didn't kick anyone when they were down...unlike *someone* I know." Dean extends his fist in my direction, which I bump with my own.

"Ooh, this one's a keeper," I say to Klair, which makes them both smile.

"Isn't he?" she says quietly, turning toward the kitchen.

Is she blushing? Since the game is over and Graham has stood up to help Klair, now is as good a time as any to bombard Dean with all sorts of prying questions to see just how much of a keeper he truly is.

124

"So Dean...we haven't had the opportunity to really get to know one another without *these two* knuckleheads around," I say, tilting my head in Klair and Graham's direction. "Tell me everything there is to know about you in five words or less."

He rubs his hands together, a wolfish smile growing on his handsome face. "Too easy— architect, Boston, dogs, pizza, lucky," he rattles off without giving it too much thought.

I knew he was an architect; Klair had mentioned that after the first time they hung out. I picked up on Boston by the subtlety of his accent, but it also explains how he knew that NBA question. And anyone who defines themselves by dogs and pizza is automatically golden in my book.

"Lucky?"

"Hell yeah, have you met Klair? I'm the luckiest man in the world," he says, leaning closer so his comment is just for me. "It's probably crazy or far too soon to be saying things like that, but honestly? I can't help it, man. I'm sure you can relate, huh?"

I turn toward the kitchen, taking in the scene of my best friend and boyfriend laughing hysterically while throwing grapes at one another. Klair dodges Graham's fruit strike as she releases a handful of grapes in his direction, almost all of them bouncing off his face and scattering across the floor—the exact opposite of cleaning the kitchen.

Is this real life? It certainly isn't one I've ever thought possible or even one I believe I've deserved, but seeing the two of them like this—my two worlds colliding this way—fills me with more hope than I've felt in a really long time.

"It's not crazy at all, Dean...I know *exactly* what you mean."

"Y'all didn't think we were *just* having a quiet night in, did you?" Klair shouts, her voice struggling to cut through the horrifically off-tune voice coming from the stage in front of us.

After another cut-throat round of trivia, she convinced the rest of us to go out for another drink and somehow, we've found ourselves in the middle of a very crowded and very familiar karaoke bar in Brooklyn—the same spot that Klair and I used to sneak out to in high school with our barely-passable fake IDs.

"I feel like I've just taken a step back in time," I say, noting that not a single thing about the packed bar has changed in the last decade. From the random collection of flashing neon bar signs to the always-sticky tables, it's exactly how I remember it.

"It'll be just like old times. Dean—you and Graham go grab that table," she says pointing at a vacant four-top near the stage. "And we'll grab some drinks." Grabbing my hand, Klair leads us toward the bar, knowing that the only chance the four of us will get served on a night this crowded is if it's her ordering.

After catching the eye of the handsome, grungy bartender, she leans forward, lingering slightly as she whispers our order of whatever concoction she thinks will be strong enough to get any of us on stage. Within minutes, the bartender has prepared two small serving trays of drinks for us—one of mixed drinks, one of shots. *Both are equally mysterious.* I settle our tab and we each take a tray as we carefully head through the throngs of people to where Dean and Graham are waiting for us.

"Alright, boys—" Klair says as we place the trays of liquid courage in front of our handsome dates. She grabs a shot, and we all follow her lead, raising our glasses together ceremoniously.

"Cheers...I pray *this* goes down better than what's about to happen next," she says before downing the shot and slamming it back down onto the table. Raising my own glass to my lips, I give her an inquisitive look which she dismisses with a shrug of her shoulders. She's up to something. *Per usual.*

"Let's give a warm welcome to our next performers..." The

DJ's voice booms throughout the crowd as I struggle to swallow whatever the hell was just in my glass. "It appears that we've got a dynamic duo up next...put your hands together for Dean Adams and Teddy Graham!" A boisterous round of applause erupts around us. If only I had my camera present to capture the range of emotions making their way across *Teddy Graham's* face because it is priceless.

Extreme confusion followed by immediate disdain. So much so that I can feel the tension radiating off his body as we all slowly turn our heads toward Klair who's now innocently sipping on her cocktail and doing a very poor job averting her gaze.

"I mean, it would be rude of us *not* to do this, right?" Dean asks in Graham's direction. It's easy to see he's unbothered by most things in life and I get the sense he'd do *anything* if it would make Klair smile.

"You can't be serious." Graham's tone is laced with anxiety but there is a smile tugging at the corners of his lips.

Dean extends a fist to Graham. "Come on, dude...we're in this together. I've got the perfect song!"

Oh. My. Gosh. Is this happening? I shoot Graham a sympathetic glance, desperately hoping he knows he doesn't have to do anything he isn't comfortable with—even though I'm shaking with excitement at the idea of Graham rocking out on stage.

Graham leans in, his lips nearly brushing mine and everything else fades away. Between the burn of the liquor and the infectious energy of everyone around us, my head begins to spin at his sudden closeness.

"You *will* be making this up to me," he says against my lips, pulling away when he knows I want more and firmly bumping Dean's fist with his own. "Let's get this over with."

Leaving the safety of our table, Dean and Graham make their way to the stage after sloppily downing their drinks, each with shoulders slightly hunched as they make their way through the rambunctious crowd. A group of girls, adorned with bachelorette party swag, shriek in perfectly horrible harmony as the two of them step onto stage. They huddle around the DJ booth discussing their song choice, and I watch as Graham shoots daggers at Dean when they head to the waiting mics.

"Are we sure about this?" I ask Klair as the cheers of the waiting crowd noticeably increases, the whole situation causes *my* anxiety to skyrocket and I'm not even the one performing.

"Oh *absolutely*," she says, raising her phone and pressing record as the music starts. The iconic intro of "Pour Some Sugar on Me" by Def Leppard blasts through the speakers while Dean belts along enthusiastically like a seasoned front man, forcing everyone's attention to center stage. Graham is standing there with his mouth agape in either awe or disgust at his partner's full-throttled dedication. The crowd goes wild as the guitar solo of the all-too familiar eighties classic rips through the speakers and the bass ricochets across every inch of the packed room.

There. Is. No. Way. They. Are. Singing. *This*. Song.

Dean pulls his mic from its stand, stepping directly in front of the gaggle of bachelorettes and moves his body in a way that is simultaneously awkward yet...arousing?

Klair and I look at each other, each of us completely stunned by this turn of events and begin screaming our heads off as we rush the stage.

She hands me her phone that's still recording and cups her hands around her mouth as we get closer. "Wooohooo...Take it off, baby." Dean must have heard her as he breaks into the widest grin between verses and sidesteps in our direction.

Despite the audible swoons of an endless sea of women, Klair is the only one he's serenading tonight. Dean gyrates his hips in time to the beat, only breaking eye contact with Klair to turn back to cue Graham who's standing there looking like a very sexy deer in headlights.

Graham closes his eyes as he places both hands on his mic. I can see his impressive chest expand as he takes in a large gulp of air.

He half-sings, half-talks the lyrics about taking and shaking a bottle and I cannot contain the smile that erupts across my face. He's swaying his hips from side-to-side in a way that indicates he's finally loosening up and when he reopens his eyes, he flashes me the most devilish toothy grin I've ever seen.

In perfect sync to the blaring music, he grabs his mic from its stand and storms the front of the stage. Dropping to his knees, Graham slides the remaining distance, skidding to a stop directly in front of where we are standing.

I will happily oblige as he croons about pouring some sugar on him as he's thrusting and grinding his hips in my direction. When Dean joins back in, the two of them put on the show of a lifetime causing Klair and I to cheer even louder. I know I'm not going to have a voice tomorrow, but I don't even care. This is truly the most wildly unexpected moment of my life and looking at the faces of Dean and Graham, who are clearly loving every second of their moment in the spotlight, I know tonight will be unforgettable.

Graham sings seductively about being hot and sticky and oh-so-sweet and in a shock to everyone in attendance, including me, he fists the hem of his shirt, ripping it open and exposing the most delicious set of abs as he rolls his body in such a way that makes my mouth water. The crowd loses their minds, erupting in a mixture of applause and collective *oh-my-god*'s.

My all-business man is giving every rock star a run for their money and looking like a freaking model while doing it and I've never been more attracted to him. His hair is slightly disheveled and beads of sweat are beginning to form along his tanned skin.

So when I run my hands along his exposed chest and stomach like the good groupie I am, I can't help but bask in Graham and Dean's moment of greatness.

As the crowd showers the two of them with even more applause, loud squeals and even the sprays of their drinks, this version of Graham—this carefree and achingly beautiful version of him—is one that will live rent-free in my mind for the rest of all time.

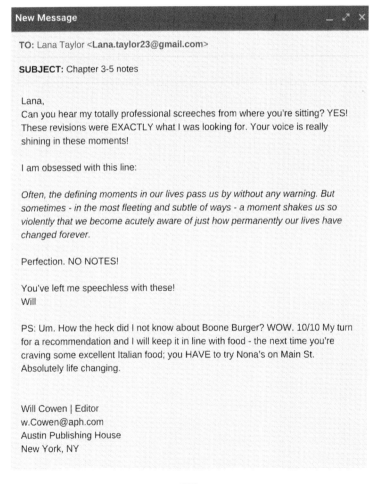

New Message

TO: Lana Taylor <Lana.taylor23@gmail.com>

SUBJECT: Chapter 3-5 notes

Lana,
Can you hear my totally professional screeches from where you're sitting? YES! These revisions were EXACTLY what I was looking for. Your voice is really shining in these moments!

I am obsessed with this line:

Often, the defining moments in our lives pass us by without any warning. But sometimes - in the most fleeting and subtle of ways - a moment shakes us so violently that we become acutely aware of just how permanently our lives have changed forever.

Perfection. NO NOTES!

You've left me speechless with these!
Will

PS: Um. How the heck did I not know about Boone Burger? WOW. 10/10 My turn for a recommendation and I will keep it in line with food - the next time you're craving some excellent Italian food; you HAVE to try Nona's on Main St. Absolutely life changing.

Will Cowen | Editor
w.Cowen@aph.com
Austin Publishing House
New York, NY

CHAPTER THIRTEEN

"WAIT...YOU INVITED LANA? TO YOUR PARENTS' HOUSE?" I thought I had mentioned that to Klair earlier. *Guess not.*

She's looking over at me from the passenger seat as we head to my parents' house, taking a break from choosing the next 90s boy band one-hit-wonder for us to belt out.

"It's really not that big of a deal." *I'm trying to not make it a big deal.* I can feel Klair's gears turning so I add, "Honestly? During our last meeting, I got the vibe that she doesn't have a local support system right now and with all of the work she's been doing on the book, I figured she could use a little...distraction?" Besides, knowing her track record, she might not even show.

"I get that. I really do..." This is unlike Klair, who usually embodies a *the more, the merrier* mentality. "But don't you think that's a lot of pressure to put onto this evening? And a little weird?"

"Yeah, aren't you already super stressed about introducing your parents to the *ever-so-dreamy* new man in your life?" Peeping his head between us, Dean physically inserts himself into our conversation. *I almost forgot he was back there!*

"Well shit, I am now...thanks for the reminder team." The three of us burst out laughing and yes, while I am incredibly anxious about the thought of introducing Graham to my parents, I know they are going to absolutely adore him. *How could you not?*

We turn down the familiar street of my parents' neighborhood in the heart of upstate New York Suburbia—a blast from the past, especially with Klair riding shotgun. After graduating high school and college, our professional lives totally monopolized everything else so it seems like it's been forever since we've been home together. Regardless of how long it's been, pulling up to my family's modest two-story always evokes the same emotion: *Home.*

Graham is leaning against his parked SUV as I pull into the driveway, a smile widening across his face when he sees us. Looking at the clock, I laugh to myself, noting that I would be concerned if Graham *hadn't* shown up twenty minutes early to an event I'd invited him to. Even though a small part of me wanted a moment alone with my parents to threaten them with a heads up to behave, seeing him here, looking gorgeous and relaxed, makes my stomach do backflips.

"Well, hello there, handsome," I say, getting out of the car and looking him up and down—failing to be discreet about it. *Whatever.*

Graham's more casually dressed than his typical suit and tie combo in the office, but he's definitely arrived ready to impress in his form-fitting, dark-washed jeans and a gray sweater underneath a sharp blazer. His eyes are hidden behind black, tinted aviator sunglasses and just when I think he couldn't get any more picture-perfect in this moment, he runs a hand through his loosely styled hair, flashing me that dazzling smile of his, and my entire body stills.

How is he real?

Pulling me into a bear hug, the intoxicating mixture of his cologne and *him* makes me melt against his strong body. "I've missed you," he says against my ear, his scruff sending multiple rounds of chills down my spine. Instinctually, I wrap my arms around his neck at the same time he grips my hips, pulling our bodies closer together than they already are. Graham plants a burning trail of kisses from my jaw, along my cheek and ever so gently on my lips, eliciting an audible moan from my mouth.

"There's a one hundred percent chance...my parents are... totally watching from the window," I say between torturous kisses.

"Good," he says playfully before giving me another kiss, letting his lips linger against mine for another perfect moment as he wraps his arms around my back. "Hopefully they can see that I make you happy."

I lean my forehead against his, tapping his chest with my hands. "I think *everyone* can see that," I admit, and it's the truth.

"Alright, lovebirds...can we go inside?" Dean yells from where he and Klair are waiting in the driveway, causing Graham and me to both laugh.

"Come on," I say, tugging at his arm. "Let's get this over with."

"One sec..." He turns and opens his car door, retrieving a bottle of wine and a gorgeous bouquet of white peonies. *Who is this man?*

"Did you bring my mother flowers?" I say through a smile so big my cheeks start to hurt.

"Of course...I want her to like me." He shakes the bottle of red. "Your dad, too." All of my previous nerves disappear as we join Klair and Dean, making our way to the front door of my childhood home. As if on cue, it swings open, revealing the ecstatic faces and loud screeches of both of my parents as they come barreling at us at full force.

"Ahhh...Will!" my mother half shouts, half cries as she launches herself at me. As much of a scene as this is, there is something so special about a mom hug. I see my dad smother Klair in a tight hug, one filled with familiarity as she spent almost every day with our family growing up, and hear her introducing Dean.

My mother has always been petite in stature but has a larger than life personality, one that has earned her the appropriate nickname *Firecracker* from my dad. He's always said it's because she fills his world with so much light, but I'm of the belief it's because she has the ability to put on *quite* the spectacle.

She places her hands on either side of my face, and looking into her eyes, I realize she looks exactly how I've always known her. Perhaps with the exception of a few wrinkles here and there and some random gray hairs in her dark blonde hair that she's informed me she's fully embracing. "It is *so good* to see you, son." I can hear the emotion in her voice as she slams me into another hug.

I give her a kiss on the cheek. "It's so good to see you, too. I'd like to introduce you both to someone..." I say, taking a step back toward Graham as my dad has now joined us. Klair and Dean have kindly stepped inside, giving this introduction some privacy. "Mom, Dad...this is Graham Austin, my boyfriend. Graham, this is my mom, Liz, and my dad, John."

"It's so nice to finally meet you both, Mr. and Mrs. Cowen. Will has spoken so highly of the two of you."

Both my parents smile at him, clearly taken by his formality and overall...*Graham-ness*.

"Oh sweetheart, please call me Liz," my mom says, giving him an equally enthusiastic hug, having to stand on her toes to wrap her arms around his neck. She winks at me from over his shoulder, mouthing *OH MY GOD*, clearly feeling the strength of his muscles and maybe lingering a little too long. *Only my mother.*

"And I assume these are for me?" my dad jokes, taking the flowers from Graham and giving his now empty hand a firm shake. "They're beautiful...you shouldn't have, Graham."

"Not as beautiful as you, John," Graham quickly fires back. Yeah, he's going to fit in perfectly with these two.

"Oh Lord...please ignore him," my mom says, swatting my dad's arm and putting hers around Graham. "Come on in, you two...the food's almost ready!"

The four of us head inside and the familiar smell of my mom's favorite sugar-cookie-scented candles greet us as we cross the threshold. No matter how much has changed in my life, coming home is like taking a step back in time. Everything is exactly how I remember it—the antique wooden bench in the entryway that used to belong to my grandmother, the smattering of gold-framed childhood photos, the lightly worn but cozy furniture. I get lost in the comforting nostalgia of it all as Graham and I take off our shoes and join Klair and Dean in the living room, who have made themselves right at home on the overstuffed couch.

"Is there anything I can help you with, Liz?" Graham asks my mom who's already begun busying herself in the kitchen. As much as I know he wants to make a good first impression, *this* is who he genuinely is—always ready and willing to offer a hand.

"Absolutely not, young man," she says, ushering him out of the kitchen. "That's why I had a kid, so that *he* could help. Go make yourself comfortable, sweetie."

Graham puts his hands up in surrender and heads into the living room to join the others, visibly uncomfortable not helping but doing his best to appear relaxed.

"What can I do, mom?"

She places a cutting board in front of me. "Can you finish the salad? Everything you'll need is in the produce drawer."

I head to the fridge, grabbing the armful of ingredients she's loaded up on and set them down in the sink. I meticulously wash the lettuce and vegetables, dry them, and place them in front of me on the counter.

"So?" my mom whispers, coming up next to me and gently nudging me with her hip.

"So, what?"

She groans dramatically, resulting in Graham briefly turning his attention in our direction. The two of us giggle but pretend not to notice.

"Don't hold out on me, Will...give me the *details.* Please, please please..." she begs like a child, tugging on my arm, making it impossible for me to cut the bell pepper I had in my hand.

"Oh my gosh, mom...okay, okay!" I say, knowing that she for sure won't let this go until I give her *something* to appease her curiosity. "Things are going really well. As you know, Klair, Graham, and I all work together and he's just..." My voice trails off as I lift my gaze to watch Graham. He's standing now, looking at the collage of family photos hanging in the living room while Dean and my dad are absorbed in a conversation about college football.

"...drop dead gorgeous?" my mom finishes my sentence with another nudge of her hip.

"I mean, *obviously*," I say, turning toward her, setting the knife down on the cutting board. "But beyond *that,* it's hard to explain...with Graham, everything just feels right. Like somewhere along the way, he and I were *meant* to find one another. Cliché, huh?"

She takes my hand in hers. "I think most people would call that lucky, son. It sounds pretty serious..." It's always been easy to talk to my mom. There are certain things that she just *knows* without having to go into too much detail. But this is a first for us...I've never had a *serious* relationship before. Definitely not one I included my family in, so part of me is thrilled at her excitement.

"It *feels* pretty serious," I admit, meeting her warm gaze. "I'm really falling for him, Mom."

She gives me another hug, her mother's intuition knowing that I probably need it. *She's right.* "I'd say the feeling is mutual..."

"How can you know that? You've met Graham for all of five seconds..."

"Oh honey...I think the entire neighborhood could feel the sparks you two were putting off in the driveway," she says, patting me hard on the cheek. "Now, can you hurry up on that salad? I'm starving."

A classic Liz Cowen mic drop.

Ah, how I've missed this. I can't help but laugh at my all-too-knowing mother as she returns her attention back to dinner prep. Graham is still exploring our family pictures, but he's now joined by my dad who keeps pointing out picture after picture, his enthusiasm growing with each one. It appears the two of them are getting along perfectly.

Just as I'm about to place the salad I prepared—*quite expertly, if I do say so myself*—on the dining room table, the doorbell rings.

"Ooh, that must be Lana." I hurry off toward the front door, the nerves I'd felt earlier slowly creeping their way back in.

"Hey...you made it," I say, opening the door a little too hard, causing it to slam loudly against the wall. Lana is dressed mini-mally in a camel-colored sweater paired with skinny jeans tucked into brown leather boots.

"I told you I would." She laughs as I raise my eyebrow at

her, remembering our history. "Okay, touché...but this is different. It's your family." Despite the confidence in her voice, I can sense her hesitancy.

"Well, come on in...I promise they won't bite. *At first.*" I step aside, signaling her to come inside.

"Ha Ha...here," she says, handing me the bowl she'd been holding as she passed. "I brought a salad." Of course, she did.

CHAPTER FOURTEEN

GRAHAM AND I ARE NOW ALONE IN MY CHILDHOOD ROOM after enjoying far too much food and even more wine. Lana left first, but only after she impressed me with her ability to field every question my parents threw her way, matching their enthusiasm. Mostly about what it was like working with me and if I was taking care of her...but they did manage to pry some interesting information from her usually tight-lipped self.

For instance, I learned she's from the Midwest originally and that she is fluent in four languages. Klair and Dean stayed a little while longer, succumbing to my mother's insistence that we all play cards. But eventually, they called it a night, taking my car back to the city so that I could conveniently ride home with Graham. I was hoping to *not* have to spend the night in my childhood bedroom, but Graham surprised me by thinking it would be fun.

So, here we are.

For as much as I was worried, tonight went exceptionally well, especially between Graham and my parents. From the second he stepped into our house, they welcomed him with warmth and the traditional Cowen enthusiasm that I was certain would overwhelm him, but per usual, Graham handled every moment of tonight with grace and charm.

Of the two of us, I think I was the overwhelmed one.

Being back here, in the home that defined so much of my early life, and seeing Graham interact so seamlessly with my family, it felt like a dream. He's honestly the first guy I've ever brought back with the intention of meeting my parents. Sure, there had been others who *happened* to meet my family, but their meetings were never intentional on my part.

With Graham, I wanted this—to immerse him in my world and pull back the curtain to a life I had before becoming the man he knows today. *Well, almost.*

Watching him now snoop through the things I cherished most as a kid...my collection of books, the random ribbons and trophies I've accumulated, he's even thrown on my high school varsity jacket. *Oh Lord, now THAT'S a sight.* And as much as that terrifies the hell out of me, the thought puts the biggest smile on my face. It leads me to walk over to Graham as he's looking at my collection of movie stubs on my cork board and wrap my arms around him, resting my cheek against his shoulder.

"Oh hello," he says in that cool and sweet tone that I love so much, placing his hands on top of mine as I squeeze him tightly.

"Did you have a nice time tonight?" I nervously ask, planting a soft kiss on his neck, inhaling the scent that can now only be described as *him*.

He turns around so we are standing face-to-face, never letting go of his hold on me, and offers a wide, toothy smile. "I had an amazing time tonight, truly." Graham reaches up and places his hand on the side of my face, stroking my cheek with

YOU & I, REWRITTEN

his thumb. "I can see where you get your cute little quirks from. And your parents are adorable. I love how much they clearly love one another, even after all these years."

Bringing my face to his, Graham kisses me in a way that instantly replaces any tension or doubt or insecurity I was feeling. I'll never not be surprised by the softness of his lips against mine, a stark contrast to the burn of his two-day-old stubble. As I deepen the kiss and press myself tighter against him, longing for more of, well, *him,* Graham pulls back. *This is a first.*

"Now that I have you alone," he says with lips still pressed against mine as I'm pulling at the waistband of his jeans. My hand slowly slides against the taut skin of his hips, feeling him tremble under my touch as my hand travels south. "I...I really did want to ask you about something." His voice sounds hesitant, nervous even, and I'm instantly intrigued. *Not enough to remove my hand from his crotch.*

"...ok? What's up?"

He leads me over to my much-smaller-than-I-remember full-sized bed. "Sit with me?" Panic instantly floods my veins. I sit next to Graham, my body rigid with anxiety having literally no idea what is going to come out of his mouth. "When you were helping your mom in the kitchen earlier, I was looking at all of the family photos your mom has hanging around."

Shit. My blood runs cold because I know *exactly* what he's going to ask me. *How the hell did I forget about that photo?*

"I noticed an older photo, you couldn't have been more than ten or eleven years old, but you were with someone who very clearly wasn't the man I met this evening. I only ask out of curiosity and absolutely respect your privacy..." his voice fading off as he looks anywhere but at me. *Is Graham anxious right now? Another first.*

My gears are turning at how to navigate this conversation

without getting too detailed, but at this point, looking at Graham—who's still wearing my varsity jacket by the way—how the hell can I possibly *not* open up to this man. Time and time again, he's shown me just how nonjudgmental he is, so the least I can do is be fully honest with him. As much as that goes against every fiber of my being when it comes to this situation, he deserves that.

Probably seeing my inner turmoil, Graham reaches over, taking both of my hands in his and says, "Forget I asked...it was an unnecessary question."

"Nothing from you is ever unnecessary, handsome..." I exhale. Graham is searching my face now, his eyes filled with concern that he's possibly overstepped. The last thing I want is for him to feel like he's done something wrong, because he hasn't. *He's perfect. Breathe, Will.* "That picture you saw? That's my biological father," I choke out through closed eyes. There. It's out in the world and seemingly nothing catastrophic has happened. *Yet.*

"Oh okay, so John is your stepfath..."

"No," I say more forcefully than I probably meant to, causing Graham to lean back. This has always been such a sensitive subject for me, especially when I was younger, and one of the reasons why I've stopped bringing my father up. *One of them.* "No...he is my dad. Always has been, always will be." My statement lingers awkwardly between us, sending waves of the most uncomfortable heat over every inch of my body. This right here is why I don't ever voluntarily bring this up. Not because of him or my past...or even how it feels, but because of the physical reaction it causes me. Thinking of *him* makes me feel like I've been engulfed in flames, a blistering burn that for the last ten years I've succeeded in avoiding.

"John and my mom have been together for as long as I can

remember," I try to explain through long, controlled breaths. "My father served in the military and was gone a lot. When I did see him, it was...it..." My mouth is dry at the memory of spending time with him. It's been years since I've seen him and the pain is still just as raw. "I've just always called John 'Dad' because that's who he's been to me since the moment he came into my life. He's my dad."

Graham, who always chooses his words very carefully, appears deep in thought, his brow now furrowed as he looks down at our intertwined hands.

"I'm sorry," I whisper. "I know this is probably weird and you probably think—"

"There is absolutely *nothing* for you to apologize for," he interrupts, his tone soft as he meets my gaze. "I'm the sorry one, Will. It was never, *ever* my intention to bring up anything that causes you pain or harm."

I lean my shoulder into him, resting my head on his and putting my arm on his leg. "This is such a me thing. Most people have no problem sharing about their families, regardless of the baggage that comes with that." I brush my lips against his jaw and say, "I just don't like being reminded of everything that comes with *him*."

"Which is perfectly fine, and again, I apologize for bringing it up," he exhales. "But I hope you know that I would never judge you or think of you any differently because of who is in or out of your life or where you come from. I understand the complexities of family dynamics, so if you *do* ever want to talk about it, I'm here."

Everything about Graham is genuine, from the way he throws himself full-throttle into every work project to the way he speaks with me. It's so easy with him—easy to be myself and easy to hope for a happier future. But this? Talking to Graham about this makes me feel like I'm shattering into a million pieces, my body left jagged and splintered, unable to be put back together. Because ever since the last time I saw my father, the only thing I've cared about, the only thing I've worked toward, is becoming the opposite of him. I look at Graham, holding his gaze and even though he doesn't know my father, I just pray he sees me for who I am, for the man I've strived so hard to be.

"Just kiss me," I say, wrapping my arms around his neck and pulling him on top of me. "I just need you to kiss me and never stop."

And he listens. Graham's lips claim mine, soft at first but then with a need that matches what I've felt all night. I don't know if it's because we are in my childhood home or the intensity of our conversation, but I want him now. I reach for the hem of his sweater, desperate to feel the warmth of his skin on my own and in one swift movement, Graham's shirt and my varsity jacket are on the floor, his muscled body on full display.

High school me would NEVER believe this was happening.

"Take your clothes off." His demand causes me to pant, knowing what's coming. *Hopefully me.*

I quickly remove my clothes, eager to have his hands over every inch of me. He hovers over me, his eyes burning with lust, and before I can beg him to fuck me, his lips are on my neck, his teeth grazing the sensitive skin, causing me to shiver with pleasure. Pinning my hands down, he trails kisses across my chest, flicking my nipple with his tongue, and down my stomach. My cock is throbbing, begging to be touched and when he takes me fully in his mouth, my eyes roll to the back of my skull.

Fuuuuuck.

He's torturing me in the best possible way. When he finally releases the grip he's had on my wrists, I grab a fistful of his hair, controlling the glide of his mouth over me, and admire the talent this man possesses.

Conflicted between not wanting to finish like this and never, *ever* wanting this to end, I reach down, placing my hands on either side of his beautiful face and pull him up to meet my wanting lips. "Fuck me. *Now*."

He moans against my lips, reaching for his pants to extract a small bottle of lube. Within seconds, he's wrapped my legs around his waist and is sliding into me with ease, the fullness of him unlocking the last bit of tension my body was holding on to.

This is where he belongs.

I slide my hands down Graham's muscled back, feeling it tighten with every thrust, and grab his ass, pulling him deeper into me. *God, I fucking need this.*

Graham is sliding into me with slow, intentional thrusts, each one threatening to bring me closer and closer to the edge. His lips are parted, breathing hard, and he's running his hands over my arms, across my chest. Leaning down, he kisses me hard, his tongue entangling with mine, the sweetness of his taste enveloping me.

"Get on top," he says, winded and full of desire.

Rolling us over, I claim Graham's cock once more, this new position allowing me to truly appreciate his size. I place my hands on his flexed chest at the same time he grips my dripping cock with one hand and my hip with the other, pushing me down deeper onto him.

He's really picking up speed now, sliding all the way out, leaving me begging for his return, only to slam back into me, deeper than before. It's too much and not nearly enough at the same time. Between his deep thrusts and his hold on my cock, I've reached the point of no return.

"Fuck...Graham...I'm gonna..." I moan, my release coating his abs and chest, sending me into a state of pure ecstasy. He grabs my hips, giving me a few more deep, relentless thrusts, before pouring into me, every spasm of pleasure I feel of his only enhancing my own.

"Holy...shit!" he grunts, pushing deeper into me, ensuring I get every last drop from him. There is no greater feeling than hearing Graham have such a visceral reaction and seeing his pleasure plastered across that gorgeous face, knowing that it was all because of me.

"Well, I am thoroughly fucked," I say, causing Graham to burst into laughter, a sight that I will never not be obsessed with. I bend down and press my lips to his. "I needed that."

"Oh, me too..." he says with a grin. "Come here." He wraps me in his arms, running his fingers along my arm. "You are so beautiful," he whispers and it's the last thing I hear before I close my eyes and give in to the weight of what today meant for me.

For us.

I'm waiting on the front steps again.

Waiting for the flash of the green Jeep to come turning around the corner and into the driveway. My bag is packed, filled with my favorite toys and stories for bedtime. I'm still waiting when Mom comes out.

"He'll be here soon," she says. Her face is sad.

The Jeep is here and I go running to meet him, dragging my bag with me. "Daddy!" But he's angry.

"No, Scott...you're not taking him like this." Mom is crying. I'm already in the car. "Scott...you're not okay to drive. Scott, if you take him, I'm going to call the po—"

Mom's on the ground. John's here now. He's with mom and then he has me in his arms. Daddy's yelling but then he's gone.

"I want my daddy."

John tells me he knows and hugs me.

I'm on the steps again. This time, I'm older, and I'm not looking forward to seeing the same old green Jeep come screeching into the driveway.

I've stopped bringing anything I like with me so my bag is just clothes and my toothbrush.

My dad is with me this time. He's let me call him that for a few years now.

The Jeep is here and he gets out. "Hey buddy...ready to go?" Dad goes over and says something to him, something I can't hear.

"Get in." He's angry again but I do what he says.

Sometimes he's happy. *Please be happy today.*

We get pizza together. He asks about school and what girl I like. *I lied.* He takes me to a movie, his arm around my shoulders.

"You want ice cream?" he asks after.

Today was a good day.

When we get to his house, he tells me to go outside and play. I ride my bike until it gets dark. When I come back in, I can smell it. He's asleep on the couch, the bottle in his hand.

I go to bed.

I'm no longer sitting on the steps.

I'm a teenager now, having no desire to see or deal with him when he gets into one of his moods. He apologizes when he gets like that, but it means nothing anymore. I tell my mom and dad

I'm not going. They try to reason with me, but I've made up my mind. I've had enough.

He's pounding on the door. *Don't let him in.* But they do, and we can all smell it. How pathetic. He pushes past Dad, his movements wild and unpredictable.

"Let's go," he yells. "It's our weekend. Let's go, *now."* He starts crying. "John, Liz...tell him. It's our weekend." He's pathetic.

"I'm not going anywhere with you," I stand up to him, my voice quivering, "ever again."

He's not crying anymore. He's livid.

That's when he punches me. That's when something inside of me breaks. That's when I know he never cared about me.

―――――――

"Will...WILL...Baby!" Graham is shaking me and I realize I'm sobbing, my arms wrapped around him, clinging to his body like a child. "Shh...everything's okay, baby," he says, holding me tight. "It was just a dream."

"I was never good enough for him," I sob. "I was never good enough for him to love, and I don't know why. I don't know why, Graham, and it kills me. Why wasn't I good enough for him?"

Why the fuck didn't he love me enough?

My words are barely audible between my sobs and no matter how hard I try to calm down, being here and being reminded of him has ripped open the crack in my chest I've tried so hard to ignore all of these years. I hate him so much. I hate him with a rage that consumes me, one that causes my vision to blur and my hands to tremble. I'm exhausted from having to pretend that it doesn't bother me, exhausted from ignoring the hurt and minimizing what he put me through. *What he put all of us through.* I can't look up at Graham right now; this is a side of me I never wanted him to see, and if I see even the faintest trace of pity on his face, I don't think I could ever recover from it.

"Why didn't he love me?" I whimper into the darkness as Graham squeezes me tighter, not knowing how badly I need that question answered, or how him just holding me through this living nightmare means everything.

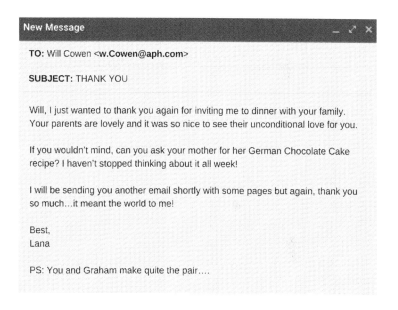

New Message — ↗ ✕

TO: Will Cowen <**w.Cowen@aph.com**>

SUBJECT: THANK YOU

Will, I just wanted to thank you again for inviting me to dinner with your family. Your parents are lovely and it was so nice to see their unconditional love for you.

If you wouldn't mind, can you ask your mother for her German Chocolate Cake recipe? I haven't stopped thinking about it all week!

I will be sending you another email shortly with some pages but again, thank you so much...it meant the world to me!

Best,
Lana

PS: You and Graham make quite the pair....

CHAPTER FIFTEEN

THE DYNAMIC BETWEEN GRAHAM AND I HAS MOST definitely shifted, especially in the workplace. Disclosing our relationship to HR wasn't nearly as stressful or complicated as I'd been fearing. We signed a few forms and confirmed that on paper, Graham wasn't my supervisor in any way and went about our business. While this didn't feel entirely necessary, it does provide a sliver of peace knowing that if things do get messy or weird, our professional lives will remain intact. I don't know if anyone else can sense the change or how much more our orbits are intentionally colliding, but throughout the day, I'm finding more excuses to be near him. Or to drag him away in the stairwell to steal a kiss from *those lips.*

Now I look forward to getting to the office early each morning, something Klair refuses to partake in. Depending on who gets there first, Graham and I have fallen into the sweetest routine of preparing coffee for one another, hoping to provide a caffeinated surprise to kick start our morning. His office light is off when I make it into the office today, so I quickly drop my stuff off at my desk and head to the break room.

Turning on the lights, I set the coffee machine to brew,

letting the woody and chocolaty aroma fill the room. I grab our mugs from the drying rack and open the fridge to grab the caramel creamer I know he loves.

"Good morning," Graham's voice comes out of nowhere, causing me to almost drop the creamer. He wraps his arms around me, smothering me in his signature scent.

I place the bottle on the counter and turn to face him. "Well hello, handsome," I say, wrapping my arms around his neck. He flashes me that smile I've come to live for. "Did you have a nice night?"

"It was fine," he says, inching his face closer to mine. "I definitely missed you." Graham presses his lips to mine, pulling me tight against his chest. I entwine my fingers in his hair, deepening the kiss that sends chills over every inch of my body. *Ugh.* I can feel his smile against my lips as he grabs my ass playfully.

"Mr. Austin, not in the workplace," I tease, causing him to laugh. "But I missed you, too." I give him another lingering kiss right in the corner of that crooked smile of his. "Coffee?"

"Please."

I detangle myself from Graham, having to make certain, um, adjustments to avoid any complaints about indecency in the workplace. After pouring the steaming brew into each of our cups and mixing in the sweet cream, we each take a mug and slowly walk back to our team's section.

"Busy day today?" I ask, watching him as he takes a sip of java mid-stride.

"Not too terrible, honestly," he says, his tongue licking a drop of coffee from his lip. *Can I do that?* "Just a few meetings this morning and then hoping to catch up on some manuscripts. What about you?" he asks with a grin.

"Hmm...Klair asked for a second set of eyes on a few projects she's juggling so I'm going to help with that, and then Lana has sent me a few chapter updates based on some revisions that I need to look over. Beyond that, it should be a pretty mellow day." *Fingers crossed.*

"How is that going by the way? Any better?"

"Definitely. She and I have established a rhythm now that we are both comfortable with and she's been churning out some really powerful stuff."

I mean it, too. Lana has been working incredibly hard over the last few weeks and I am so proud of the progress she's made. She takes feedback so well and really leans into the critiques, returning with pages that are far better than I could have imagined.

"That's so great to hear," he says, bumping me with his shoulder. "I can't wait to read more of her work." We arrive at my desk, indicating the time has come to go our separate ways. People have slowly been trickling into the office, the quiet sounds of their own morning routines fill the open office. "Well... I guess it's time to get busy. I hope you have a great day, mister."

"Likewise." I want to kiss him so badly—*so, so badly*—but I reluctantly refrain. Instead, I let my gaze linger a little too long on his strong and toned backside as he heads to his own office.

Taking advantage of my clear distraction, Klair sneaks up behind me and whispers in my ear, "Nice view, huh?"

"Ahhh, beat it, nerd!" I yell, trying to stifle my laugh.

She removes her jacket, sets her purse down, and reaches for my coffee mug, taking a big gulp of the hot liquid.

"Um, sure...help yourself."

"Thanks, bestie. It's just *so hard* coming into the office and not having a special someone make my coffee everyday, you know?" She hands it back to me, a prominent deep red lipstick ring now decorating the rim.

"You're so dramatic. You know what? Keep it," I laugh, shaking my head as I walk back to our break room to brew another cup. Between Graham and his sneak attacks and Klair, well...just being Klair, I can already tell today is going to be an interesting one.

"Knock, knock," Graham says, tapping on the side of our cubicle, pulling both Klair and me out of our individual work trances, a welcome distraction from the endless edits I was reviewing all morning.

"Hey, boss man, what brings you to our side of the office?" Klair asks, waving her arms with a flair toward our section, resulting in my favorite Graham smirk that makes my heart race. He leans against the wall, crossing his ankles.

"I actually have a favor to ask the two of you," he says to us, but he's looking directly at me. Did he just...? *Yup, he most certainly bit his lip and cocked an eyebrow.* I swallow hard. He could literally ask me to bury a body right now and I'd drag Klair with me kicking and screaming. Graham using his sex appeal on me while asking for help wasn't how I pictured my day going, but hey, who am I to complain?

"And what might this favor be?" I ask, leaning forward on my elbows. I'm intrigued considering Graham *usually* handles everything himself.

"Well, I know you are both working with newer authors right now and I really want to capitalize on that." Graham's face lights up when he talks about work, especially projects that he's passionate about, and I can't help but feel a wave of pride wash over me knowing that one of *my* books is part of his excitement. "I have a few meetings later this afternoon with my father to pitch some upcoming press events, and I'd love to have a few writing samples and talking points from both of you to start generating some buzz. Do you think you can put something together for me?"

This is actually perfect. Klair and I were *just* talking about ways to start promoting our authors and had begun putting together mini press packets, so this so-called favor is essentially done.

"Funny you bring this up," Klair says, giving me a grin as she proceeds to explain what we've already put together. "Does something like that work?"

"Look at you two...our little publishing dream team," Graham says. "If you can just make sure there is some background information on each author and print out a few copies, this will be so helpful."

"Too easy," I say, leaning back in my chair. Graham runs his eyes over my body, so I stretch my arms over my head, flexing in the process and hoping he notices. He shakes his head, rolling his eyes at the same time. *Gotcha.*

As he starts to head back to his office, Klair pops up from her chair. "Wait...since this is basically done and I'm *starving,* join us for lunch?" I don't know that I've ever seen Graham leave the office for lunch. He's usually bent over a manuscript or typing away at his computer between bites of his salad. *Boring.* I mean, I guess that's how he has the body he does.

He's contemplating Klair's invite. Briefly, he looks at me, uncertainty written all over his face. *Is he nervous?* I give him a reassuring smile; it's just lunch after all.

"Sure," he says hesitantly.

"Okay, well don't sound too excited," Klair laughs, grabbing her purse. "Come on, Will...Mr. Bossy Pants is buying."

She pulls me up from my desk and loops her arm through mine as we head down the hall, Graham walking behind us with his hands in his pockets and the cutest smile on his face.

"Damn, you were *so* right to be gawking over him earlier. Look at that bu..."

"Oh my god, woman...Will you *shut up!*" I hiss at Klair as we are waiting in line. After asking what we wanted, Graham is standing at the counter placing our order but definitely still within earshot.

"Jeez, okay. But I'm just saying...go you." she says, putting her hands up defensively but still feeling compelled to give me a wink.

She's not wrong, Graham looks *extra* sexy today wearing his slim chinos and chunky sweater, a very casual look compared to his usual suit-and-tie combo.

"Yeah, yeah...let's grab a table before he gets irritated with the pair of us." I say, wrapping my arm around her shoulders and giving her a much-deserved squeeze.

"Ughhh...Get off."

We both start laughing, way too loudly I might add, in search of a table, settling on a secluded booth in the corner.

Waiting for Graham to join us, Klair and I take seats across from one another.

"You seem really happy," she says, reaching across the table and grabbing my arm. "Like, *really* happy."

"That's because I am, silly." She's been in my life longer than almost anyone and knowing that she sees what I'm feeling means the world to me. "Beyond all of *that*," I say, waving in Graham's general direction, "for the first time in a while, everything in my life, personally and professionally, seems to be falling into place. I know you're not supposed to say things like that out loud because, you know...*jinxes* and what not, but moving back, this job...it has all been worth it."

"Well good, because selfishly, I don't think I want to adult without you again."

"It's a good thing you don't have to then," I say, as she stares back at me with that look in her eyes, the one that only friends who've been through the complexities of life together have.

Graham's timing could not be more perfect. Interrupting before either of us melt into a puddle of emotions, he slides our tray of food on the table and takes the empty seat in the booth next to me.

"Alright...I've got a turkey club and a side of fries for you," he says, handing Klair her sandwich. "And an Italian Panini with a cup of autumn squash soup for this guy." He passes me my lunch, brushing his hand against mine. "What did I miss?"

"Oh nothing," Klair says, her mouth already full of her sandwich that I'm kicking myself for not ordering. "I was just threatening Will with his life if he ever decides to move away from me again."

Turning his attention toward me, I see a look of panic momentarily cross his face.

"Relax...I'm not going anywhere." I put my hand on his thigh, giving it a reassuring squeeze. "What Klair *meant* to say is that we were just talking about how good this move has been for me." My clarification causes Graham to visibly relax, but his reaction gives me butterflies the size of pterodactyls. *So he wants me to stick around, huh?*

"Well, I'm definitely happy to hear that you're enjoying your move to the company," Graham says, picking at his sandwich. "While I have you both here..."

"No way, mister...You're violating lunch-break rules. No work chat until *after* we've finished eating." Klair teases, throwing a French fry in his direction, which Graham picks up and throws it right back at her, causing us all to burst out laughing.

"He's new to the lunch club so I'm granting him a one-time pass," I say, before this turns into a full-blown adult food fight. "What's up?"

Graham clears his throat, straightening his back in his seat. "I guess I just wanted to ask if either of you have noticed that the morale in the office seems to be...off?"

We're both silent.

He looks at me, then across the table at Klair. "It's that bad?" he asks, as his voice softens, a sense of defeat in his tone.

"No!" Klair and I both say at the same time.

"It's definitely not *bad,* just a little...intense?" she says.

Pressing my thigh against his, I add, "And I don't think that's a bad thing. Has the office ever planned some sort of fun, group outing?"

Klair snorts.

We're both looking at her, clearly waiting for her to explain.

"Come on, Will...you know Mr. Serious over here wouldn't know fun if it bit him in the ass," she teases. *I volunteer to bite his ass.* "Graham, I adore you...you're the best editor and colleague I've ever worked with, but do you do *anything* for fun?"

Graham's expression is unreadable as he stares Klair down from across the table. Leaning forward, he rests his elbows on the table and places his square jaw on his fists.

"What is this *fun* you speak of?" he asks, breaking into a grin, causing Klair and I both to laugh.

"I'm serious," she giggles. "What do you do for fun? Working out doesn't count...and neither does reading, because let's be honest, none of us can read for leisure anymore."

"Hmm...I can think of a lot of *fun* things I enjoy doing," he says, turning to face me. *Oh fuck.* His hand trails up my leg, ever so softly grazing my bulge with the back of his hand.

"Holy shit, *that*...doesn't count either," Klair adds, throwing another fry in our direction.

Graham smirks, taking his time responding to her very demanding inquiry. But while he's figuring out his answer, I'm thinking of my own. Is this what getting older is? Working and eating and not really doing anything *fun?*

"Um...I like to bake," Graham says quietly, looking down at his barely-touched food. His demeanor changes, like a bashful child sharing a secret. There are moments when I'm with Graham where he says or does something, moments like this one, where I catch myself wondering how the hell someone like him exists.

The three of us spend the rest of our lunch break sharing stories of the past. Graham spends a significant amount of time interrogating Klair about our high school adventures, which causes me to make a mental note to smother Klair later for going over my "awkward phase" in excruciating detail.

After walking back to the office, full of food and way more laughter than I was anticipating, we all go our separate ways, settling back into the workday. Between the edits I was previously working on and finalizing the favor Graham asked for, my mind keeps wandering to the sweet visual of a certain tall and serious man I know baking in the kitchen.

I concoct a plan for some mid-week fun, hoping to put a smile on Graham's face and see him in his element. After wrapping up my tasks for the day, I sneak out of the office to get everything I'll need to pull this off.

I ring the buzzer of Graham's building with my elbow.

After making a quick pit-stop at home to change, my hands are now full from my trip to the grocery store, the canvas totes I brought with me filled to the brim with an arsenal of essentials.

"Hello?" Graham's voice chimes through the voice box, clearly not expecting visitors.

"Hey...it's me! Can I come up?" I hear the pop of the door unlocking and shifting the weight of bags, I pull open the door and head to the elevator, taking it up to the twelfth floor. I'm now realizing this is the first time I'm showing up to his place unannounced.

Is this a bad idea? *Probably.*

Well, I'm here now, so there's no turning back. I knock on Graham's apartment door, hoping my impromptu visit doesn't make me come across as weird and clingy.

Graham opens the door almost instantly, standing there casually dressed in soft joggers and a plain white t-shirt. *Um... he's barefoot.* "Well, hello...I was just thinking about you," he says with a smile. Okay, thank GOD he's not totally turned off by my visit. Seeing the bags I'm carrying, he quickly takes a few from me. "Come in," he says, stepping aside so I can cross the threshold into his apartment.

Taking my shoes off, I follow him as he leads me into the immaculately clean and spacious kitchen, placing the canvas totes I'd been carrying on the large island.

"What did I do to deserve this fun surprise?" he asks, coming over and wrapping me in a tight hug. He smells clean, like he recently took a shower, but I can still smell the sweetness of his cologne.

"I was hoping you'd be up for a little fun," I say, kissing him on the neck, his stubble tickling my lips.

"Is that so?" He gives me a questioning look and pulls me tighter against him, the conversation we had with Klair obviously fresh in his mind.

"Down boy." I push away from him but take his hand in

mine, leading him over to the bags I brought with me. "I thought we could do some baking…Maybe bring in a sweet treat for the office tomorrow?"

"Did you buy the *whole* store?" he asks, laughing while putting his arm around me.

"Okay, in my defense, I don't have a lot of experience baking and I wasn't sure how stocked your kitchen would be…which, thinking about it now is dumb because it's *you.*"

He starts rifling through the bags, pulling out a bottle of my favorite red I snagged at the last second, raising his eyebrow at me.

"That's for me, duh." I snatch it from him as he pulls open a drawer and hands me a wine opener. After removing the cork with a *pop*, he sets two stemless glasses in front of me, which I fill with the delicious wine.

He raises his glass. "To random…*fun*," he says, clinking his glass against mine, his eyes bright and filled with mischief.

"Cheers." I watch as he takes a deep pull from his glass, his lips parting ever so slightly. A rogue drop of wine remains on the glass which he slowly retrieves by sliding his tongue along the rim, making eye contact with me the entire time that sends waves of desire through my veins. He knows exactly what he's doing. *Lord, help me.* Get it together…we're here to bake.

"Anyway," I say, putting some distance between us. "I may or may not have selfishly picked out these ingredients?"

Reaching into the bag, I grab the chocolate chips I'd refrained from snacking on on the way over here and toss it to him, which he catches in one hand.

"Chocolate chip cookies?" he asks.

"My favorite *and* a fail-proof way to ensure office morale is boosted, killing two birds with one stone." I hop on the counter next to him. "Actually, three birds."

"Oh yeah? How's that?"

"Because you, my sexy little baker, will be having fun." I say, planting a kiss on his cheek. "Now come on, chop chop."

He rolls his eyes at me, taking out the remainder of the ingredients and placing them on the counter, clearly separating what he's going to need from what was unnecessary for me to buy. Before I know it, he's already meticulously measuring out ingredients and combining them into a big, glass bowl. Sipping on my wine in his kitchen and in his world, my heart melts for the man who told me that baking brings him joy, especially seeing the smile on his face when he pauses what he's doing to look over at me.

"Wanna help me mix?" he asks, holding the wooden spoon in my direction, which of course I do because I'm realizing there isn't a whole lot I wouldn't do for this man.

Taking the spoon from his hand, I let my fingers linger, feeling the warmth of his touch against mine. Our eyes meet and the electricity I always feel around him buzzes around us, my own personal lightning rod.

Setting the spoon on the counter, I take him by surprise when I lunge at him, crashing my lips to his and wrapping my arms around his neck. I take a deep inhale of him, the chocolate and sugar accentuate his natural sweetness causing me to deepen our kiss, taking his tongue in my mouth as I force our bodies closer to one another.

"Well hello," he whispers against our lips, his hands frozen at his sides, traces of flour on his fingertips. "What was that for?"

"Oh, no reason," I say, picking up the spoon and sliding in front of him, claiming my spot at the mixing bowl. "I'm just having a lot of fun, that's all."

He laughs, putting his arms around me and kissing the side of my head. "So am I."

"Did you bring them?" I ask, unable to hide my excitement. I raced to the conference room to ensure I was the first one to our weekly staff meeting that morning. Well, besides Graham.

"Can you please *shut up?*" he hisses at me, though not even he can keep a straight face. Lifting a bag from beneath the table to his lap, he slides a large container to the center of the table. The rest of the team starts filing in, taking their usual seats. Klair, who's in on the surprise, sits down next to me, both of us leaning back in our chairs with our arms crossed.

"Ooh...are those cookies?" Audra inquires.

As soon as she lifts the lid of the container, filling the conference room with the mouthwatering aroma of the baked goods, it's game over. I don't know what it is about chocolate chip cookies that turns offices into a feeding frenzy, but it happens *every time* without fail. I know these are some of the best cookies I've ever had so when I hear the disturbingly close to sexual noises coming from the rest of our team, I smile knowing they are in agreement.

"Thank you *so much* for the cookies, Klair," Mark says, his mouth stuffed with the chocolaty goodness, his eyes closed in enjoyment.

"Um. These are *amazing!*" Jane says, echoing his sentiments.

"Actually, I didn't bring the treats today," Klair says, raising her eyebrows in Graham's direction.

The entire team swivels their head at Graham, who's sitting quietly, twirling his pen between his fingers, clearly uncomfortable with all the attention suddenly on him.

"Graham, this was so nice...thank you so much," Audra says, stealing another cookie from the container and placing it on her notepad.

"It was nothing, honestly," he says, straightening in his chair. He looks around the conference table, looking each of our team members in the eye. "I just wanted to do a little something to show my appreciation for the hard work you all have been doing. It doesn't go unnoticed, not by my father and definitely not by me. So, load up on some sugar, and unless anyone has anything super pressing, let's use this time to just relax, have some more coffee, and chit chat." He grabs a cookie, taking a big, dramatic bite, the smallest smudge of chocolate sticking to his upper lip that I literally have to force myself to keep from leaning across the table and licking off.

I can feel the mood in the conference room noticeably shift, the cookies doing the morale magic I'd hoped they would, and seeing Graham being so casual with the rest of the team makes my heart soar. While the cookies were just a small gesture of appreciation, it was his genuine and kind words that seemed to cause a much-needed thaw within our team's dynamic, and for that, I couldn't be prouder.

New Message — ↗ ✕

TO: Lana Taylor <**Lana.taylor23@gmail.com**>

SUBJECT: Tomorrow's Press Event - 9 a.m.

Good morning, Lana - I just wanted to share with you the interview questions for your conversation with Hannah tomorrow. This is a low-threat event and I will be with you the entire time. Take a second to review the questions and if you have any concerns, please let me know!

EXHALE.

I can totally picture you starting to freak out but you got this! You're just going to talk about the book, your inspiration and your excitement for its release… everything will be perfect!

I believe in you!

PS: If you need a moment of calm tonight, put *The Light* by The Album Leaf on repeat. Trust me.

Will Cowen | Editor
w.Cowen@aph.com
Austin Publishing House
New York, NY

CHAPTER SIXTEEN

"DON'T WORRY." I REACH OVER AND GIVE LANA'S ARM A reassuring squeeze. "This is nothing to freak out over. Our office has worked with Hannah and her team for years, so I assure you, this is very low-threat and will be over before you know it."

Lana's looking at me like she doesn't believe a word I'm saying, but nods her head anyway. She's wearing a casual but chic jewel-toned pantsuit and her dark hair is pinned neatly back. She looks strong and feminine and ready to shake up the literary world.

The two of us are sitting in our conference room waiting to be called into Graham's office which has been transformed into a make-shift studio. I'm focusing my efforts on remaining calm for her sake because by the way she's picking at the mocked-up cover of her book, I can tell her nerves are all over the place.

"Besides, you've created something pretty special. The world is going to love it as much as I do," I reassure her, knowing that if I were in her shoes, I'd need to hear it.

She looks up at me, her smile warm, but those piercing green eyes of hers are a million miles away. "Thank you, Will. That means the world coming from you."

Before I can give too much thought to how *off* Lana seems right now, Graham comes through the frosted-glass doors, flashing me that signature smirk, looking every bit the man in charge today. I smile back at him and notice he's followed by his father, Mitch, who's in lockstep with Hannah.

Sliding our chairs back, probably harder than we both intended to, Lana and I both awkwardly stand up at Mitch's impromptu arrival, insinuating a more serious meeting than either of us anticipated. *If Lana wasn't nervous before, she sure is now.*

"Lana, I don't think you've had the chance to meet my father yet," Graham says as Mitch takes her hand in his. "Dad, this is Lana Taylor...our newest author whose book we're here to talk about which is guaranteed to be a smash." He turns his head slightly in my direction, giving me a secret wink. *Swoon.*

"It's so nice to meet you, Mr. Austin." Lana's voice is reserved, but she meets his gaze with a kind smile.

"Oh, Lana...please call me Mitch! I hope our team has been taking care of you."

From my limited interactions with Mitch, I've realized he has a way of making everyone he's talking to feel like the most important person in the room. *Like father, like son.* There's something undeniably sweet about his demeanor. Where others have built their businesses on ruthlessness and savvy, Mitch, and now Graham, have built theirs on kindness, and respect. It was one of the reasons I applied for this position.

"How are you feeling about today? Are you ready?" he asks.

"Ready as I'll ever be with this kinda stuff." I can hear Lana's introverted tendencies hollering in protest about the interview, but she's putting on a brave face because it's just what has to be done.

"Well...we all know you're going to knock it out of the park."

Directing his attention to me, he asks, "Can I steal you for a second?"

Shit. Hannah and Graham are deep in a discussion about last-minute details, but this causes Graham to momentarily shift his focus our way.

"Absolutely." I follow him out of the conference room, completely unsure of where this is going to go. I've always admired Mitch, and if I'm being honest, I would give anything to have the type of career he's had. So, if I've somehow disappointed him, I don't...I can't fathom how awful that would make me feel.

"We haven't had a lot of alone time, just you and I." *Please don't fire me. Please don't fire me. Please don't fir...* "That meddling son of mine is always around," he says, laughing and flashing me a grin that has me looking into Graham's future. "Before you get back to it, I want to really see how Lana is doing...the poor girl looked like she was going to pass out," he adds, his voice riddled with concern.

"I know. Through all of our prep, she's expressed her challenging relationship with public speaking and feeling like the attention is all on her." Mitch crosses his arms, leaning against the wall. How have I never noticed how much he and Graham emulate one another? "But we worked out a plan in case she feels uncomfortable or anxious at any time. Besides, if she can survive Graham's version of feedback...*on top* of mine, she totally can handle this."

"Good," he laughs. "Because *Lana* is our number one priority here. There will be other opportunities for press and interviews, but I don't ever want to push one of our authors to do something they clearly aren't comfortable with, so keep an eye on her like you have been." A statement like this from the boss carries a lot of weight. *Another reason I adore working for this man.*

"Yes, sir...I promise that this is *my* number one priority, as well."

He puts his large hand on my shoulder. "And what about you, Will?"

Me? Why would he want or even care to know how I'm doing? *That's weird, right?*

"I'm ...good?" I say, my confusion and hesitation put a smile on his face.

Taking a step closer to me, he says, "Son, I know this is your first book with us, and from what Graham has told me..." He puts his hands up, clearly seeing the signs of panic begin to form on my face. "Nothing personal—he would never do that. He's just expressed to me how deeply moving this book is. And boy, do I know from personal experience how taxing working night and day on projects like these can be."

He can't help but come across as fatherly. Not in a *let me tell you how to do your job* way, but out of concern for the well-being of his team. It's another reminder of the incredible family Graham comes from.

"I appreciate the check-in...I really do. But I'm great." Who am I trying to convince, Mitch or myself? His cocked eyebrow answers that for me. "My primary focus is helping Lana take this thing to the finish line..."

"And I have no doubt you will," he interrupts. "Do me a favor, though, just make sure you're *also* focusing on taking care of yourself and lean on your team—including my son—when it's too much, okay?"

Lean on Graham professionally? Personally? *Ugh. This is getting confusing.*

Before I can respond, he continues, "We should probably head back in, huh? We've left them alone for *way* too long now, so who knows what sorts of trouble they're getting into!" With that, he pats me on the arm while turning to head back into the conference room. Was I anticipating having this kind of deep fatherly conversation with my new boyfriend's father who also happens to be my boss? Nope.

"Well...this'll be interesting," I laugh to myself as I follow him back into the conference room, ready to get this over with.

———

Hannah and Lana have been talking for almost half an hour and everything is going perfectly. Lana is answering Hannah's questions with charisma and sincerity, her responses are thought out and articulate.

See? You had nothing to worry about.

As Lana continues the charm campaign, I sneak a glance over at Graham who is standing behind Hannah's cameraman. He's listening intently, a smile tugging on the corner of that mouth of his. In the dramatic lighting they've set up in his office, his features look even more defined.

He's so damn hot when he works.

"So, Lana, your book suggests sympathy for alcoholics, right? Or insinuates their actions are redeemable?" I hear Hannah ask, her tactless question lingering in the air and met by an uncomfortable silence from everyone in the room. I remove my gaze from Graham, his expression formidable, and lock eyes with an uncomfortable and seemingly frozen Lana.

What the fuck did she just ask? Rage and panic flood my veins. This was supposed to be a "fluff piece" to generate some buzz about Lana and her book, but the directness of Hannah's question crossed a professional line that no one is happy about. *Least of all Graham.*

I don't know how much time has elapsed, but I feel myself rising from my seated position behind the lighting that's been set up. Graham shoots me a questioning glance that I ignore.

"What a weird and inappropriate question to ask, Hannah."
I didn't even intend to say anything but seeing the hurt radiating
from Lana's gaze compelled me to speak. "Especially in a room
full of strangers where you have *absolutely* no idea what people
have going on behind the scenes." I'm standing directly behind
Lana now, my gaze narrowing at Hannah, fully aware that I've
just ruined whatever shot the cameras were trying to capture.
"While Lana most certainly can speak for herself, I hope that
somehow *you* aren't suggesting that people, regardless of the
struggles they've faced, aren't deserving of grace and compassion when seeking absolution? That those who struggle with
mental health issues or are plagued with addiction aren't worthy
of redemption?"

Hannah, her face pinched in horror, realizes her misstep,
and attempts to back pedal.

"I...No, I wasn't insinuating..."

I wave off her feeble attempt to regain control of this situation. "Oh no, Hannah, that was rhetorical." I place both hands
on the back of the couch Lana's sitting on, leaning toward
Hannah now. "That type of insensitive and dated thinking has
no place here, so unless Lana has anything else to add, I think
this interview is over." I extend my hand to Lana, which she
takes, a smile forming on her lips.

"Nope...I think that covers it," she says, allowing me to pull
her up from her seated position and throw my arm around her
shoulders.

"Have a good rest of your afternoon, Hannah...Make sure
you get this all cleaned up so Mr. Austin can get back to work.
Thanks." I call nonchalantly over my shoulder as Lana and I
walk side-by-side out of the office.

I know I should be doing the right thing by Lana's career right now. I know that the right thing is to smooth things over between Lana and Hannah, to make sure that her career isn't at risk of being tainted by this interview. But right now, I don't want to do the right thing and judging by the way Lana stormed out of the office, shrugging off my offer to join her, I don't think she cares about the so-called "right thing" any more than I do.

Instead, I just sit alone in the now-empty conference room, Hannah's question on a loop in my mind. *But are their actions redeemable?* Doubling over in my chair and putting my head in my hands, I just want this day to be over.

"You doing okay?" I didn't even hear Graham come in. *Sneaky bastard.* I look up and see he's leaning casually against the head of the conference table; his demeanor is soft but I can see the tension he's carrying. Clearly, this afternoon's events didn't sit well with him either.

Am I doing okay? Is this a joke? I know Graham isn't responsible for how I'm feeling right now, but what the hell kind of question is that? Of course I'm not doing okay. I single-handedly just tanked Lana's career before it even began, embarrassing Graham, and his father, in the process.

"I'm fine," I say with as much calm and grace as I can manage while fighting the urge to scream.

His jaw tightens, locking his eyes on mine, a dark fire burning just beneath the surface. "It's okay if you're not fine." He slowly crosses the room until he's standing before me, his powerful frame looming over me. "Because I don't feel fine at all, Will. I'm enraged, quite frankly."

Fuck, I knew I messed up.

His hands reach for the lapels of my suit coat, gently tugging so I'm forced to stand, our chests pressing against one another. I catch a whiff of his spiced cologne, the scent instantly spiking my desire. *What is he doing?*

Graham's expression softens. "Have I told you lately how impressed by you I am?" *Wait, what? I thought...*But before I can continue thinking, his hands tangle in the hair at the base of my neck, pulling my mouth toward his. "Will...I am....in awe...of *you*," he breathes against my mouth, those intoxicating lips crushing over mine between the words I didn't know I needed to hear until now.

"But I..." I try to interrupt in between the need of his lips. "Graham...I don't understa..." *Oh hell.* His tongue dips into my mouth, sending intense flashes of arousal coursing through me so I do what my body clearly wants and kiss him back with everything I have.

He presses my back against the wall, deepening our kiss. His hands are on my waist and I moan at the feeling of his erection pressed against my thigh, his hips colliding with mine.

"Take off your pants." *Here?* He eases back ever so slightly, just far enough to look me in the eyes. "Everyone's gone for the day. Take. Off. Your. Pants. *Now*," he says, kissing up my neck between every word. When his mouth finds mine again, I know I'm going to do what he says.

I fumble with my pants, a hunger now replacing the confusion I initially felt, and when they drop to the floor, pooling over my shoes, Graham drops to his knees, pulling my briefs down with him. My throbbing dick springs free, begging to be touched. *Now.*

Graham looks up at me as he plants a soft kiss on my tip, letting his lips linger for a moment before fully taking me in his mouth. His hands grip my hips and ass as he takes me in deeper, causing me to drop my head back, growling in ecstasy. *More, fuck, so much more.*

"You like that?" he teases.

"More than you'll ever fucking know." I'm panting as he trails his lips along my hip bone.

He gives my cock a squeeze, sliding his sweet tongue over me ever so slowly, all while peering up at me, his eyes hooded with desire. He stands, his hands pushing up the fabric of my shirt, the burn of his fingertips on my bare skin making me tremble. When his urgent lips claim mine again, he's driven by a need that's only matched by my own. "Fuck me, Will. I need to feel you inside of me," he whispers in my ear, his lips causing my body to shiver as he grinds his hips into mine, the fullness of his bulge begging for release.

My eager fingers pull at his suit pants, unfastening the buttons at the same time he quickly removes my shirt, his lips never leaving mine. I throw my entire weight into every ounce of our kiss, reveling in the hard planes of his body and moaning when my hand cups his throbbing cock. Graham's breathing is heavy, his rising and falling chest creating the only distance between us now.

"Come here," I say as I guide him back to the conference table, both pairs of pants still around each of our ankles. *Classy.* Turning him around, I run my hands over his chest as he pushes back against me, his head resting back on my shoulder.

"Tell me what you want, baby," I gently whisper into his ear. "Tell me what you need." My words cause his back to arch, his hands reaching back to pull me somehow closer to him. He turns his head toward mine, our lips barely touching.

"Please, Will...give me all of you," he begs against my lips.

I press him forward, his hands now resting on the table in front of us as I plant kisses across his shoulders and down his back until I reach the band of his briefs. Pulling them down to meet the pants at his ankles, I run my hands over the beautiful sight of his now exposed ass, causing Graham to push back against my touch and my own cock to twitch. *Someone's eager.*

Bringing my hand to my mouth, I coat my fingers in spit, ensuring there's enough to not cause him any discomfort. "This is going to be fast and hard, baby," I say, standing, slapping my dick against Graham's opening. Running my slick fingers over my cock, I push myself against him, his body momentarily tensing at the pressure of my touch. There is nothing quite like sliding into Graham, as he commands every ounce of my attention.

"I'm fine, babe...come on," Graham pants, reaching back and pulling me deeper into him.

Oh my god. He's rocking his hips, increasing the friction against us so I match his movements, thrusting harder as I feel him open up for me.

"You feel so *fucking* amazing." I'm pinning him down against the table, one arm planted across his back, the other gripping his hips tighter with each stroke. Reaching around, I find his dripping cock, my strokes match the timing of my thrusts. "I want you to come with me."

I'm right on the edge, each plunge deeper into Graham threatens to obliterate me in a way I've come to love.

Now slick with sweat, Graham leans back, pressing every inch of his delicious frame against my chest and turns, finding my lips with his."Come for me," he says, his need palpable. "Please baby, I need you to come." Crashing my lips to his, I slam into him deeper, my grip tightening its hold on him, willing his release.

"Graham, I'm going to...*holy fuck,* I'm going to fucking come..." I moan against his mouth, throwing myself willingly over the edge, spent and battered and slumped against this gorgeous man. My release sets forth a chain reaction, feeling Graham tighten around me, his body convulsing.

"Oh god...Baby." I furiously jerk him off, the anticipation of his release making me ache. "Don't stop...I'm right there...I'm..." he says as he finishes, falling against me, his legs unable to support the weight of his orgasm.

I reluctantly slide out of him, both of us left ragged and gasping for air. *Our poor conference table.*

Turning to face me, Graham wraps his arms around my neck, planting a lingering kiss on my lips. "Still feel just *fine?*" he whispers with a smirk. We are both still in some variation of undress, our skin still covered in remnants of, well, one another.

"Shut up," I laugh.

Tightening his hold on me, he places kisses on my cheeks, along the lines of my jaw, my neck, and on my forehead. "I'm going to say it again...in case you had any doubt the first time I said it." He's holding my face between his hands, his eyes filled with passion and sincerity and all the beauty in the world. "Have I told you lately how impressed I am by you?" His question falls differently on my ears after how we just abused the conference table.

"If that's how you're going to tell me...you can do *that* more often." I kiss him once more.

I know there are important things to discuss about Lana and the book and probably even about my unprofessionalism toward Hannah, but right now, I just want to cling to this moment for as long as I can. The real world can wait.

"So, how bad is it?" Clearly, the real world couldn't wait *that* much longer.

Graham and I dress quietly, our movements slow and slurred thanks to the intensity of what we just did in our conference room. *Another first.* My cheeks will forever burn in the best possible way any time I am forced to sit through another meeting in here.

"There was *nothing* bad about that," Graham says, shrugging on his suit jacket and straightening his tie. "That was...something."

"You absolutely know that's not what I meant." I roll my

eyes at him, but smile knowing Graham enjoyed himself as much as I did.

"I know, I know." He pulls out the chair I'm fairly certain he was just bent over, taking a seat and getting more comfortable. When receiving bad news, I prefer to stand. "Could it have gone better? Of course." *Ugh.* "But I don't really think this is going to have the repercussions you think it will. I've worked with Hannah for years, which is why I'm both confused and annoyed at her manner of questioning."

"I feel like I completely ruined any and all early buzz we had with Lana's book." I look down, not wanting to see his expression. "I crossed a professional line."

He reaches over and grabs my hand, pulling me closer to him.

"Hey...come here," he says, his tone soft. "I meant what I said, babe. You thoroughly impressed me by how you defended your author. I'm a firm believer that right is right. Not that you need to hear that, and I hope you don't doubt it, but honestly, the way you conducted yourself was *far* better than I would have."

I remember Graham's expression darkening when Hannah asked that question. *She wouldn't have stood a chance with him.* He stands, letting go of my hand but wrapping me in his arms. "I told you a while back that nothing is more important than our people. Not sales. Not so-called 'buzz.' And certainly not a silly interview." He kisses my temple, squeezing me tighter. I inhale his delicious scent, trying to force the words he's saying to make me feel better about the whole situation.

"For what it's worth, I do feel like the whole drama of today, and the events leading up to it, brought Lana and me closer." Maybe she'll finally be less guarded with me. *I hope so.*

"See? There you go." I feel Graham smile against me. "Listen to me, no one is going to fault you for coming to the defense of an author. Not me, not my father..." I tense when he mentions Mitch. I've been so focused on how Graham would react to this; I hadn't really thought about his father.

"I should probably make it a point to talk to him, huh?" *Please don't make me.*

"That can wait until tomorrow." He takes my hand, leading me toward the conference room door. "Come on, let's grab something to eat and get cleaned up." Turning and giving me that mischievous grin of his, he says, "Well...let's get *dirty* again first," which sends every molecule of my being into overdrive as we walk hand-in-hand into what will undoubtedly be a very eventful evening.

I'm awkwardly lingering outside of Mitch's office. *Creep.*

I rushed this morning to make sure I made it into our building early, hoping to catch him before his day got too hectic. Not taking into consideration just how close Graham's place is to APH, here I am, lingering like said creep.

Waking up next to Graham after an evening full of...well, *Graham*...started my day off perfectly. We've gotten in the habit of "sleeping over" on a more routine basis, something I never thought would feel so... normal? *Especially this quickly.* But with Graham, everything feels normal and right and not like we're rushing into something neither one of us are ready for. Honestly, we haven't really even had these conversations yet— we're either too busy ripping one another's clothes off or eating. *I've never met anyone who can match my cheeseburger intake, so consider me impressed.*

Just as I'm thinking I should head to my desk to start working, Mitch rounds the corner, his face lighting up into a smile.

"Well, well, well..." Mitch's voice is amused and chipper

first thing in the morning. "I assume you're waiting on me?" He points to himself as he passes me, opening his office door and turning on the lights. "Come on in, Will. You want some coffee?"

"I'm alright, sir, but thank you so much." *I need this to go well.*

"*Please* knock off that 'sir' nonsense,' he laughs, his casual demeanor instantly calming my nerves. "It's Mitch from now on, okay?" He proceeds to brew himself a cup of coffee, the comforting aroma filling his office.

"Sounds good, si—Mitch," I laugh, embarrassed by my rigid ways. *Ugh. Why am I like this?*

"So," he says, taking a seat behind his impressive desk. Mitch's office is much like Graham's in the sense that it is filled to the brim with photos and personal memorabilia. My snooping tendencies are itching to explore. "To what do I owe the pleasure of this early morning meeting?" He casually leans back in his chair, crossing his legs.

"Truthfully, I just wanted to come and apologize for what happened with Hannah yesterday." *Breathe,* I remind myself. I take a seat directly opposite him. "I acted out of line and out of character...period. So, I want you to know that I take *full* responsibility for whatever consequences come from this situation."

He takes a sip of his coffee, mulling over my words. Mitch is an intimidating man, both physically and professionally. But it's the intensity of his gaze, much like Graham's, that leaves me wondering what the hell he's thinking.

"Son, while the sentiment is appreciated, truly," he says, leaning forward on his elbows, "it's not necessary. I spoke with Hannah last night and informed her that our professional relationship would be over if she didn't reconsider how she approached my team, especially when it pertains to issues as deeply personal as Ms. Taylor's book touches on."

Relief floods my body and I visibly exhale, letting out the breath I'd been holding since first stepping foot into his office. "I appreciate you saying that, and for your understanding of what this book means to Lana." *To me.* "I am still sorry if my actions put you in an uncomfortable position."

Mitch chuckles to himself. "In all my years in this business, I've realized that hardly anything worth doing, and doing right, is *comfortable.*" Okay, well that was profound. "The stories we tell, the ones that we are privileged enough to be the keepers of and share with the world, sometimes those stories, and the authors who write them, need protecting."

This. This right here is the reason why I wanted to come to work for this team. What we do is so much *more* than just business, and to hear Mitch articulate it this way only makes me admire him that much more.

"I hope you know how rare that is...and how lucky I feel to work for a boss who thinks that way." My compliment causes him to put his coffee down, rising to step around and join me in the matching chairs across from his desk.

"That's kind of you to say," his tone softens. "I wasn't always like this. Oh man, I used to be focused on all the wrong things when I was first starting out. As our company began to grow and proved itself to be a major competitor in this industry, all I cared about was building on that momentum." Mitch steals a glance at the framed family photo on his desk. "All I cared about was making money."

I feel the weight of his words, the honest emotion and truth behind them. *God damn it, don't cry!* What is it with these Austin men and their ability to skyrocket my emotions like this?

"But then Graham grew up and he—" his voice cracks. *No, please don't do this.* "—and he came out. All of a sudden, my beautiful boy had this bright and new story to share with the world. One that needed protecting." He chokes in a way that only proud fathers do. *He did it.* My eyes sting with tears. Hearing him talk about his son this way—seeing the love he has for him—overwhelms me in a way I wasn't prepared for on a Thursday morning. *Or in general.*

Afraid that if I open my mouth to speak, I'll lose my inner battle against my tears, I remain firmly planted in my seat, my gaze looking everywhere but at Mitch. *Should I hug him? Do I leave?* I'm the worst.

"Woah...sorry," he says, clearing his throat. "Didn't mean to get all emotional on you this bright and early. That usually only happens after happy hour." He gives me the signature Austin family wink as he stands back up, patting me on the shoulder. "All of that to say, you did the right thing yesterday, Will...and I'm very proud to have you on our team."

I swallow the lump that's been lodged in my throat since this conversation took an emotional turn. "Thank you, Mitch. That really means a lot." I turn to exit his office, hoping he doesn't say anything else that'll punch me in the gut.

"He really cares about you." I stand frozen, stuck between the door and the father of the man who drives me wild. "I'm probably overstepping, but that's just who I am. I've never seen him this happy...this *himself.*"

This has to violate some human resources document we've all signed. *Thou shall not sleep with the boss's son.* But no HR training could ever prepare you for a moment like this.

"I really care about him, too," I blurt out.

More than he knows, I think as I forcibly remove myself from his office, needing to put as much distance as humanly possibly between Mitch and the tears that are now streaming from my face.

New Message — ✗ ×

TO: Will Cowen <**w.Cowen@aph.com**>

SUBJECT: um...WTF?

Well, that could have gone better...

I hope that this doesn't cause any issues for Graham or his father...but I have to say how much it meant to me that you stepped in the way that you did. I was completely thrown off guard by Hannah's line of questioning.

Fully aware that I owe you revisions but I think I need to take the evening to clear my head...

Best,
Lana

CHAPTER SEVENTEEN

OVER THE LAST SEVERAL WEEKS, BALANCING MY GROWING workload and my time with Graham, both in and out of the workplace, has been keeping me on my toes. During the day, we're able to work closely on several projects and that professional collaboration has quickly become the highlight of my workday. Our nights, on the other hand, have now been filled with dinner dates, movie marathons, and the most delicious time spent "collaborating" in far more fun ways. Graham even earned an infinite amount of Boyfriend Brownie Points by showing up with late-night tacos, so all in all, life is good.

Starting and ending my days with him has fulfilled me in ways I don't think I've been capable of fathoming. Even though we haven't been officially *dating* for that long, I know my time with Graham is something special. He is strong, filled with seemingly endless knowledge, and the most passionate man I've ever met. He asks thoughtful questions and listens intently, and there is a subtle confidence in the way he goes through life, knowing what he offers the world without appearing overly cocky or full of himself. It's quite admirable, honestly, and sexy as hell.

Last night was the first night in what feels like forever that we didn't spend it together. Graham had a family thing he had to go to, so it gave me the opportunity to have a much-needed friend date night with Klair, even though she left me after an hour or so to do some "collaboration" of her own with Dean. I would have done the same thing if the roles were reversed.

Walking into the office this morning, I can't help but smile at the thought of seeing Graham. It's crazy how quickly I've become dependent on seeing his handsome face first thing and after waking up without him today, I know for certain that that is not something I want to get used to. It feels too early to say I've fallen for him, but I've *really* fallen for him, and that thought scares the shit out of me.

My phone pings as I step into the elevator.

A text from Graham lights up across my screen. He's taken a selfie of himself in his office holding a mug of coffee. *Ugh.* He's so dreamy.

> Hurry up & get into the office.
> Can't wait to smooch you xx, G

I'm instantly a puddle of mush and my face hurts from smiling. This man knows how to pull at *allllll* of my heartstrings and it doesn't even seem like he's trying.

"Hold the elevator, please," a voice calls out right before the elevator doors close. I instinctively jam my hand through the opening, forcing them back open.

One of the most glamorous women I've ever seen rushes

through the now open elevator doors, shooting me a smile of appreciation as she stands next to me.

"Thank you so much...floor 21, please." I detect a beautiful and alluring accent in her voice. Italian? Is it weird that she's spoken a handful of words and I desperately want to just sit and listen to her talk all day? I'm obnoxious.

She's dressed impeccably. Her petite frame is wrapped in a long gray overcoat with a simple satin blouse underneath that's been tucked into deep olive, wide-legged trousers. Very similar to how Klair wears hers, this lovely and stylish woman has her long, thick, dark hair loosely curled, framing her dark features. *She's gorgeous..*

The doors open and I step aside, letting my glamazon companion exit first. "Have a nice day," I say in her direction before heading toward my desk. "Oh, and I love your coat."

She smiles, her entire face radiating warmth. "That's sweet of you to say. Thank you!" she says, winking at me.

We both seem to be heading in the same direction, which makes me feel foolish for saying a farewell. Well, that's uncomfortable. Slowing my stride so that I'm not in lockstep with the woman, it is now that I realize just how awkward of a human being I am. *Why am I like this?* I laugh to myself, shooting her a quick glance to make sure she's not gawking at my weirdness. The repetitive punctuation of her killer heels is every bit the sound of authority as she rounds the corner into our office section, familiar with where she's heading.

I spy Graham leaning against his office door, coffee mug still in hand. He's looking down, his attention pulled to whatever book he's reading, but at the increasing volume of my new friend's heels, his head pops to attention and he flashes an enormous grin in my direction.

"Mama," he says warmly, the greeting clearly not intended for me.

Mama? I turn toward who I am now learning is Mrs. Austin and, seeing the two of them side-by-side, the resemblance is uncanny. While Graham is a near spitting image of his father, seeing him next to his mother highlights everything I've come to adore about him has been inherited from her. His piercing eyes, full and thick hair, and that poreless skin of his that makes me green with envy.

"Buenos dias, mi amor," she says, giving him a hug and a kiss on the cheek.

"¿Qué haces aquí?" he says back, catching me off guard. I don't think I'll ever get used to *that*. The two of them continue going back and forth as they step into Graham's office, with me trailing behind them like a love-sick puppy. The closeness of their relationship is wildly obvious despite having no idea what they are saying.

Turning his gaze back to me, Graham sits on the edge of his desk. "I'm so sorry, Will. This is my mother, Dr. Camila Austin-Rojas."

"*Ay, mijo,*" she says, swatting at his arm. "Please, call me Camila. So, you're the famous Will? Que guapo!" she says to Graham. I know that one. "Do you speak any Spanish, Will?" she asks, taking a step closer to me and putting her hand on my arm.

"Eh..." I'm kicking myself for taking French in high school. "Donde está la biblioteca?" I stammer out, my Spanish accent about as American as it gets.

Graham and Camila both burst into laughter, and I can't help but join them.

"Really? Where is the library?" Graham teases, shaking his head.

"Hey, that just seems like a practical phrase to have in my back pocket in our line of work," I say, defending myself, only slightly embarrassed.

"Okay, well we're going to have to work on...*that*," she says, her voice filled with a warmth that somehow only mothers possess as she gives me a tight embrace. "It's so nice to finally meet you." She smells of lavender and vanilla, a sweet aroma that feels familial and welcoming. Mom hugs are the best.

"Likewise," I say, trying to hide my nervousness. I didn't have "Meeting the mother of the man I'm sleeping with" on my vision board this morning.

"I know you boys have a lot of work to do and your father is expecting me, so I won't keep you." Camila walks toward the door but pauses before leaving, turning back toward Graham. "I just stopped by to remind you one more time about our charity event this evening. You haven't given me a definitive answer, so I figured I'd get your RSVP in person." Mom guilt, I love it.

Graham runs a hand through his tousled hair, giving me a sideways glance as he does. "I'll be there, Mama. I wouldn't miss it for the world."

"Ah, perfecto. I look forward to seeing you *both* later. It was so nice to meet you, Will!" she states over her shoulder, heading out the door with a flourish, her voice and the sound of her heels echoing down the hallway once more.

Turning my attention back to Graham, I put my hands up in question. "What the heck just happened?" I laugh, setting my bag down on his chair.

"The ever-persuasive Camila just happened," he says, shaking his head. Closing the space between us, he wraps me in a tight embrace. "Good morning, handsome. I missed you last night."

"Yeah, let's not make a habit of that," I say, pulling him tighter to me and planting my lips quickly on his. Even though it is still early and hardly anyone is in the office, we keep visible public displays of affection like this brief. After all, perception *is* reality, and I would hate for anyone to think I was receiving preferential treatment because of our relationship.

"So...what did you think?" Graham asks inquisitively, handing me a waiting cup of coffee.

"Of your mother? I mean, talk about glamorous. Tell your father I'm sorry but it's evident where you get your good looks from." I take a sip of the delicious liquid, loving the fact that he's perfected my coffee-to-cream ratio, but then a wave of insecurity rushes over me. "Were you *planning* on inviting me to the event tonight?"

Sitting on the edge of his desk, Graham looks down at his hands. "I wasn't planning on going myself, but thanks to my mother's drop-in visit, I guess I no longer have a say in the matter." That makes me feel a little better.

"She's a psychiatrist and devotes a lot of her time advocating for mental health initiatives city-wide...especially for children and families impacted by addiction." There's something loaded in his tone, like this is somehow irritating. It feels personal, but I'm not sure if it's my place to ask. "Every year, her and her closest colleagues and friends put together a charity fundraiser to raise money for said initiatives."

"Graham, that sounds amazing," I say leaning against his desk next to him.

"This year's theme is *Hearts for Change: Facing Addiction Head On*," he whispers as he raises his eyes to meet mine.

Is it possible for my heart to speed up and melt at the same time? We hadn't talked about my father since that night at my parent's house, but clearly, Graham was going out of his way to shield me from a potential trigger.

"Is that why you didn't invite me?"

He leans his head on my shoulder and wraps his arm around my waist. "I didn't want to subject you to something like that so unnecessarily. These events have a way of being overly emotional, and despite the worthy cause, they can also be draining. I didn't know how you'd feel about it."

I go to respond but he doesn't let me.

"Before you say anything, please know that I wasn't trying to make decisions for you or even protect you. I know you're not a man who needs protecting; I know you can take care of yourself. I just didn't want to..."

I crush my lips to his. "Just please shut up and kiss me."

Which he does, in a way that makes me not give a single care in the world about public displays of affection and makes me want to immediately rip him out of his clothes.

"I guess I need to figure out an outfit, huh?" I say after finally breaking my lips from his, lightheaded and breathless.

"You always look perfect so don't worry about it."

I laugh. "Um, hello? Have you met me? I worry about *every-thing...*" I lean forward and give him one last kiss on those addictive lips of his before grabbing my bag and heading toward the door. "Besides, I literally just met your mother, so yeah, I'm definitely going to need to figure something out."

I blow Graham a kiss and exit his office to the sound of him laughing as I head to my desk in a hurry, knowing there is only one person on the planet who can help me now.

"Klaaaaiiiir! Stop whatever you're working on...your expertise is needed," I hiss as her perfect little head snaps up from behind her computer.

"Damn...did the pants have to be *this* tight?" I groan, trying to fasten the button to the satin dress slacks Klair's handed me. I'm being dramatic, of course, because staring at my reflection in my floor-length mirror, I love how these pants accentuate my, um, assets?

"Okay, first of all, mister...you gave me all of two hours to make sure you were dressed to the nines for a black-tie event, so you'll take what you get," she says as she opens my bedroom door. "Second of all, you look amazing, per usual. Here, let me," she says, watching me struggle with styling my bow tie.

"What would I do without you?"

"Honestly? Probably wither away or worse, wear cargo shorts." She slaps her hands on my chest. "There...perfect. Do you have time for a drink?"

I check my phone, seeing that I have at least twenty minutes before Graham is supposed to get here. "You know it."

After heading into our kitchen, I grab everything I need from our bar cart to whip up some simple vodka spritzers.

"You're my lifesaver, you know that, right?" I say, raising my glass to Klair.

Our glasses clink. "And you're mine...always."

The bite of the cocktail stings my throat as I take a big gulp. "Let's talk about something, anything—anything at all—to distract me from the fact that I'm going to be spending an entire evening with Graham and his family. Go!"

She snorts into her glass. "Someone's nervous, huh? Okay, let's see...things with Dean and I are going really, *reallllllly* well." She blushes while looking down at the counter, which tells me everything I need to know. Klair is totally falling for this guy, and I love having a front row seat to it.

"Aww, Klair! That makes me so, so happy. The two of you are beyond adorable together." I say, adding, "Honestly, I don't think I've ever seen you this happy."

"Um, I could say the same to you, sir."

We both are quiet for a second, reflecting on whatever

cosmic juju is in the air allowing us *both* to be this happy simultaneously.

"It's funny...when I moved back home, I had no intention of starting anything with anyone, you know?" I say, taking another sip of my cocktail.

Klair hops up onto our kitchen island, her drink spilling slightly. "Oh, I know *exactly* what you mean. I guess it's true when they say people come into your life when you are least expecting it."

"Amen to that," I say, tipping my drink in her direction. "Everything with Graham feels so..."

"Sexy?" Klair interrupts.

"Ha Ha," I mock. "Okay, yes...obviously sexy. I'm *not* blind. But...no, it's just that with him, it feels like exhaling. That's the only way I can describe it. Like I've been holding this breath my entire life," I point to my heart. "And then this man comes along, and he sees me for who I am, and for the first time in my life, I can just *be*."

I look up at Klair, who is wiping tears from her eyes. "That's all I've ever wanted for you, Will. I know the weight you've carried, so seeing yourself opening up like this with Graham...it's something special to witness."

"I'm going to... need you to cut that out right now," I say, my voice catching in my throat. "Have you noticed that all of our toasts have turned into these sob fests lately?"

"I don't even know who we are anymore," Klair says, sending us both into a mix of laughter and repressed tears. "Anyway, I know I'm supposed to be distracting you from thinking about tonight, but are you at least excited?"

I've been thinking about this all afternoon. Graham's mood seemed to be off from the moment his mother left his office. I didn't want to pry because it didn't feel like my place to inquire, but I could definitely tell something was on his mind.

"You know me in social settings...especially ones that include dressing up and impressing people such as the parents of the guy I'm seeing." Instantly, my stomach is in knots.

"I know, I know," Klair says after taking another sip from her drink. "But hey, plus side? You get to drool over Graham wearing a tux all evening."

Our doorbell rings at the mention of Graham. "Speaking of," she says, hopping off the counter and all but running to the front door, opening it with dramatic flourish. "Well, well, well... don't you clean up nice, mister boss man."

Standing in the doorway looking like a freaking magazine cover model, Graham is mouth-watering in his all-black ensemble.

"Hey, handsome," he says, completely overlooking Klair and locking eyes with me, his voice soft but compelling and my need for him is immediate. There's something *so sexy* about Graham when he is this dressed up, but man, what I would give to rip him out of these expensive clothes. *Now.* "Shall we?" he asks.

"Oh no you don't!" Klair says, grabbing Graham's forearm and keeping him rooted in place. "I'm not letting the two of you leave looking *this* good without taking a picture." She grabs her phone from the coffee table and heads out the front door.

"Come on, you'll thank me later." I roll my eyes at her because when Klair says she wants to take a picture, that usually means a hundred. I mouth *I'm sorry* to Graham as she leads us onto the front porch and aggressively positions us as if we are heading off to prom.

"Okay boys, three...two...one...smile!" Klair says as she snaps away. "Can y'all maybe do something different? I get it...you both are handsome and broody and masculine and..."

"You mean like this?" I say, abruptly pulling Graham by the hand causing our chests to collide, the sudden movement making a loud laugh escape from his lips. Our faces are close, this new proximity allowing me the opportunity to appreciate the beauty that is Graham fully smiling. It's...mesmerizing.

"Perfect," Klair declares, her voice ripping me from a Graham-induced trance. "Now get out of here and go have some fun."

"After you," Graham says, extending his arm outward in the direction of the street. We both turn and start heading toward Graham's black SUV.

"Don't do anything I wouldn't do," Klair yells before closing our front door behind her.

I hear Graham's throaty laugh directly behind me. As I round the hood of the car and go to open the passenger door, he grabs my waist, squeezing slightly as he turns me around and pulls me closer to him.

"You look very, very sexy," he whispers against my ear, pushing me firmly against the side of the car. Graham grazes his lips against my neck, along my jawline. His hands move from my waist to the front of my pants, the tight material doing nothing to contain my growing erection.

I wrap my arms around his neck, cementing my hold on him. "Um...so do you, stud. This whole black-on-black-on-black vibe totally suits you."

He pushes his groin against my thigh, highlighting his own state of arousal that makes my eyes roll back into my skull. *Fuck, I want that in my mouth.* Driven by lust, I pull his mouth to mine, sliding my tongue through his parted lips. It is then that the all too familiar buzz of electricity rings in my ears, overpowering every sense with urgency. I *need* him.

"As much as I desperately want to take care of *this*," Graham says between kisses, giving my now throbbing member the most delicious of squeezes, "...we should probably get going."

He opens the passenger door and I steal one last kiss before hopping in. "Oh, you'll definitely be taking care of it later, don't you worry."

"Get in the damn car, Will," he says with a laugh, closing the door behind me with the biggest smile on his face.

CHAPTER EIGHTEEN

"So...are we going to go in?"

We're standing outside the lavish double doors of the West Chester County Country Club after making the thirty-minute drive just outside of the city. Graham let me play DJ, and consider me thoroughly impressed by his vast lyrical knowledge of today's pop divas. I'm pretty sure riding shotgun with Graham belting out every word of my personal favorite songs by the one and only Taylor Swift will be a relationship high point. No question.

Looking over at him, I can tell he's anxious. His brow is furrowed, and he keeps adjusting his suit coat. "Hey...look at me," I say, standing in front of him and putting my hands on his broad shoulders. Graham lifts his gaze to mine, worry filling his beautiful eyes. "Let's just go in there, mingle, and have some fun with your family, okay? I will be right by your side the entire evening."

He gives me a small grin. "Look at you being mister calm, cool, and collected."

"We can't *both* be anxious wrecks," I say, tugging on his arm in an attempt to lighten the mood. Walking through the double doors, the hum of mingling people fills the air. "Come on, let's grab a drink and go find your parents."

"Ah, about that...I forgot to mention that seeing as this is an evening raising money for addiction, it's a *completely* dry event." Duh. That totally makes sense, but there goes my plan of having a little liquid courage before spending the evening attempting to charm Graham's family. "But hey, I have an idea." He grabs my hand with a mischievous grin on his face and leads me down a hallway off the side of the grand hall's entryway.

Graham clearly knows where he's heading and when the sounds of the event's attendees die down, he pulls us into a secluded corner out of sight from anyone walking by. Reaching into his suit jacket and procuring a small, silver flask, he unscrews the top and raises it to his lips, taking a long pull. "Bottoms up!"

His spontaneity is infectious and so unlike the controlled man I've come to know, but after seeing how hesitant he was to come to this event in the first place, I can't ignore my gut feeling that *something* is off with him. Graham licks the remnants from his drink off his lower lip and offers the flask in my direction. Not wanting to completely blow him off, I take the smallest sip before handing it back to him, the hard liquor burning my throat as I quickly swallow.

Bringing the flask to his lips once more, Graham takes another deep pull of the liquid, double the amount he had the first time.

"You doing okay?" I have to ask, because the more he drinks, the more I know something is going on with him.

He wipes his mouth on his suit jacket. "Oh yeah...just wanting to make this evening more enjoyable," he says, tipping the flask back in my direction.

"I'm alright, thanks." I look at my watch, realizing we're

running late. "How do you feel about joining in on the festivities? I don't want your parents to think we're bailing on them."

"Oh please, they probably haven't even noticed we're not here," he says, his voice sharp but muffled by the flask at his lips, again. Screwing the top back onto the flask, he stashes it back in his jacket pocket. He steps closer to me with a look I've come to know so well plastered all over his face.

Ever so slowly, he raises his hands to my waist, pulling me gently to him. "Will, I think I need to reiterate how insanely handsome you look..." he says, his breath warm against my ear, the cloying trace of liquor mixes with his usual spicy scent. "*Sexy...enticing...mouthwatering...*" he says between lingering kisses along my neck, burning every inch of my skin along the way.

"Flattery will get you everywhere," I pant, my voice thick with desire.

"Mmmm, good boy." He slides his hand down inside the waistband of my trousers, bypassing my trunks and firmly grabbing my throbbing erection. *Kill me.* "You said you wanted me to take care of this, right?" He brings his lips to mine, taking my lower lip between his teeth and tugging. A literal moan escapes my lips and if I wasn't minutes away from having to spend the evening with his parents, I would let him slam me against the wall right now and have his way with me.

"I didn't mean *here*," I hiss, waving my hand in our general vicinity. "Are you stalling?"

"Depends...is it working?" he asks, giving me another squeeze.

"Um, you're fully aware of how well it's working." I lean my forehead against his, fighting against the targeted torment he is oh-so-expertly delivering with everything I have. "But if we don't leave *right now,* I won't have any willpower left." I playfully shove him off of me, enjoying the way it causes him to laugh, and head back to the direction of the party. "Come on, my little avoider...let's get this over with."

The moment we step out from our quiet corner and join the growing crowd, I can immediately feel Graham tense next to me. Despite not knowing where I'm going, I take his hand, leading him through the throngs of charitable do-gooders in search of his family. Before he even comes into view, I can hear Mitch's thunderous voice plain as day, overpowering the sounds of a room full of casual chit-chat and pleasantries. There's a small break in the crowd, just enough so that I can see both Mitch and Camila at the center of a gaggle of patrons, all immaculately dressed for the occasion.

"There they are," Mitch booms as we make it closer to their group, interrupting whatever conversation he was in the middle of. "I thought you boys were going to make me deal with all of *this* by myself," he says, waving his arm in the direction of the mingling guests. Clearly, Graham takes after his father in this regard.

"*Ay amor*," Camila says, swatting his arm after breaking away from her friends. She looks absolutely radiant in a floor-length, black gown slung off of one shoulder with a dramatic slit revealing her toned leg. "I'm so glad you both could make it. It means the world to me. Mijo, déjame..." she says, reaching up to adjust Graham's bow tie, which he stoically obliges. I blush slightly, knowing I'm responsible for Graham's somewhat disheveled appearance. *If you could even call it that.*

"I told you we wouldn't miss it, Mama," Graham says as she wraps him in a tight embrace, her appreciation evident by the beaming smile across her face.

"And look at you. *Que guapo*," she says, releasing Graham and giving me a tight squeeze, extending the same warmth she showed her own son.

"Camila...you look absolutely stunning!"

She places a warm hand on my cheek, her eyes bright with excitement. "And you two make *quite* the pair," she says with a wink.

"Darling, it's almost time," Mitch says, suddenly at her side. "Do you have your notecards? Can I get you anything?" He's in full-blown supportive husband mode, and it's beyond adorable to witness.

"It's time already? Dios mío...okay, wish me luck boys," she says with a wink.

Mitch places a quick kiss at her temple. "Knock 'em dead, love."

Camila makes her way to the grand staircase toward the back of the room and is handed a microphone from a nearby server after carefully climbing a few stairs to be sure she can be seen by all.

"Excuse me, ladies and gentlemen. If I could just take a quick moment of your time..." she says, her voice echoing throughout the room as people quiet down. All eyes are on Camila now as she continues. "My name is Dr. Camila Austin-Rojas, and I want to thank you all for attending the tenth annual Hearts for Change fundraiser." The crowd responds with bois-terous applause, clearly happy to be a part of an event for such a good cause.

"When we first started this foundation, our goal was to find some small way to give back to children and families impacted by addiction. In the last ten years, however, we've been able to expand our efforts and outreach into a much broader umbrella of mental health initiatives." The crowd erupts into applause once more and Camila pauses before she continues.

"As some of you may know, my own family has been where a lot of the families we serve have been..." her quiet voice cracks. *Wait...what?* I feel Graham tense once more behind me. "I'm sorry...I can't help but get emotional because I know first-hand the powerful grip that addiction and mental health challenges can have on our loved ones. Witnessing your child suffer in this way is one of the most insurmountable pains as a parent, and if we didn't have the resources and the community that we did, I can guarantee you we wouldn't have survived it."

The room is silent, mesmerized by Camila's raw transparency. Is she referring to Graham? I don't want to make assumptions, especially without knowing the context or the full story, but maybe this would explain why he didn't want to come tonight. Maybe it was *too* personal of an event to invite me to.

I'm suddenly overwhelmed by the feeling that I shouldn't be here. If Graham had wanted me to know anything about this, he would have told me, right? It's not like we haven't had ample time and opportunity to discuss something like this. Lord knows I've opened up to him in ways that I usually don't...I can't help but wonder if I have done or said something that has given him the impression he can't do the same.

This isn't about you, idiot.

"It was then, once we were safely on the other side, that I knew there was so much more that we could be doing. That's how all of this came to be," she continues, her voice strong and filled with conviction once again. "Each year when we gather, I am blown away by the collective kindness and generosity of this beautiful community. Families are able to come together, learning from one another and sharing in each other's recovery. As I say to my family, there is no shame in admitting you need help, and when we face our challenges head on, and we face them together, there is nothing we can't accomplish. From the bottom of my heart, thank you for being here and supporting this cause, and I hope you have a wonderful evening."

Mitch, Graham, and I all join the room in enthusiastic applause, which leaves Camila beaming. It's clear just how much this organization and fundraiser mean to her, and while I don't feel it's my place to pry about what she alluded to in her speech, I'm eager to get Graham alone to see if any of this comes up. *If he's even willing to talk about it.*

The music begins to play as people resume their mingling. Mitch hurries off toward his better half, wrapping her in a tight embrace before the two of them are quickly swarmed by well-wishers, leaving Graham and I together. I steal a glance at him, his expression strained and the opposite of relaxed. Before I can say anything, he places a soft touch on my back. "Excuse me for just a moment," he says quietly, his voice filled with tension and what sounds a lot like sadness.

Watching him walk away, my own anxiety starts creeping back in. I started the evening telling Graham that we both couldn't be anxious wrecks and here I am going back on that. I was a fool for thinking I could be the so-called strong one of the two of us for a change. I glance over at where Graham and his parents were just moments ago and I see they've been swallowed up by the crowd, so instead of just awkwardly standing alone, I decide to take a lap, looking for some sort of distraction. *Any* sort of distraction.

The room has been lined with banners and informational signs for various programs and resources. There are flyers for support groups and organizations, all geared toward providing families and children access to care they so desperately need. It's refreshing to see the emphasis organizations are placing on mental health initiatives. Continuing my path along the wall, I browse the numerous handouts, pocketing a few I find interesting. Who knows, I may just find some new techniques for dealing with my own issues.

"This is all quite impressive, huh?" A strange voice pulls my attention from the pamphlet I was reading about the benefits of emotional support animals for children. Looking up, I meet the eyes of a tall, slender man, easily in his early to mid-thirties. His features are dramatic, with pronounced cheek bones and tired eyes, but despite his sullen appearance, he's definitely naturally handsome. He stands slightly shorter than me, his thin frame almost lost in the sharp suit he's wearing, and as he runs a hand through his dark blonde hair, I can't help but notice a subtle shake to his movements.

"It's certainly an inspiring cause," I say through a smile, not wanting to be impolite. I realize I've ventured away from the main crowd so my new friend and I are almost entirely alone. I'm normally never one to turn down small talk, but right now, I just want to clear my mind.

"I don't know...Don't you feel like it's all too much? Like, let's all get together and *raise awareness* so that we can say we helped in some way, but then we all go back to our perfectly normal lives. It seems rather selfish to me." His tone is laced with a disdain that makes me uncomfortable.

I think of Camila's genuine emotion and take a step back from him, putting distance from whatever negativity he's giving off. "I don't think there's anything selfish about wanting to help those who are struggling. Especially if you've been in their shoes before."

"Fair enough," he says, putting his hands up in surrender. "So, how do you know the famous Graham Austin? I saw the two of you come in together." There's an unexplained annoyance in his voice, one that I can't quite put my finger on but it's definitely there.

"I'm sorry...who are you?" I know I'm coming across more direct than necessary, but I'm not going to start answering personal inquiries by some stranger.

Before he can respond, I'm suddenly joined by Graham, his presence larger than life at this moment. Oh god, did he think I was flirting or being hit on?

"What are you doing?" Graham demands, his voice sharp.

Initially, I thought the question was directed at me, but looking up at him, I see now he's staring daggers at this man whose identity is still unknown.

"Hello, brother," he responds, a smirk forming across his long face as he crosses his arms. "Didn't good ol' mom and dad tell you I'd be here? I'm Luca," he says, turning his attention back to me and extending his hand. I take it, giving him a brief but firm handshake, which I can tell bothers Graham, but I'm not going to be outwardly rude to someone I just met. I'm still reeling at the fact that his *brother* hasn't come up in conversation before. *Brother, huh? What the hell?*

"I'm Will." I look between the two of them, noting the subtle similarities that weren't apparent until seeing them side-by-side like this. While Graham has darker features, his mother's genes so clearly on the surface, Luca must take after Mitch's side, his complexion and hair much lighter than the rest of the family's.

"Alright, you've had your introduction or whatever this was, Luca." Graham puts his arm firmly around my waist, pulling me slightly closer to him. I can tell he's angry, his body is basically vibrating with tension at this point.

"Oh, come on," he says, playfully punching Graham's arm, but judging by the way it makes him scowl, I know there's nothing playful about it. "It's been what, two, three years since we've seen one another? Let's catch up and have some fun tonight. It's a shame we can't have a few drinks to celebrate this epic reunion."

Graham takes a quick step forward, now just inches away from Luca' face. He may be the *little brother*, but there is nothing little about Graham's stature. He looks massive compared to Luca.

"Do you think that's funny? After all these years...after everything that they've done for you...you think that *tonight* is the night to make a joke like that?" He's furious, and part of me is prepared to intervene in case this turns into some sort of brotherly brawl.

Luca laughs but doesn't move an inch. He's got guts, I'll give him that. "Lighten up, little brother...is he always this intense?" he asks over Graham's shoulder in my direction.

Graham grabs him by the suit jacket, pushing him backward into a nearby cocktail table and sending several glasses crashing to the floor. If people weren't looking before, they most certainly are now. "I mean it, Luca...this isn't fucking funny," he roars, drawing the attention of even more curious eyes.

"That's enough," I hiss, stepping between the two of them, placing a hand on both of their chests and pushing hard. "Look, I don't know the history between the two of you, but now is not the time and most *definitely* not the place to rehash it all. Do *not* do this to your mother."

My words snap Graham from whatever frenzied state he was in, causing him to drop his hands to his side and take a step backward. Out of the corner of my eye, I see a worried Mitch and Camila making their way toward us.

"Yeah, Graham...you should probably listen to your boyf...."

I whip around so that I'm now the one in Luca' face. "You should *probably* shut that mouth of yours." Rage fuels every cell in my body and honestly, I'm prepared to do whatever it takes to get Graham out of this situation. Even if that means knocking out his brother.

He looks me dead in the eye, gauging the seriousness of my tone. Opening his mouth once more, I take another step forward, our chests now touching.

"Try me." I refuse to break eye contact and I can see his uncertainty increasing as he assesses his options here. Between Graham and I, just based on size alone, he must know that he's no match for us together. Not that I would ever want it to come to that, especially with a member of Graham's family, but I'm relieved when he takes a step backward, glancing between the two of us before slowly turning around and disappearing into the now growing crowd. I don't take my eyes off his frame until he's completely out of my sight.

When I finally turn back to Graham, his head is lowered as his parents are questioning him about everything that just transpired.

"Son, what was that about?" Mitch doesn't sound or appear angry, but there is serious concern in his voice. Graham doesn't respond but just shakes his head.

I look to Camila, who's standing quietly with tears in her eyes, which causes a lump to form in my own throat. "I'm so sorry...I don't know exactly what just happened, but I just didn't want anyone to get hurt."

"No, Will...you did the right thing. Thank you," she says quietly, grabbing my hand and giving it an affectionate squeeze. "Come on, *amor*...let these two have a moment." Camila reaches for Mitch as the two of them walk arm-in-arm through the crowd.

Graham still hasn't lifted his gaze, so I quickly close the distance between us. "What can I do?" I ask, placing my hand on his arm and ignoring the not-so-subtle stares of the lingering guests. He slowly raises his head, his eyes meeting mine for the first time and I see it all—shame, betrayal, anger, sadness. My heart breaks for him without even truly understanding why.

"I...Will, I need to get out of here, *now*." His eyes are red, tears threatening to betray everything he's keeping bottled up, and all I want to do is wrap him in my arms and shield him from whatever is impacting him this profoundly.

"Then let's go," I say, extending my hand toward him, which he seems happy to hold on to, as if it's the only thing keeping him here in the moment. Once again, I lead us through the swells of the crowd, back through the lavish double doors and into the night's darkness.

———

I turn Graham's SUV onto the quiet highway. When we left the country club and made it back to his car, he willingly gave me his keys when I asked for them, both of us realizing that he was not in any sort of mindset to drive safely. Graham is leaning with his head against the passenger window and his back slightly turned to me like he doesn't want me to see him in this state.

His breathing has finally slowed to a normal rate, which allows me to put the fear of him having a panic attack out of my mind. We drive in silence, the dimness of the street lamps illuminating our way as I replay this evening's events over and over in my mind. From Graham's hesitation about joining his family in the first place to his mother's revealing speech to finally meeting a brother I had no idea existed, tonight was filled with one too many surprises that I was not mentally prepared for. But again, I have to remind myself that none of this is about me and that my priority right now is making sure Graham is okay.

For someone who is normally so in control of his actions and reactions, it was a whole new experience to see Graham go through such a wide array of emotions. The passion and spontaneity he exhibited when it was just the two of us. The rash behavior his brother seemed to pull from him. And then the deep sadness that I hope to never see again. Ugh, *my sweet Graham.* I wish there was something I could say or do to make this better for him, but based on his body language, I get the sense that he just wants to be left alone with his thoughts. *I think?*

At the risk of doing something contradictory to what he

needs in the moment, I lay my hand on his thigh, gently running my thumb back and forth against the smooth fabric of his suit pants. If nothing else, he'll know that I'm here.

"Are you hungry?" I hear him ask, straightening in his seat. "I'm just realizing we were supposed to have dinner tonight."

"I'm fine...don't even worry about that," I say, doing my best to reassure him that the last thing on my mind right now is food or anything related to me. But of course, my empty stomach decides now is the time to stab me in the back and let out an audible rumble, which I know he hears because he's now staring at me from the passenger seat.

"Pull off at the next exit...I know a place," Graham says, a faint smile forming on his lips, the sight alone making me want to pull over and do cartwheels up and down the street. I follow Graham's instructions as he quietly but competently navigates me through the outskirts of downtown Brooklyn. After we find a parking spot, Graham takes my hand in his as he leads us down the street, his demeanor starting to normalize.

"Do you trust me?" he asks as we arrive at a cluster of food trucks that are radiating the most mouthwatering smells. I know I'm hungry, but these people clearly know what they are doing.

"Always."

"Perfect...go and grab us a table and I'll be right back." He gives me a quick kiss on the cheek before padding off toward the growing line of people placing their orders. I've never seen this little area before, but it's definitely a place I want to come back to. There are probably six or seven food trucks lined up, offering a wide variety of items. They've made a make-shift seating area on a nicely manicured patch of lawn with warm bistro lights strung overhead. The entire space exudes social-media-worthy date-night and I'm so glad I'm experiencing it for the first time with Graham.

I choose a semi-secluded table and sit down, taking out my

phone for the first time since leaving earlier this evening and see that I have several messages from Klair who's desperate for an update. I just finished typing out a quick *I'm not dead, but I'll fill you in later* message when Graham returns, his hands full of food boxes and two beer bottles.

"That was fast!" I say, reaching up to grab the ice-cold beers from his hands so that he can set the rest down between us. He slides over one of the grease-covered boxes in my direction, a smile spreading across his sweet face.

"I wasn't sure what kind of beer you liked so I just got you my favorite...I hope that's okay," he says, lifting his bottle to mine so they clink together. He appears to be back in control of his emotions, but I know he's the master of bottling up his feelings.

"This is great...cheers." I bring the bottle to my lips; the crisp amber ale is refreshing in all the right ways.

"Okay, I know how much you love burgers, so let me present you with my submission for the BEST burger in the city," he says enthusiastically, opening the box in front of him as I do the same that releases a scent that literally makes me drool. He's charming me with burgers...it's like he knows the way to my heart or something.

More brownie points.

"Ooohhhmgosh," I moan after taking a massive bit of the cheesy and bacony deliciousness placed before me, ignoring the condiments I can feel now dripping from my fingers. I inhale a few more bites, breaking to take a swig from my beer. "This is probably one of the best burgers I've ever had."

"Right? I need to figure out their secret." Graham says through a genuine smile, the kind that always stops me in my tracks. I pause in appreciation of this moment. We must be quite the sight right now—still dressed in our formal attire, crammed together at this small table, and bent over a couple of burgers and beers. I wouldn't change a thing.

In no time at all, we've both finished our burgers and wiped their remnants from our mouths and fingers. Leaning back in my chair, I take a slow sip of my beer, completely content.

Graham picks at his fries and I can tell his gears are turning. "Will, I cannot apologize enough for the complete disaster that our evening turned into," he says, remorse filling every inch of his face.

"Are you kidding? I just devoured the most orgasmic burger with the most handsome man in the world. I'm a happy camper."

"That's awfully gracious of you, but you know what I mean." Graham reaches across the table, taking my hand in his. "I never would have gone tonight, let alone taken you, if I knew *he* was going to be there. I also realize that I should have told you about him before all of this went down, but you can see now why I didn't."

"You don't have to apologize to me, Graham. Honestly, I was and still am just worried about *you...*" I look down, tracing the lines of his strong hands. "Trust me, you're talking to the king of wanting to keep certain parts of his family hidden. Without crossing any lines, can I ask what the situation is between the two of you?"

"First of all, you can always ask me anything you want. I know this is contradictory to tonight's events and you must have a million questions now, but I do try to be an open book with you." Graham shifts in his chair. Letting go of my hand, he takes a deep pull from his beer, and I watch him exhale.

"Second of all, Luca is just...he's just a dick, to put it bluntly. He is charming and kind when he needs something, but the second he gets it, he lashes out at those who are closest to him, specifically my parents. He's a user and an addict, but worst of all, he's selfish."

Knowing that we have this shared experience makes me all the more appreciative of the way Graham handled my own family drama. Going through all of this with his brother has made him more empathetic to those around him.

"That must be incredibly hard on the entire family, especially your mother."

"It was...it is. It kills me to know that he's struggled all these years and I would give *anything* to take that away from him. But it's heartbreaking to watch him take advantage of my parents' kindness, because he knows what he's doing."

He leans back in his chair, crossing his muscular arms across his chest. As he's describing his brother, I can't help but think of my father and the rollercoaster his so-called love was.

"Growing up, nine out of ten holidays or family occasions were always turned into mini-interventions for him," he continues, bitterness dripping off every word. "I love my parents, more than anything in this whole world, but *he* is their weakness, and he always has been. No matter the cost or the lengths, they will drop everything anytime he needs them. How can I fault them for that? Isn't that what any good parent would do? But, well... they have two sons, and I needed parents, too." Tears return to Graham's eyes, the same ones that compelled me to wrap him in my arms earlier. His confession shatters my heart into a million pieces.

"Did you have a bad relationship with your parents growing up? The three of you seem so close now."

"Of course not...my parents were and still are my biggest champions." He takes another sip from his beer, and I do the same, the fullness of the ale doing nothing against the growing lump in my throat. "But I didn't want to ever be another *problem* for them as they were drowning in the toxic chaos that was Luca. So, I vowed to be the perfect one...the one who was holding it all together no matter what was going on in my personal life, to ensure that they didn't feel like they needed to parent me."

"I don't think anything you could do would ever classify you as a *problem*."

"Will, I was the gay one...not that they knew it at the time, because I didn't either," he says, his voice cracking, "but I didn't want to give my parents a single reason to not love me, so I kept all of that buried deep inside of me and just focused on being the perfect and reliable son. The one they could depend on."

I have no words. I fight the urge to get up and hug him because hearing how he viewed himself as a child is devastating.

"I was so jealous of him," he continues, the tears now flowing freely. "My entire life has been spent feeling jealous of an addict. And I hate myself for that...I still do. I played everything safe so as not to take a step over this imaginary line my parents had, but Luca on the other hand, he just ran wild with the life he'd been given. He caused chaos and drama and didn't seem to have a care in the world about who he hurt along the way. Looking at it through my lens, that unbridled belief in himself...that unwavering faith in who he was despite all of his shortcomings...*that* is what I was jealous of. I never had that growing up, and to be honest, I don't know if I ever will."

I've never felt so connected to another human being before this very moment. This is by far the most honest Graham has been with me, and the fact that he feels comfortable enough to be this vulnerable and trusting with his deepest truths is not lost on me.

"I can't imagine how this heavy burden at such a young age made you feel or how it's shaped the man you are today, but I hope you know that your life...the one that *you* built and made for yourself...is yours to live as you see fit. You get to be the adult that *you* want to be." I reach back across the table and take his hands once more. Bringing them to my lips, I take in the man before me as I kiss them. The soft glow of the bistro lights is reflected in his watery eyes and in this moment of openness, he's never looked more beautiful.

I stand up, forcing him to join me and wrap my arms around his waist. He buries his head in my neck and I inhale the sweet and spicy scent of him that I've come to love so much.

"Who you are is worthy of a life you love, my handsome man," I whisper against his ear. "Who you are is someone to be proud of...I know I am. Despite everything that you've shared with me tonight and everything you've overcome to get to where you are today, *that* man is someone I am in awe of."

I gently place my hands on either side of his gorgeous face, moved by his vulnerability, and place my lips to his. It's quick and tender but full of all of the feelings I don't yet have the words for. With him firmly in my arms and the lights around us starting to dim, I know definitively the lengths I would go to protect this man.

No matter what.

New Message — ∠ ×

TO: Lana Taylor <**Lana.taylor23@gmail.com**>

SUBJECT: Final Edits :)

Good morning, Lana,

I hope you're having a better week than I am...long story but I will definitely fill you in on our next phone call!

Attached you will see my notes on this final draft. I have to ask, is everything okay? I say this in the NICEST way possible but these additions feel "off." Take a look at my notes and see if you agree with the changes to the flow.

OF NOTE: I think you can completely omit the that last paragraph from chapter 21. Honestly? It feels insincere for an apology like that to be coming all these years later...that could just be me but why don't we delete for now and save it for future use.

Keep up the amazing work and never forget WHY you started writing in the first place. This story is worth telling and you are SO CLOSE so just keep moving forward and we will get there. I'm proud of you!

-Will

Will Cowen | Editor
w.Cowen@aph.com
Austin Publishing House
New York, NY

CHAPTER NINETEEN

AFTER THE INTENSITY OF LAST NIGHT'S FUNDRAISER AND
the surprise introduction to Graham's brother, Luca, I happily
welcome the monotony of a busy morning at work. Graham
spent the night with me, instantly passing out the moment our
heads hit the pillow. And while I will never grow tired of seeing
his gorgeous frame stripped naked and cuddled up in my bed, I
stayed up half the night worrying about the weight he's been
carrying on his heart all these years.

For most of the morning, Graham has been behind closed
doors with his father, which I can only imagine has been incredibly emotional for the two of them. While it's definitely not my
place, I'm a little disappointed that Mitch and Camila would
tolerate that type of behavior. Even if it was by their son.

In between back-to-back meetings, my mind has involun-
tarily wandered to how growing up the way that he did
impacted the man Graham is today. It explains so much, and my
heart melts at the fact that he feels comfortable enough with me
to be as open and vulnerable as he was last night.

Walking back from the conference room and discussing the

remaining items needed for Lana's book with Klair, the soft *ding* of the elevator catches my attention.

What the hell?

"Dad?" I say, confused as the elevator doors spring open and out walks out my dad dressed in a very sharp suit and tie. "What are you doing here?"

"What? Can't a man just come to check in on his boy?" he says, wrapping me in a tight bear hug, his eyes bright. I highly doubt he's just popping in to check on me, but it's great to see him regardless. "Hey, Klair Bear. Well aren't you just a sight for sore eyes," he says, releasing me and quickly replacing me with his adoptive daughter.

"Oh, stop it, John," she says in an old-timey accent when he finally releases her. Klair theatrically strikes a pose, flailing her long black jacket in the process, which sends my dad's thunderous laughter echoing down our office hall. *Ugh, people are most definitely watching.* "I practically threw this on in the dark." Her accent is even more pronounced on that one. *Liar.*

"Alright you two...that'll be enough of *that*." I don't know how or when it exactly started, but whenever my dad and Klair get together, they bring out one another's inner *thespian*. And if I don't put a stop to this charade they do, it will never stop. *Nerds.*

I see Graham emerge from the opposite end of the hall, his face pinched and his shoulders raised, but when he finally lifts his gaze to mine, his body seems to relax ever so slightly. I watch as he runs a hand through his already perfectly styled hair and quickly adjusts his tie as he approaches.

"It's so good to see you again, John," Graham says, extending his hand toward my father.

"The Cowens are huggers, young man...get over here," my father says, pulling Graham into a tight embrace. I could be completely making something out of nothing, but it looks like

Graham visibly exhales in my father's arms...like he needed this moment, and he didn't even realize it.

"No flowers this time?" he teases, his hands still on Graham's shoulders.

Graham pats his pockets, playfully looking around confused. "I know I left them somewhere around here." The natural and easy banter that quickly formed between the two of them has blown me away. I knew everyone would adore Graham, but honestly, I never imagined it would be like *this*.

My father turns his attention back to me. "I actually had a meeting downtown this morning and figured I'd see if you had time to grab a coffee with your old man...the two of you are more than welcome to join." he says to Klair and Graham.

"You know I love a good excuse to annoy Will with you, John...but I actually have a mountain of work waiting for me that *this one* will kill me if I don't finish today," she says, nudging Graham gently in the side with her elbow. I think Graham and I have matching eye rolls for once as she waltzes back to our section.

"And I have to get back to *my* dad to discuss a few things," Graham says, his smile is genuine but fades slightly, just enough for me to notice, as he tilts his head back in the direction of his father's office. "Thank you so much for the invite, but you two have fun."

He turns away from us, quickly walking back toward Mitch's office door. I watch as he shoves his hands in his pockets, using his shoulder to push open the heavy door and when it's fully open, I can see Mitch isn't alone as he stands there with his arms crossed and head lowered.

Luca.

Of course *he's* here, which explains Graham's demeanor and instantly causes my heart to ache for him.

"Looks like it's just you and me, buddy," my dad says,

throwing his arm around my shoulder and leading me into the waiting elevator. I'm conflicted whether or not I should leave the office right now...what if Graham needs me?

Don't be ridiculous. I know he can take care of himself but after everything that went down last night, my boyfriend senses are tingling.

"Your mother says hello," he says, hanging up his phone before I can say hello back and placing it in his suit jacket pocket as I set our coffees down in front of us.

We made the quick walk to my favorite café around the corner from our building and of course, he had to call my mom on the way to let her know that we'd met up. I swear, the two of them narrate every single second of their days to one another, but I'd be lying if I said it wasn't the cutest thing ever. Truthfully, I've always aspired to have what they have—a loving partner who is *also* my best friend.

"Everything alright, son? Is Graham okay?"

John Cowen is many things and intuitive is unquestionably one of them. Then again, I can feel the worry lines on my forehead so...

"He's just got some family stuff going on at the moment." It's not my place to speak for Graham, so I am careful not to overshare.

"Well, I pray that everything will work itself out as things tend to do. Just make sure you're there for him." My dad takes a long sip of his coffee, then another, before speaking again. "He's the one, isn't he?"

My father's question completely catches me off guard, causing me to nearly choke on my coffee. "What do you mean *he's the one?*" I ask, playing with the coffee creamer containers in front of me instead of making eye contact with him.

"William Michael Cowen, I raised you to be *honest* with your feelings, so don't play dumb. Not with me."

I know his sudden tone change isn't serious, but he's got a point. I have been tiptoeing around my feelings for Graham for months, and while I know I love spending time with him and am deeply attracted to him, I also know there's more to it than that.

"I'm scared, Dad," I quietly admit, the safety of this father-son conversation pulling the truth from my heart. I've never said the dreaded *L word* to anyone before. But Graham? It's different with him. He has shown me time and time again how different he is to anyone I've ever known.

"Of course you are, son...falling in love can be terrifying." He leans forward, grabbing my forearm. "But it's also the most beautiful and thrilling thing in the world. Everything changed the moment I met your mother, and there's not a day that goes by that I don't appreciate the life that I have because of her."

My dad has always worn his heart so proudly on his sleeve—it's this quality of his that I admire most and not once have I questioned his love for us. It's that type of brave and unnerving faith in love that I want so desperately for my own life, and for the first time ever, I've found someone I can see myself having it with.

"What are you scared of?" he asks, his empathetic eyes pouring into mine.

The truth is I'm not sure what scares me more...choosing to take that leap of faith and go there with Graham, only to find out that he doesn't feel the same way. Or letting myself be open to love, only to have it walk away down the road...and what it would mean if it did.

"The life that I've had—the life that you and Mom have

given me—has been an incredibly blessed one." I put my hand on top of his, hoping he knows how genuine my words are. "But I think at some point, I gave up on looking for something real... something worth living for...because for the longest time, I woke up every single day feeling unlovable and not worthy, and I felt so guilty feeling that way because of you."

Tears pool up in my father's deep brown eyes and I take a moment to really take in the man before me. While his dark hair and beard have grayed slightly and his expression lines are more noticeable, I still see the man I met when I was three years old. The same man who kept me safe and put my mother and I back together over and over again.

"Because of me? What do you mean by that, son?" his voice cracks slightly.

"Dad, you loved me like I was your own blood—no questions asked—from the very first moment you met me. You've raised me and been by my side every step of the way and you made sure that I knew I was loved and safe and special. Yet there I was begging for the love and approval of a man who couldn't care less about me."

He clears his throat, quickly trying to wipe away a few stray tears. "You know...I would do...everything the same, Will. You are *my* son," he says, leaning over and awkwardly trying to hug me with a bistro table between us. "Always."

I do my best to hug him back without spilling our coffees. "I know that, Dad...trust me, I've never *not* known that. But the last thing I'd ever want is for you to feel that I love or appreciate you any less due to how broken I feel because of *him*."

"I could never think that, son," he says, doing his best to compose himself. "What you have been through—at such a young age I might add—will always weigh heavily on your heart, Will, and for that, I am truly sorry. But look at the life you have built: the career, the friends, your future with Graham. Don't risk living a life wondering what could have been because of someone else's hurt and pain."

He's right, and if anything, I know that I don't want to keep living life with the future I so desperately want at arm's length. *I want this life with Graham...whatever that looks like.* While the thought of losing what we have is paralyzing, I know that it's worth the risk.

"Well, that got real heavy, *real* quick," I say as the both of us dab our eyes with the rough, café napkins.

He laughs, his big, goofy smile taking its normal place on my father's face. "I swear that wasn't the intention of my visit!"

"Mhmm."

"Here, let's change the subject...how's work been going recently?"

My phone begins buzzing on the table and I see it's Lana calling me, which is odd because we normally communicate via email. Maybe she has some thoughts about the edits I sent her way earlier this morning.

"Speaking of...hold that thought. I need to take this." I excuse myself from the table and quickly step outside to answer her call.

"Hey, Lana...how's it going?"

There's a long pause before she responds. "Will, I'm so sorry for this abrupt phone call, but I can't do this any longer."

Wait...what? She's speaking so fast that I don't think I understand her correctly.

"Hold on, Lana...what's going on? Is everything okay?" There has to be something up to make her have such a sudden change of heart.

"I've already sent over the voided contract and had documents drawn up to handle the advance. I'm really sorry."

"I don't understand, Lana...Have I done something wrong? If that's the case, Klair or Graham would happily take over to make sure your book can be published." I can't let Lana hear me fall apart on the phone. I need her to know that I'm professional and can do a good job for her.

"I no longer wish to proceed with the book, Will." This *cannot* be happening.

The line goes dead.

Everything we've worked for over the last several months... everything I *fought* for...is gone with a single phone call. Leaning my forehead against the cold windowpane of the café, I focus on calming my breathing, but all I want to do is scream.

So, I do.

CHAPTER TWENTY

I can't tell you how long I stood outside that café.

My dad took one look at what I can only imagine was pure panic splashed across my face when I finally returned to our table and practically ushered me out the door. He was completely understanding of my need to cut our impromptu coffee date short amid the full-blown work crisis I was now smack in the middle of. Walking back to APH was agonizing and each step toward our building was more strenuous and emotionally damaging than the last.

Because the closer I got to my office, the closer I got to Graham.

And the closer I got to Graham, the closer I got to having to admit that I was a failure.

There was no sense sugar coating it at this point—I *had* failed. My one job was to ensure Lana was supported through publication and somewhere along the way, she started having doubts. How did I not see this coming? Did I allow myself to get too distracted by Graham and somehow miss something? Every interaction with her shuffles through panicked thoughts but I truly can't pinpoint any sort of shift in our dynamic. My heart sinks as I force myself through the front doors, up the elevator and when I stumble out onto our floor, the panic attack sets in— I've made it as far as I can physically go.

Slumping against the cool wood paneling of the hallway, the blood begins pounding in my ears and my vision blurs and distorts everything in front of me, creating a soft and dizzying vignette. This forces me to push harder against the wall to ensure I remain semi-upright. I know I need to get my breathing under control but the vice-like grip that my anxiety has on my chest right now is making that nearly impossible. The more I think about trying to breathe the more I realize that I just might never be able to breathe again. My chest rises and falls rapidly as I struggle to force air into my reluctant lungs and when it's clear that I'm a failure at that as well, I claw the collar of my shirt, physically preparing to rip it off of me in the off chance I can't jumpstart my traitorous lungs.

"Just breathe, Will," Klair—who I could have sworn was just at her desk when the elevator doors opened—says, wrapping an arm around me. "I need you to breathe. Come on, Will...breathe with me." She takes my hands in hers and looks me in the eye, physically forcing me to do what she says because it's Klair and of course I can breathe when she tells me I have to. I mimic her dramatic inhales and long exhales until I'm somewhat in control again. Embarrassment barges to the forefront of my mind as I've just publicly had the worst panic attack I've ever experienced— in my place of work, no less. Luckily, no one from our team seems to have noticed the two of us huddled in the hallway loudly exhaling into one another's face.

"Tell me three things you can see, hear or smell." Klair hasn't had to do this for me since high school when I'd found out my grandmother passed away on our way to Chemistry. Much like now, the two of us sat, forehead-to-forehead in the middle of our crowded school hallway, until the relief of air rushed through me again and brought me back to a somewhat manageable reality.

I take a few more inhales, letting the air flow slowly and purposefully through flared nostrils. "I smell..." Exhale. "Um, I can smell your perfume," I say, taking in the familiar sweet and floral scent that's always been a Klair Thompson staple.

"That's good...You gave that to me as a birthday gift years ago and I've worn it ever since, remember?" I do—she's always been someone who's incredibly moved by the smallest of gestures. "What else, Will?"

"Um, I can hear Audra..." I say, straining to hear her calm but strong voice over the cubicle wall. "Yeah, she's on the phone talking about..." Exhale. "...an upcoming marketing campaign." Frankly, she doesn't sound too happy but that's neither here nor there.

Klair gives me a little space, perhaps sensing that I'm breathing somewhat regularly at the moment but still keeps my hands in hers. "Excellent...what else?"

Movement just beyond her head catches my attention just as my vision returns to normal. Graham is pacing from one end of his office to the other with an open manuscript in his hand. His sleeves are rolled casually, showing off his strong forearms and it seems that he's undone a button or two at his collar.

Graham.

Just when I thought I'd removed the lump lodged in my throat, it returns with a vengeance like no other at the sight of Graham. I have no idea how I'll be able to tell him about this.

"Lana terminated her contract."

Confusion ripples across Klair's face. "Wait...what?"

"Yeah, she called me when I was grabbing coffee with my dad," I whisper, afraid to say it all out loud because once I do, there's no going back.

"She said she's done with me."

Klair sits back on her heels and her expression softens. "Okay, first of all, she's not done with *you*, Will. I don't know what could possibly be going on—and I'll be honest, I've held my tongue for quite some time now about the vibe I've been getting from Little Miss Lana, but there's got to be an explanation. Something you're not seeing."

I look back over at Graham, who's now sitting on the arm of the leather chair across from his desk. He's tapping a pen against the pages he's holding, his subconscious tell that he's irritated and instantly, I'm terrified he's going to be upset with me. Or worse, disappointed.

"I don't know. Like...I honestly did *not* see this coming, and I have no idea how to fix it."

"Honestly, Will...this isn't something you have to *fix*. Especially right now." She stands up and brushes off the blush slacks she's wearing. "Come on," she says, extending a hand in my direction which I grab. Despite our substantial size difference, Klair yanks me to my feet with ease. "We clearly don't have the full picture here, but I think it would be best to give Lana a few days to mull all of this over. Give her the space she needs—because I know you, Will. I know you're dying to pick up the phone or show up at her place unannounced to smooth things over and that is the last thing anyone needs right now."

We start walking toward our desks but Klair has never once let go of me. For most of my life, Klair has been the one constant, the hand that is always most comforting when held. Despite what I've now found with Graham, that hasn't changed. She understands this side of me, free of judgment, and has always known how to step in and help me find my way back through the darkness.

Graham may be my epic love, but Klair will always be my person.

"You're right," I say before being forced to part ways at our desks. "I know you're right—I just really felt like this was *the one*, you know? The one that takes off and soars. The one that means something to someone." I lean against our shared cubicle wall, resting my head against my forearms and feel the tension circulating throughout my body.

"And it still can be. Just trust me on this, Will...give Lana a moment to think this all through and give yourself the peace of mind in knowing that there is literally nothing that can be done to fix the situation right now." She rubs my back before returning to her desk.

"I know it's hard but do your best to just put this out of your mind today and wait until tomorrow to figure out what's next, okay? Can you do that for me?"

We're both liars if we think I'll be able to do that but I nod my head in agreement anyway before sitting down at my own desk and willing something—anything, to distract me from the fact that my professional life feels like it's hanging on by a thread.

After enduring more back-to-back meetings I truly feared would suck the life out of me, I slump down in my chair and give myself permission to momentarily think about Lana's phone call. I know Klair is right and that something is going on that I'm not privy to, to warrant this sudden change. All I can do is hope that a little time will sort this all out. In the meantime, I owe it to Graham to fill him in—but with everything he's got going on with his brother, I don't want to be yet another thing he needs to deal with right now. Honestly, I don't think I have it in me to even address it. I rub my temples, the beginning of a migraine threatening to wreck any and all of my plans for the remainder of the day. Ugh. Why do *both* of these things have to be happening simultaneously? All I want to do is nose-dive into my bed, turn my phone off and just let the world fade away for a while. Is that too much to ask for?

Leaning back into my chair and stretching my arms and back, noting the stiffness from sitting for so long, I see the pop of pale yellow and an all too familiar script adhered to my desk phone out of the corner of my eye.

MEET ME AT
825 SURF AVE NEAR
HARBOR PARK - 8 P.M.

DON'T BE LATE...XOXO, G

"Hey Klair, have you heard of Harbor Park?" I ask over our shared desk wall. She's yet again bent over another manuscript and just shrugs her shoulders. *Yeah, me neither.* After a quick internet search, I see that Harbor Park is near Coney Island, the famous and historical New York amusement park where I'd spent many nights as a kid with my family.

I glance at the clock, noting that I have over three hours until I'm supposed to meet Graham. Despite my earlier desire for a relaxing evening, whatever he has up his sleeve sounds far more interesting.

"Are you sure this is the right place?" I hesitantly ask my taxi driver, taking in the very dark and very sketchy parking garage she's just pulled up in front of.

"Yeah man...this is *definitely* 825 Surf Ave." I reluctantly pay her and as I stand on the side of the dark street watching the glow of her taillights disappear into the night air, I realize that hers might be the last face I see tonight in the event she's dropped me off to be murdered. This is fine—*everything is fine.* Looking down the street, I see there's what appears to be a taco truck parked a block or so away. *Ooh...our luck has changed!* I head in that direction...

"Hey, you..." Graham says from out of nowhere. *Ahhh. That sneaky bastard.*

"Okay *not cool,* mister," I hiss as he steps closer. I may or may not have wet my pants a little. "Hi handsome...this is such a, *um,* romantic date night spot." I tease as he wraps me in his arms.

"Shush..." he says, his hand now cupping my face as he brings his lips to mine. There's an urgency to Graham's kiss—the burn from his scruff dances across my lips, sending scorching waves of desire crashing through every nerve ending. His tongue, hot and full of need, dips into my mouth as he pulls me even closer to him, deepening our kiss and pressing his hard body against mine. *Dear god.* Instinctively, I reach for the throb I feel pressing against my thigh which results in a throaty moan to escape Graham's lips against mine.

He puts his forehead to mine, our breathing ravaged from the quick escalation of our kiss. Will it always be like this? The intense need and want I feel for him? *Of course.*

"Come on...I want to show you something," he says, placing a soft kiss against the corner of my mouth, a beautiful contrast between the immediacy of his first kiss and tenderness of this one.

"You mean this *isn't* where you wanted to take me tonight?" I tease once more, waving my arms around before taking his outstretched hand. Graham rolls his eyes at me. I don't know how he puts up with me but I'm so glad he does. I take his hand as he leads me a little further down the road before turning down a discreet side street. When we get to a door with a big *Employees Only* sign plastered across it in authoritative red letters, Graham removes a random key from his pocket and opens the door.

"Oh okay, so you *are* murdering me tonight...got it. Well, Teddy Graham...this was fun while it lasted," I say, leaning into him as we both stand in the doorway.

"Someone's been watching too many crime documentaries with Klair," he says, giving my hand a squeeze. "Do you trust me?"

"Duh."

"Good...I promise you're going to love this." There's an excitement growing behind his eyes, one that only solidifies the fact that I would follow him anywhere—even down a dark and musky hallway. *Probably to my death.*

The only light from the streetlight disappears as he closes the door behind us, but Graham leads us forward down the narrow hallway. There's a subtle chill to the air and as my eyes begin to adjust to the vast darkness, I can see a soft, blue glow illuminating an open space further ahead. I sneak a glance in Graham's direction as the glow grows brighter and I'm met with the most beautiful smile known to man. Now I'm *definitely* intrigued as to what has him smiling like that.

Our path begins to curve slightly, and our destination comes into focus, stopping me in my tracks.

"Graham..." The words get lost in my chest and all I can do is take in the scene before me. He's led me to an expansive glass room that has been transformed into our own personal date night. Centered in the open space, he's laid out a thick blanket with dozens of pillows scattered around, creating an intimate escape. There's wine and a cheese board and small candles on nearly every surface.

I slowly turn toward him, unable to contain my shock and total surprise. "You did all of this? I don't..."

"You missed the best part," he says, closing the distance between us. Graham lifts his gaze upward and I follow suit...the sight literally leaving me speechless. We are completely surrounded by thousands of jellyfish moving ever so slowly in their larger-than-life tanks, their iridescence casting a stunning glow across the dark room.

"It's mesmerizing, Graham...how did you do this?" I inquire, wrapping my arms around his waist.

"My family has worked extensively with the Wildlife Conservation Society for years, so I felt it was okay to call in a favor." He places a warm hand against my cheek. "Do you like it?"

Between the cozy spread he's created for us and the spell-binding jellyfish, I am completely blown away. "Graham...it's absolutely perfect. Is it silly that I wish I had my camera?"

"Ah...I figured you'd want to take a few photos, so I had Klair sneak this from your room this morning just in case," he says after breaking away and rummaging in a bag I hadn't noticed. He places my favorite digital camera into my hands, leaving me even more stunned than I was initially. He's truly thought of *everything*. "Go ahead, my little shutterbug...I'll pour us some wine."

Graham leaves me be momentarily and I quickly immerse myself in the beauty he's set up for me. I take a few test photos of the luminous creatures floating all around me and adjust my settings to account for the low lighting. *Click.* The jellyfish make the most alluring subjects, their long tentacles weightlessly trailing behind them as they float in and out of frame. *Click.* Placing my eye to the viewfinder of my camera, I hone in on a rather large and ominous looking jellyfish and follow my new translucent friend with my lens as it slowly floats along the edge of the tank. *Click.*

Zooming out, Graham's beautiful face has found itself in my frame illuminated by the hue of the soft light. He's patiently standing there, two wine glasses in his hands with his gaze turned upward, completely entranced by the intricate dance these sea creatures are putting on. *Click.*

I've never seen anything more breathtaking—despite being surrounded by some of the most beautiful species in the natural world, I am completely overwhelmed with adoration for this man. A thought, no...a thunderous tidal wave of emotion that I've tried to make sense of and explain away since the moment we met comes crashing over me.

Putting my camera down, I walk over to where he's standing—a crooked smile spreading slowly across his face as I take the wine glasses from him. Graham raises an eyebrow at me but doesn't say anything as I take both of his hands in mine.

"I need you to know how much I appreciate all of *this,* Graham...no one has ever done anything like this for me before and it's a memory that I will cherish for the rest of my life."

"I'm just glad you like it," he says, taking a step closer to me, our chests nearly touching. The weight of the words I'm about to blurt out send my body into overdrive and I can feel it begin to tremble.

"I love it...I love it almost as much as I love you." His eyes widen as I take his face in my hands, the trembling having stopped the moment I spoke the truth that's been growing only stronger in my heart. "I love you, Graham Austin and I think I have been slowly and undeniably falling in love with you since the moment I saw you. All of *this*. All of *you*...it's far more than I deserve but I need you to know how mu..."

Graham crashes his lips to mine, stunning my senses with the heat of his passion while wrapping me in an inescapable embrace. His hands interlock behind my neck pulling me even closer to him as he slows our kiss, sending time screeching to a halt. The soft glow that surrounds us fades even farther into the background as the love I feel for Graham washes over me and it is then that I know just how much he means to me...just how much I needed him.

He leans back ever so slowly, putting just enough distance between us so he can stare directly into my eyes. "You have no idea how badly I needed to hear that, babe..." he says, his lips still pressed to mine.

"I've never believed in fate or in happily ever after's. At least I didn't until you came along, Will." His voice is soft as he cups my face. "But loving you and knowing you love me back has fundamentally changed me. It's like being seen for the first time ever. Like I am free of the man I thought I needed to be and I *finally* get to be who I've always wanted to be—happy, spontaneous and so hopelessly in love with the man of my dreams."

Graham leans forward, gently bringing his lips to mine once more, a whisper of a kiss but full of so much love and tenderness my heart might explode.

"I'm sure you've noticed that I struggle connecting with people." I don't have the heart to make a joke about that being an understatement. "But you came barreling into my world out of nowhere, forcing me to see and feel things differently than I ever have before. You, Klair and even Dean...you all have made me feel *whole* in a way that has never made sense to me. In the books that we publish, the idea of found family and meeting your person never really resonated with me. Until you."

I'm his person—his words and the emotion behind them

make me visibly sag against him. "Oh baby, I've known from our very first kiss that I was a goner. What we have..." I say, my lips now pressed against his neck. "...it's the kind of love I've been silently praying was in the cards for me. The kind of love I'll never stop being thankful for."

Graham kisses my temple, wrapping me tighter in his arms and begins to sway ever so slightly to the peaceful sounds of the water tanks surrounding us.

"You had the audacity to come rushing into my life with your big and beautiful feelings, Will Cowen, and you decided that I was worthy—worthy of your time and your heart." Graham places his large hand across my chest, his warmth flowing straight to my core in a moment I know will be ingrained in my mind forever.

"And if I have any say in the matter, I hope to be worthy of every second of your always."

CHAPTER TWENTY-ONE

"Mmm...where do you think you're going, *guapo?*" Graham wraps his arms around me, pulling me tighter to his chest, kissing my shoulder and nuzzling deeper against me. I will never get sick of hearing him call me handsome in Spanish. His warmth envelopes me, creating the coziest of cocoons, but I *really* have to pee.

"I'll be right back," I say, extracting myself from his deliciously naked body, which he responds to with the cutest sounds of objection. I hear the buzz of one of our phones vibrating on the nightstand as I head to the bathroom. *It's probably nothing.*

Last night was everything I could have ever hoped it to be. My lips and skin are still tingling from the trails of kisses Graham left as we made love, slowly and intentionally. *He loves me.* His words play over and over in my head...words I've been waiting my whole life to hear, and now that I have, I know I'll never be the same. The moment Graham told me he loved me, something shifted. He wishes for a forever with me and while that scares the hell out of me, spending the rest of my life with

Graham, and now knowing the depth of his love for me, I can't think of anything else I'd rather do.

I pad back to the bed, eager to be in Graham's arms. We have zero plans this weekend, and if I have anything to say about it, we will not be leaving this bed.

"Your phone keeps ringing, babe," Graham groans, throwing an arm over his head. He's usually such a morning person, but *someone* had a little too much wine last night.

I reach over, grabbing my phone. *Holy shit.* Thirteen missed calls from the same number? A slight panic begins to creep in.

"Does this number sound familiar to you?" I ask him, repeating the number. "They called me a bunch of times."

He shakes his head. "Just call it back."

At that precise moment, my phone vibrates in my hand, signaling another incoming call from that same number.

"Hello?" I quietly answer, unsure of who is going to be on the other end.

"Good morning, I'm trying to get a hold of William Cowen," a rushed voice says, her tone soft but laced with urgency.

I swallow. "Yeah, this is him."

"Mr. Cowen, my name is Anne, I'm an ER nurse at New York Memorial Hospital. We've been trying to contact you this morning regarding your father who was recently admitted..."

Dad's hurt. Admitted? I don't...what? I'm not sure I'm hearing her correctly.

I sit on the edge of the bed, feeling woozy. I look back at Graham, who must have sensed a change in my body language, and see he's now sitting up, his naked torso on display.

What's wrong, he mouths.

"I'm sorry, I don't understand. Is my mom with him? Can I talk to her?" Surely, she would have called me.

"No...your father came in alone." I can hear a commotion in the background, Anne's focus is pulled. "Mr. Cowen, it's imperative that you come to the hospital as soon as possible. As his next of kin, there are forms that need to be signed and medical decisions to be made."

I am so confused. My mom and dad *never* do anything without the other. Utter fear rushes through my veins. "Is everything okay with my mom? I don't understand why she isn't with him." My voice is trembling, and I can feel myself beginning to shake. Graham places a hand on my back.

"Hold on," Anne says. I can hear the clicks of her keyboard. "No, we don't have any record of your mother. Just to confirm... Scott Russell is your father, right? You're listed as his next of kin."

My heart stops. *Scott Russell.* My father, Scott Russell. He's in the hospital. *But for what? Did she even say? How did he get my phone number?*

I let out the breath I'd been holding since I picked up her call. *Thank god.*

"Oh, I'm sorry...there seems to be some sort of mistake." Pure relief floods every ounce of my body. "I don't have a relationship with that man. I haven't in years."

"But sir, you don't understand. You need to deci—" I hang up, setting my phone back on the nightstand.

"Will, what's going on?" Graham's voice is full of concern. I crawl back into bed, claiming my spot against him. I can feel him looking at me, his body tense and rigid.

"Everything's fine." I start kissing his exposed chest, running my hand slowly over his hip.

He stops my hand, taking it in his. "But is everything okay with your family? That sounded really serious."

"Graham, everything is *fine*...it was a miscommunication, that's all." Confusion and compassion are all over his face. *Ugh.* He's clearly not going to drop it. "My mom and dad are fine, but I guess my biological father landed himself in the hospital and he had me listed as his next of kin or something..." I hear the indifference in my tone. *Graham must think I'm a monster.*

"Oh handsome, I'm sorry." He's hugging me. *Why is he sorry?* "Is there anything I can do?" he adds, rubbing my back.

"Like I said, everything is fine." I'm getting frustrated. Why isn't he understanding this?

"Okay so should we get ready?" Graham says as he gets up, leaving the comfort of the bed. "Do we need to get going?"

He's in full-blown hero mode, swooping in and standing by, ready to reconnect me with my sick, long-lost father. I didn't ask for this, and I *definitely* don't want this.

I get up, meeting him at the foot of the bed, our eyes locking as my body squares in front of his. "I don't know what all of *this* is..." I say waving my hands in his general direction. *Unnecessary.* "But I'm confused as to how or why you think I'd go rushing off to see someone who I feel nothing for."

"I just—"

"Graham, I'm not going. End of conversation," I cut him off before he can get another word in. As I walk to the bathroom again, closing the door behind me, I know just how big of a dick I'm being. *He doesn't understand...how could he with his perfect family?* I know that thought couldn't be farther from the truth, but I don't care. I'm livid.

The pain this man has inflicted on not just me but my entire family, on Klair, even. It's not something that just goes away with time. It's a wound that is just as raw today as it was back when I was younger. Back when I first realized how cruel and pitiful my father is, when I realized he's never cared.

I yank open the shower door, turning on the water as hot as it'll go. I need to think, and I need to do it away from Graham and his compassionate gaze and comforting touches. I don't want to be comforted; I want to be angry. I *am* angry. Whenever I think about my father, which, to be fair, isn't often, I am ripped right back to that very last time I saw him, the dull throb of where he hit me still so present like it happened just moments ago. I've never understood, and honestly never will, how after all these years, he couldn't just choose his family over his need to drink. People do it every single day...they overcome their addictions, face their demons, and move on with their lives. Why the hell couldn't he be one of them? *Why didn't he want to be?*

Leaning against the shower wall, I let the sting of the water envelope me. Almost instantly, my body is fatigued, vibrating through a wide range of emotional distress I'm not even sure I have a name for. Rage? Confusion?

And sadness. I can no longer deny the devastating sadness I feel. As soon as the admission fills my head, a sob I didn't know was building in my chest erupts, doubling me over in a pain I've been running from for years.

My father, one of the few people on this earth who is genetically programmed to love me, could not or would not choose me. An act that has left a scar on my heart so deep, so profoundly mangled, and unfixable, that I've convinced myself I'm unworthy of love from anyone, unless I'm this perfect version of who they want me to be. Love has always felt conditional.

Until now.

Graham has shown me just how off my thinking has been. That I *am* worthy of love. His love—his unwavering and overwhelming love—is unlike anything I've ever experienced, and time and time again, I make a mockery of it by retreating to these toxic habits.

Like father, like son? The thought sickens me.

He doesn't deserve this. *More like I don't deserve him.*

Turning off the water, I wrap myself in a towel, not even bothering to dry myself off. When I open the bathroom door, I see that Graham is standing in the same spot he was when I stormed off. He looks up at me, his eyes wide and tired, and when he opens his mouth to say something, I launch myself at him. Wrapping my arms around him, pressing my dripping body to his, I hold on to him for dear life.

He exhales, squeezing me tighter in the process. "I'm so sorry for assuming," he says, placing a kiss on my soaking wet hair. "I truly only wanted to help." His voice is soft, filled with uncertainty, and it kills me to know that my actions, my behavior has made him feel this way.

"I'm the one who needs to be sorry," I cry, the shower no longer concealing my tears. "I'm so sorry, babe. I should never have snapped at you like that."

"Shh, I know," he says, causing the tears to flow even harder. "Come on, let's get you dried off."

Graham pours me another cup of coffee then proceeds to sit directly next to me at the kitchen island. I take a deep sip, savoring its richness and warmth, the sharpness of the caffeine comforting me. I know he wants to talk, I can all but hear his inner monologue going crazy right now. Turning to look at him, I put my mug down and put my hand on his thigh.

"I can feel you biting your tongue," I say, my tone much softer than it was earlier.

"I am not." He takes my hand in his, gliding his thumb over my knuckles. *Liar.*

"Graham...I overreacted earlier. You *know* that I value your input and opinion." I lean over, planting a kiss at the corner of his mouth. He smiles in return. "Talk to me."

Turning toward me, I can see his hesitation. *I'm such an asshole.*

"Just hear me out, okay?" he says, staring at our entwined

hands. "But before I say anything, please know that *you* are my primary concern in all of this."

"I know that babe."

"I just want you to think long and hard about what *not* going means." His body tenses, anticipating my reaction. "And I don't say that to imply what it would mean for your father, because Lord knows you don't owe that man anything. But think about what it would mean for *you* to not go."

I hadn't thought of it that way. When the subject of my father comes up, I guess I get tunnel vision, and I hadn't really thought about how I'll feel down the line.

"You've carried the weight of your father on your heart for years," Graham continues, his voice filled with sincerity. "Don't you want an opportunity for closure? To turn the page on this chapter of your life?" He squeezes my hand. "This sounds serious, Will...how many times did they call? Ten?" *Thirteen, actually.* "What if you miss an opportunity to get any questions you have answered? Or to scream at the top of your lungs about how pissed off you are? I know it's been years and so much hurt has been caused, so I get it...I don't know how I'd be feeling right now if I was in this situation. But just think about the dreaded *what if* moment, okay?"

He puts his arms around me, pulling me into a hug I so desperately need. "And if you still don't want to go, I hope you know that I support you in that decision. I just feel like I owe it to you, as someone who cares so deeply about you and your happiness, to offer another perspective."

In my heart, I know he's right. Of course he is. However, does it even matter? The thought of seeing my father...*Ugh.* And what if it is as serious as Graham says? Does that change anything? This whole situation is too much to think about and I hate how much it's conflicting me. *Damn it, I don't want to do this.*

Graham, with his strong arms still around me, whispers in my ear, "Regardless of what happens today, know that I love you." Even in the midst of *everything* going on, hearing that word come out of his beautiful mouth again stills my heart.

It's in that moment, looking up at the man who I love so intensely, that I know I'm going to go see my father. *I have to.*

"Will you come with me?" I whisper.

He takes my face in his hands, wiping away the last remaining tears.

"Always."

Graham pulls into midmorning traffic with ease.

We haven't really spoken much, but he's got his hand on my leg and is humming along as his music shuffles, so I think *we're* okay. I don't know what to say. Part of me wants to beg and plead with him to turn around and take me home, to express what a horrible idea this is. Another part of me wants him to hurry the hell up and drive faster.

And another part of me wants to vomit, so that's where we're at.

I steal a glance over in Graham's direction, admiring his profile. He's completely focused on the road, on getting us to the hospital. Of course, he's amazing in a crisis; calm, supportive, kind. *Sexy.* Despite all of that, even though I know Graham would never and has never judged me for the situation with my father, my anxiety is spiking at the thought of the two of them meeting. Do I want him to know that part of my life? I'm not even prepared to see *him* after all these years, let alone introduce my boyfriend to him.

Hi, Deadbeat Father? This is Graham, the love of my life. Oh, and by the way, I'm super gay. I shake my head; I hadn't put too much thought or energy into my father's reaction to me being gay. He was out of the picture when I officially came out, but I'm sure on some level, he had to have known.

I reach over, running my fingers through the hair at the base of Graham's neck and put my head on his shoulder, causing him to smile. "Thank you for driving...and for coming. It *really* means the world to me."

He reaches for my hand and brings it to his lips, his focus still on the road. Planting a kiss on the back of my hand, he says, "There is nowhere I'd rather be."

He keeps my hand in his for the remainder of our drive, slowly tracing small hearts on my skin, the simple act doing wonders to subdue the fear and anxiety I'd been feeling.

We pull up to the loading zone at the main hospital entrance.

"Why don't you go ahead while I park," Graham says, giving me a reassuring smile.

I exit the car, my breathing accelerating as I close the door behind me. Walking through the motion-activated doors, my legs feel like lead, each step closer to the information desk feels like I'm dragging the weight of a freight train.

More like ten plus years of abandonment and daddy issues, get it together.

The hospital is buzzing with all the sounds you'd expect it to—pages for doctors, ringing phones, the subtle beeps of medical equipment. Behind the desk, several nurses are carrying out their business, each one diligently taking calls, addressing patients and family members and everything else that's thrown at them. *I don't know how they do it.*

When I finally make it to the charging station, noting that none of them appear to be judging me for my slow-motion entrance—*thank god*—I place both hands on the cool veneer of the desk.

"Hi." My voice is swallowed whole by the cacophony of background noise and instead of displaying any sort of adult competence, I stand there like a child waiting for an adult to handle all of my problems.

"Can I help you with something, hun?" a tiny and friendly looking nurse asks, clearly aware of how lost I am. She's looking at me with pity in her eyes, like she's trying to figure out if I need medical attention or if I'm utterly useless. *Maybe both?* I glance at her name badge: Heather.

"Hi," I repeat. "I received a call about Scott Russell?"

"And you're family?"

"He's my father." I hate calling him that, the disdain drips from my lips. Sure, we share some genes, but this man is *not* my family.

"Okay, let me see where he is." Heather turns toward the computer and begins typing when another nurse comes around the corner.

"You said you're here to see Scott Russell?" she asks, stepping around the desk that separates me from them. "I'm assuming you're Will Cowen? We spoke earlier. I'm Anne." She extends her hand, which I take, noticing the softness of her skin. "Let's chat over here." Her deep, brown eyes offer a kindness I can only assume comes with years in this field—cheering alongside patients during happy and healing moments and grieving with them during the hard ones. I follow her to a quiet seating area, away from the hustle and bustle of the main entrance, sitting only because she does, my body on autopilot.

"Mr. Cowen, what I was *trying* to tell you earlier on the phone was that your father's condition is very serious," she speaks so softly, but the severity of her tone reminds me of a disappointed parent dealing with a difficult child. "He came in last night after noticing traces of blood when coughing, which is always concerning, but coupled with the treatment he was receiving at the VA to try to combat his liver failure, we weren't presented with many options."

Perhaps seeing the confusion on my face or remembering my comment about not having a relationship with the man, Anne puts her hand on my arm. "Your father drank heavily for many years, which I take it you know." That's an understatement. "Well," she says, patting my knee as she continues, "that level of drinking has caused severe damage to both his liver and his esophagus."

"Okay, so can you point me in the direction of his room? I'd like to speak with his doctor." I have a basic understanding of the human body thanks to many Grey's Anatomy marathons, so I know how serious liver damage can be, but it would be great to hear all of this directly from his medical team.

"Will, your father isn't here. He's..."

"What do you mean he isn't here?" I shout at her and immediately feel like an asshole. "This is where *you* told me to come!"

"Like I mentioned on the phone, as his next of kin, there were medical decisions that only you could have made." Anne stands, crossing her arms, clearly irritated by my demeanor. "With that being said, as your father's condition worsened—very rapidly I might add—he required emergency surgery, and at that time, without you here to tell us otherwise, his doctors concluded there wasn't any more they could do for him here."

I jump up, causing my chair to screech against the linoleum floor. "So, if he's not here, where the hell is he?"

"He was airlifted to the University of New York University Medical Center about thirty minutes before you got here." *Shit.* That's about an hour away with traffic.

I take off running toward the door, not able to make out what Anne shouts after me. Sprinting across the lobby and

243

through the main entrance, I race into the parking lot, my eyes scanning for a sign of Graham's black SUV with each stride.

There. Spotting his car, I weave through the packed parking lot, making my way down the aisle. Ripping open the passenger door, I jump in, my return surprising Graham who was typing away on his phone.

"Hey, I'm sorry...I was just finishing an emai..." His voice trails off when he meets my gaze. "What's wrong?"

"We need to go to NYU Medical Center. He isn't here." Graham reaches over and tries to take my hand. "Graham, we have to go. RIGHT NOW."

He throws me his phone. "Plug in the address," he directs, throwing his car in drive and peeling out of the parking lot, seemingly understanding the urgency in my voice.

"Can we go any faster?" I've asked this every couple of minutes and I'm sure I'm driving Graham insane. Beyond that, we've ridden in silence.

"I'm going as fast as I can go, babe...but we're almost there. Just a couple more miles."

My leg is tapping uncontrollably and if we don't get to the hospital soon, I think I'm on the verge of a full-blown panic attack. *I fucked up.*

I feel sick to my stomach. Why didn't I take this seriously? Am I really *that* proud that I scoffed at the thought of my father being in the hospital? I know the man he is—*well, was*—and nothing has changed, but deep down, I know I feel some semblance of love for him. I was desperate for his love and attention for years. Even after I cut him out of my life, he was central to every decision I made as an adult in my attempt to *not* be like him. I do love him almost as much as I want him to love me.

I repeat Anne's words in my head. *He was airlifted about thirty minutes before you got here.* Thirty minutes. Would being there thirty minutes earlier change anything? Who knows? He would have at least known I was there, but would he have even cared? *Of course he would.*

"We're just around the corner," Graham's voice snaps me back to reality. Looking out the window, I can see the hospital entrance. He pulls into the driveway, but I can't wait any longer. I force open the door, not even caring that Graham is still driving, and shoot out.

"Will, oh my God!" he yells after me, but I'm already gone, sprinting as hard and fast as I can toward the hospital entrance. I underestimated how far away we still were, the burn in my lungs threatening to slow me down. *Come on, Will...MOVE!*

My body is moving on pure adrenaline alone. *And fear.* Because I need to see him. After all of these wasted years, time that I could have tried harder to fix things or to be better or to get him the help he needed, especially as I got older. I *chose* to not have him in my life, and right now, I'm willing to give just about anything to see him. *Almost there.*

I crash through the hospital entrance, my breathing ragged and a sheen of sweat covering every inch of my exposed skin. "I'm here...I'm here to see... Sco...my father, Scott Russell." I can barely get the words out. My abdomen muscles cramp, doubling me over the front desk, alarming the poor nurse. "What room? Please, *please* just tell me what room he's in?" I beg with tears streaming down my face.

The man in front of me types away on his computer. "Your father is in room 423. Take the elevator to your left up to the fourth floor, and it'll be a straight shot," he informs me, his voice filled with compassion. I yell thank you over my shoulder as I'm already half-running, half-limping toward the elevator.

Everything around me is moving in slow motion—the speed of the elevator, the endless seconds it takes for the doors to *ping* open, the time it takes to travel up four floors. I can feel my heart beating out of my chest.

Floor 2. My mouth is dry and I'm really struggling to breathe. I can't think of a time in my life where I've ever been this scared.

Floor 3. I need him to be okay so that I can yell at him for missing so many of my life's moments. For not being the father I deserved. I need him to know how badly it hurt when he wasn't there. How desperately I wanted him to be. I need him to know that I love him.

Floor 4. The elevator doors open, and I barrel forward, looking to the nearest sign to see how much farther I have to go still. Just a few more rooms. The spike of adrenaline I'd been running on is gone, filling my body with a cold emptiness that sends a chill down my spine with every step forward. Looking down the hall, I can see the blurred movement of medical staff at work, their movements fast and rushed, their urgency calls me forward.

*417, 419, 421...*I'm almost there. *423.* The hall goes momentarily silent and then the long, piercing tone—the one you hear in all the movies—shatters through the void. That's when I know.

He's gone. I know without knowing. The only thing I can hear is the tone that's replaced my father's heartbeat and I'm left standing in the doorway, staring at the chipped tile, unable to look into the room.

"I'm his son," I whisper, unsure if anyone even cared to hear me. "I said I'm his son," my voice louder this time. Nothing. *You have to look up. Look up, Will. You have to.*

So, I do. And I immediately wish I hadn't.

Gone was the muscular man who served his country all those years ago, and in his place, a stranger who looks vaguely familiar but entirely unrecognizable. His face is gaunt, his body bloated, gorged in an almost cartoonish manner. His skin, once tanned and full of life, is tinted yellow, a sign of his liver failing like Anne mentioned. Every tube known to man is sticking out of him, a living pin cushion, the remnants of the doctors doing everything in their power to save him. The sight of him like this causes bile to fill my throat, the sting of the sterile environment filling my nostrils causes the room to spin.

I collapse to my knees, a sob ripping through my chest, threatening to tear me in half and slam my fists into the ground.

"I'm his son," I cry, unable to hold it together any longer.

"I'm his son." The room goes black; the sound of the heart monitor drowns me into oblivion.

Dad, I'm here...I'm here, Dad. I'm sorry I'm late, but I'm here.

"Mr. Cowen? Can you hear me?" A murky voice breaks through the ringing in my ears. Are my eyes open? I feel like my eyes are open, but I can't see anything. "Mr. Cowen, can you open your eyes for me?" *That explains it.*

Opening my eyes, I'm staring into the faces of several concerned doctors and nurses, their expressions change slightly once I'm alert. I realize I'm still on the floor, the coolness of the tiles causes me to shiver.

"Come on...let's get you up in this chair." I couldn't have been out for more than a few seconds, but I feel like I just woke up from the deepest sleep and everything is resonating with a cloudiness that only adds to my confusion. *What the hell?* I'm lifted up into the chair across the wall, my body tense and limp all at the same time.

When I'm placed in a seated position, the doctor to my right checks my pulse, her fingers sure and strong against my wrist. "Sir, my name is Dr. Sharvina Ziyeh. Can you do me a favor and follow my fingers? I want to make sure you didn't injure yourself."

I nod my head as she begins moving her fingers slowly in front of my face, my eyes compelled to follow. She examines my head, gingerly tracing her fingers along my skull.

"Dr. Ziyeh, I'm okay. I don't think I hit my head," my voice hoarse.

Satisfied with her examination or possibly just taking my word for it, she takes a step back, her gaze softening. "Still, I'd like to give you something for shock."

"I don't think that will be neces—" It hits me like a ton of bricks.

My father is dead.

I stand a little too quickly, my legs buckle but find their balance, and push past her.

"Mr. Cowen, please take it easy," she says, her hands on my arms. I need to see him for myself, not trusting the nightmarish mental image now playing on repeat in my mind.

But there he is, lifeless and empty, a physical depiction of how I'm feeling on the inside. I place my hands on the foot of his bed, afraid to touch him but feeling compelled to be near him. They made quick work of the tubes and wires while I was out. He looks more human now, peaceful even. His facial hair has grown in and is flecked with gray. His hair, normally cropped short and close on the sides, has been left untouched for a while. I look at his hands, the same ones that used to bring me so much comfort and then so much pain and see the thick calluses that have been present my entire life.

I feel numb.

"If I promise to sit down, can I have a moment alone with him?" I ask, my voice cracking.

"Of course, take all the time you need." She gives my arm a reassuring squeeze, one that tells me she knows this moment all too well and turns to leave with the rest of the medical staff.

Reclaiming my seat against the wall, I bow my head, placing it in my hands and grabbing fistfuls of hair which helps release some of the tension. A dull throb has been present all afternoon but has reached the point that I feel like my brain is going to erupt from my skull. The doctor was right; I am most *definitely* in shock. I look back over at my father, the stillness of his body is beginning to become unsettling, but I don't know what to do or what to say.

I was too late. My selfish behavior caused him to die alone and honestly, despite everything this man has done, I don't know how that makes me feel. This morning, I was so sure that I didn't want anything to do with him and now...I look at his face, the muscles relaxed...now I'll never know what could have been.

I'll never know.

The thought causes the tears to return, harder and with more force than before because I'm fairly certain this moment will remain with me for the rest of my life. The regret and the pain and the endless guilt will haunt me forever and there's nothing I can do to change that.

I hear footsteps getting closer between sobs. "I said I need a minute," I say, hiding my face away.

Silence.

"Please, can you just give me a min—" I turn, facing my visitor. "Lana?"

Did I accidently call her? I'm so confused. *How mortifying.*

I attempt to wipe the tears and snot from my face, self-conscious at how disgusting I must look. Looking up at her face, I see her eyes are red, too. *Has she been crying? Maybe she was here visiting someone?*

"Is...is everything okay?" I ask, my voice cracks as I do my best to stand up.

She steps toward me, preventing me from doing so, and wraps her arms around me. Returning her hug, I can feel her shaking.

"He wanted you to have this," she whispers, placing a kiss on my cheek. *He? Who?* She pushes an incredibly thick and worn envelope into my chest. "Please don't hate me." Her voice is a whisper. Without saying another word, Lana turns without looking at me and exits the hospital room as quickly as she entered.

I turn the envelope over, feeling its weight in my hands. *What the hell?*

"Lana!" I yell, knowing she's probably already long gone. How did she...He wanted me to have what? I'm so confused.

Getting up from my chair, the stability finally returning to my limbs, I tuck the envelope under my arm, not having the heart or the mental capacity to deal with it right this second. Walking toward the door, I stop before crossing the threshold into the hallway, my body frozen in place.

I can't say goodbye.

Instead, I quickly turn around and walk back to my father's bedside. Looking down at the man before me—the man I once admired and feared so much—my heart is conflicted. I don't physically think it's possible to shed another tear, but I feel a bubble of rage building. He could have prevented this. *This* didn't have to happen.

I lean down, putting my forehead to his with my eyes closed like I used to when I was little. I picture him young and full of life, happy and laughing on one of our good days. *That's* how

I'm going to choose to remember him. While those moments were fleeting, they were there.

"I pray that whatever battle you've been fighting is over, Dad," I whisper, a final tear rolling down my cheek onto his.

Pushing away from his bed, I keep my eyes closed as I walk out the door so that my final thought of my father will be a happy one, one of my own choosing.

Goodbye, Dad.

I can't be in this hospital anymore.

Riding the elevator down to the lobby, my body begins to shake, the weight of today, of this moment, is too much to bear. I've never felt this mentally and physically exhausted before in my life, and somehow, it still feels like just the beginning.

I blink and suddenly, I'm in the lobby.

Cramped in a chair that is much too small for his stature, Graham's sitting with his long legs out in front of him, crossed at the ankle. His head slumped to the side with his eyes closed, clearly feeling the same level of exhaustion I am. Even dozing off, he's truly the most beautiful sight I've ever seen, a welcome one after everything that just went down behind the hospital doors.

I would give anything to be wrapped in the warmth of his embrace, but right now, all I can think about is how I'm surrounded by death. The need for fresh air pushes me past him, attempting to put as much distance as possible between myself and this damn hospital.

Turning too quickly in the direction of the front entrance, I collide directly with a random hospital worker pushing a cart of supplies, causing both to crash across the lobby. In a fog and completely out of my body, I push past the mess I just created, choking out a muffled apology.

Graham, who snapped to attention at the chaos in the lobby, jumps to his feet.

"Will!" he shouts after me as I race forward, forcing open the sliding doors in my way, the much-needed cool air waking me from a paralyzing fog. "Babe, slow down." I hear him but I can't stop. *Not yet.*

I keep walking—past the parking lot, where I know his car is waiting somewhere, past the hospital's entry sign off the main street. I keep walking once I reach the side of the road, the rush of the speeding traffic sending gusts of wind in every direction. Graham has been silently following me, always just a few steps behind.

Finally, I stop.

I feel him behind me, his breath on the back of my neck. He places his hand ever so gently on my shoulder, his warm touch makes me want to curl into him and melt in his arms. But I stand rigid. "Talk to me, love...what can I do?"

"He's dead."

My words hang between us, a deafening silence that makes my skin crawl.

"My father's dead, Graham," I roar, turning to face him. His face falls, his tired eyes searching mine for...I don't know what exactly, but his gaze pierces through my heart.

"I...God, Will...I'm so sorry." His apology physically hurts me. *He did nothing wrong.* From the very start of all of this, Graham had been the one pushing me to be here, and me being the asshole I am, didn't listen. "What do you need? Do you want to talk about it?" He takes a step toward me, attempting to pull me closer, but I'm being suffocated right now. Choked by guilt and remorse and so much hurt that I can barely see straight.

"What do you want me to say, Graham? That I miss him?" I

yell, take a step back and put my hands up in front of me. He looks like I just slapped him, but he stands his ground.

"Should I say how badly I fucked up and should have been there? Or how about the fact that I hate him? Because I do. I hate him so much that sometimes it's all I can think about. I'm feeling *all* of those things right now. I'm fucking livid. I'm numb. I'm heartbro..." My voice fails me as the pain in my chest explodes, shattering me into a state of hysteria. It hurts to cry but it's killing me to hold it in any longer, so I let it all out, falling into Graham's waiting arms. *God, this poor man.*

He holds me tight, his arms shielding me from the world and the heartache. Even in the midst of the pain I'm feeling right now, I know that I love this man in a forever kind of way—it's the most powerful emotion I've ever felt.

"I hate him so much, Graham." I cling to his shirt, burying my face in his neck. "But I hate myself more for how much I want him to tell me that I was enough and that he loves me. That he's proud of me. And now he's drunk himself to death and he'll never be able to. He chose THAT over me."

Letting go of his embrace, he grips me by the arms. "Look at me, Will." My head is slumped against his chest. "Look at me," he repeated, more forcefully this time. I lift my gaze to his, my vision blurred through the tears.

Graham takes my face in his, forcing our eyes to lock.

"This will mean nothing to you right now or even tomorrow or over the next few days and months, but I promise you this, my sweet and beautiful man, you are so much more than enough." He kisses my cheek softly, lingering in the most tender and loving way. "There are no words to take away the pain you're feeling, but I need you to know that I will be here for you every single step of the way."

He looks at me with tears streaming down his beautiful face, pulling me back into his arms once more.

"I will spend the rest of my life telling *and* showing you that if you need me to, because I love you, Will. I am so sorry you are hurting, but I will help you through it with every ounce of love I have."

Despite the insurmountable ache in my heart, I know he will.

CHAPTER TWENTY-TWO

I KNOW I NEED TO OPEN IT.

Since the moment Lana placed the envelope in my lap, her words—*He wanted you to have this...please don't hate me*—have been repeating over and over again in the disjointed fragments that is my mind. The unknown meaning of her statement only adds to the immense grief and anger I'm feeling. I cannot take it any longer. Not knowing is threatening to send me into a deeper state of madness and heartbreak.

Grabbing the envelope from Graham's coffee table, I sit in his oversized armchair, running my hand along the soft but worn gray fabric. He's left me alone, if only momentarily, but I can hear the faint sounds of the shower echoing down the hall. Every fiber of my being wants to be with him right now, to let the warmth of the water release the tension I've been feeling all afternoon. But I know that if I don't get this over with now, I'll only be prolonging the inevitable.

I turn the envelope over, feeling its weight in my hands. I feel numb, like whatever is in this envelope is going to gut me to my core. Ripping its seal, I empty the contents into my lap. There's a smaller envelope with my name written in slanted handwriting. Even though it's been years, I slowly run my fingertip over my father's distinguishable script, feeling the indents of each letter as he firmly pressed them onto the page.

Tears fill my eyes. *He wanted you to have this.* I'm not ready to read what I'm assuming is a letter from my father. I can't. So instead, I set his envelope down and grab the thick stack of papers bound together with a black clip and my heart stops. The words *I Should Have Told You Then* are centered on the front.

Why the *hell* would my father have a copy of Lana's novel? That's when I notice it at the bottom of the page, right aligned in a small font.

Written by Scott Russell.

This must be some sort of a sick joke. I quickly turn the pages through my fingers, realizing that this is *definitely* her book. I feel sick to my stomach. *No.* Lana and I have been working on this together for months. We've spoken *in*-person about it...I know she wrote this. I look back to the letter. Confusion and rage surge through my veins as my hands begin to shake.

"*No, no, NO*...There is *no way* this is real," I yell fanning through the pages one more time, knowing no one is there to hear me. My head pounds as I try to go over every interaction I've had with Lana over the last several months. She was private and shy, sure. She mentioned how being in crowds wasn't her thing, but this? I...I don't understand. She knew my father? Why *would she do this to me?*

I feel betrayed, both personally and professionally. Lana was welcomed into my life from the very first moment I met her. I invited her home, for fuck's sake. *God, she met my parents.* The ache in my chest is debilitating. My heart feels like it's been punched out of my chest and the more I try to make sense of this situation, the more confused I become.

The tears fall now, burning hot on my skin. I defended her.

I fought for her. I fell in love with her words. How the *hell* am I going to explain *this* to Graham? *Oh shit...Mitch!* The publicity, all that money spent, how did I not see a *single* red flag?

I clutch the manuscript to my chest, crumpling its pages against my sobs. This is too much. After everything that happened today, *this* is too fucking much, and I don't know if I'll survive it. I turn the letter over and over between unsteady fingers, the tears now falling so rapidly that I can barely see, but I need an explanation. I need to make sense of all of this.

My heart pounds as I tear the letter from its envelope, running my thumb along each fold of the pages. I slowly bring the letter to my nose after opening them and inhale. I know it's the grief and there's no way this is not all in my head, but I swear I can smell *him*. That same musky and tobacco-infused scent that once brought momentary comfort when I was younger now overwhelms my senses, causing the tears to fall even harder.

Dad.

I've never felt pain like this before. The immensity of this raw and all-consuming pain coupled with anger and confusion feels never-ending. For as much as I loathe the man, I have to know what his letter says. I need to know what his final words are...were.

I notice he dated the letter almost a week ago.

Dear Will,

I have been putting off this letter for years, hoping that someday we'd have this conversation face-to-face. Time is one of the most precious things in this world, but unfortunately, it appears that I've run out of it.

I have failed you in more ways than I can even begin to count and the fact that you are reading this letter means I have failed you a final time, and for that, my son...I am eternally sorry. It should come as no surprise to you that I am an alcoholic. I know you know this and have lived through the worst of it, but as part of my recovery, I need to feel the weight of those words pass my lips to all of those I've hurt. The decisions I made in life were mine and mine alone...I cannot blame alcohol for the actions of my damaged soul.

I'm sorry that I wasn't strong enough to reach out to you when I still had time. Lord knows I wanted to, Will...with every fiber of who I am I wanted to, so badly. But I didn't think I was deserving of even having a conversation with you. After everything I put you through...after everything I put your mother through. I know that in not doing so, I robbed you of the opportunity for some semblance of closure, if you even wanted or needed it. Saying "I'm sorry" just didn't feel significant enough for what I put you through. But I am, Will. God, I am so sorry, and I will be for the rest of my days and for whatever hell awaits me. Because as broken as I am, you never deserved to be treated the way I treated you. You never deserved to be subjected to my demons.

My entire world revolved around being the perfect Marine. Outside of you, serving my country is the thing in my life that I am proudest of. It's who I am...or was. But it's taken me years to understand the toll that the war took on my mental health. Growing up, there wasn't as much of an emphasis on mental toughness like there is today. You came in, did your job, and never complained about it, and then went about your business. Over the years, watching my friends, my military family die around me on deployment after deployment, the unimaginable things I witnessed all in service of this great nation...they all piled up, and I think I reached my mental breaking point. All the while trying to be some version of a good husband and father. Yet time and time again, I failed. I turned toward alcohol to numb the pain instead of turning toward your mother. I turned toward anger instead of turning toward compassion. And the thing that I will have to live with for the rest of my miserable life is that the anger I felt...that rage and that pain I tried so desperately to suppress, led me to lay my hands on you.

In the vilest and most unforgivable of ways.

In a way that replays over and over in my mind.

I am not asking for your forgiveness, because I know I will never and can never deserve it. You deserved a father you could be proud of...someone who you knew without a shadow of a doubt loved you and would protect you at all costs, and unfortunately, my horrific actions and behavior allowed you to grow up not knowing those things. That kills me, Will. Knowing that my weakness and my own shortcomings may have caused you to question your worth or if you were loved.

Because son, I have loved you since the very first moment you came into this world. You are my only child, my flesh and my blood, and the day that you were born changed my life forever. I may not have been there or in your life these last few years, but I've always kept up with how you're doing through your mother or the internet, and I can't tell you how proud I am of the wonderful man you grew up to be. Despite your upbringing and despite having me as a father, you have thrown yourself into the world unapologetically and have led a life filled with kindness, strength, and humility.

Something I have never known.

In your hands is something years in the making. What started off as random letters here and there or journal entries from my recovery has turned into this book. One that was never supposed to see the light of day—until I met Lana. I am in no position to ask anything of you, but please don't be mad at her. All of this... all the deceit to get this into your hands in a roundabout way was my idea. From what she's told me, the two of you have formed a genuine friendship. If you believe anything I ever say, please let it be that she is one of the good ones. She has her own story to tell, one that is woven with mine yet not mine to share...the irony of that comment is not lost on me, but please don't turn your back on her. Not now.

I didn't know if I would ever have the opportunity to share with you how I felt. I never knew if you'd be able to understand my dark pain and insurmountable regret, so I wrote it—at least some fictionalized version of it—in the hope that one day, when you were ready, and on your own terms, you'd be able to read it. Not to absolve me of what I've done or even to make sense of it, but to learn from it. To have something tangible that speaks to the depth of my love for you. Because these last few months have been the most agonizing and bittersweet months of my life. Having the opportunity to work with you, even though you were unknowingly doing so, was a dream. You pushed me to be more honest and open with my pain and guilt. You forced me to face those demons head on instead of burying them. And you made me realize that despite the worst version of me, you somehow grew up to be this incredible man who treats everyone with dignity and respect. Someone who honors their life experiences, no matter how painful, and shows them unwavering support.

There are no words to describe the pride I have in my heart knowing you became who you are, Will. Never lose that.

My time is coming to an end. I know that and am at peace with it—no matter what comes next. But I need you to know, Will...you will be my last thought as I leave this earth and the last name on my breath, because you, my beautiful and strong son, are the only good thing that has come from my life. I pray that one day, the immeasurable pain I've inflicted on your life subsides, and that as time goes on, you can look back on this book and know that you were and will forever be loved.

Remember...rise, heal, overcome.

No matter what, I will always love you.

I clutch my father's words—the words I so desperately needed to hear—against my heart. Words that have left me hollowed out, emptied of all emotion and reason. The realization that my alcoholic father, my dead father, is secretly one of the most profound authors I've ever encountered feels like an unimaginable reality. A cruel and sick version of everything I thought I knew and believed in.

I reread his letter, over and over again, each time ripping open my heart even wider. The only thing I can do, the only thing keeping me from drowning in this moment, is to curl myself into this chair and let every ounce of pain and heartache, every repressed memory and emotional response to his words wash over me.

"Babe? What did it say?" Graham asks, his soft voice filled with concern as he pads back into the living room. I meet his gaze, seeing the love and empathy in his eyes and am filled with an overwhelming sense of appreciation.

For the man he is and the man he most certainly isn't.

How could someone I love more than anything possibly make sense of all this? Because I sure as hell can't. Where do I even begin?

I have no idea what comes next, but as Graham slides in next to me on this oversized armchair, wrapping me in his arms that I now call home and enveloping me in the most comforting scent in the world—*him*—I know that whatever it is, we'll be okay.

All of us.

EPILOGUE
SIX MONTHS LATER

THE SCALDING WATER POURS OVER ME, LOOSENING THE stress that's been threatening to eat me alive for days. Even though months have passed since my father's death, there are moments where I find myself moving in slow motion, almost paralyzed by the what ifs, and nearly drowning in the immense guilt that refuses to subside.

Moments like today, where I let routine and habit autopilot my every movement. Everyone has told me it's not my fault. *There wasn't anything you could have done, Will.* Of course, I know that. I didn't force an alcoholic to drink all those years. I didn't choose this life for him, nor did I have any part in it. But...

I hesitated.

I didn't listen to Graham when he said I should go to the hospital right away and I'll never know if that would have made a difference. For me or for my father. Would I feel differently if I had gotten the opportunity to say goodbye to him? Would it lessen the guilt I feel, regardless of how illogical it is?

I'd like to think this is an *everything happens for a reason* kind of moment, but honestly? I can't accept that. Choosing to not go to the hospital...choosing to not go see *him*...is what I must live with every single day. Some days, that choice is easier to swallow than others. Some days, I remember why I distanced myself from my father for all these years, choosing self-preservation and happiness above all else, including blood.

But other days—days like today—I agonize over not just getting in the car and driving to him. I missed the one opportunity to tell him how I've felt all these years—alone, never good enough, unwanted. *Broken.* I missed the chance to tell him how angry and consumed with self-hate I am for still loving him and desperately wanting him to love me back. And the thing that really makes my heart tear open even more is the fact that I will never have that moment. Whether it was pride or anger or fear, I hesitated, and that's something that will always be with me.

The shower masks the tears that have become a new constant in my life. Despite moments of pure happiness and genuine love with Graham, the support of my family and friends, my job, the ache in my chest is always there; a constant and painful reminder of that hesitation and my choice just brimming beneath the surface.

I've been mentally preparing for today for quite some time now. Because after months of planning and back and forth discussions with our entire team, my father's book will officially be out into the world. After the dust settled and I was able to return to work, I was initially adamant that I never wanted his words to see the light of day. He didn't deserve it.

I was angry and embarrassed, ashamed that I had been so publicly played the way that I had. Lana had disappeared into thin air, and truthfully, I wanted nothing to do with her. The betrayal and confusion I felt in those moments after my father's passing drove my every move, and since that day, I know I'll be forever indebted to Graham for his constant and unwavering kindness and support; even when I know I didn't deserve it at times.

As our team began brainstorming ways to move forward with my father's work, making the necessary adjustments to the timelines and drafting updated releases, it was Mitch who convinced me to take a step back, putting my own feelings aside to let other readers be moved by the power of the words my father's book contained. He reminded me of how passionately I defended it when I was under the impression it was written by Lana. How fiercely I fought for its contents to be shared across the globe. I was so appreciative when Klair offered to step in. She handled the remainder of the editing and publishing process, allowing me to put some distance between my father and my grief. I'll never be able to repay her for continuously being one of the strongest pillars of strength in my life.

That distance allowed me to pour my heart, soul, and pain into another project—one that felt right given everything that had transpired. I couldn't get my father's letter out of my head, especially the part where he talked about his post-traumatic stress disorder related to his time in military service. The more I thought about it, the more curious I became about how many other service members were suffering with similar demons. It became an obsession of mine...something I literally couldn't put out of my mind, and at Graham's urging, I finally did something about it.

I've spent the last few months contacting veteran organizations and shelters searching for veterans who've struggled with PTSD and other invisible wounds. As their stories of trauma came pouring in, it became abundantly clear just how serious the stigma of seeking mental health help was for this generation of service members. Story after story told the unimaginable pain of watching their brothers and sisters in arms die in senseless wars, these poor men and women haunted by the things they'd witnessed throughout their careers...all while being told seeking help would be detrimental to their future in the military.

It was heartbreaking, and as someone who hadn't served a day in his life, I knew there was no way I could ever truly understand the struggles they'd faced in service of our nation. But there was something I could do in my position.

I coordinated with military installations across the globe and worked with their public affairs teams to interview and photograph these veterans from every branch of service to honor their stories and share their struggles. Together, we compiled enough content to assemble a gorgeous and gut-wrenching coffee-table book filled with stunning photographs and harrowing recounts of their resilience, which both Mitch and Graham enthusiastically threw their support behind.

I even had the opportunity to attend one of these interviews and get behind the lens. Even if it was just for fun, the experience was truly one of the most life-affirming and rewarding moments I will hold in my heart for the rest of my days on this earth.

What started out as a project to help take my mind off the loss of my father and the confusing circumstances surrounding his reemergence into my life turned into something powerful and important. Something that I pray will make a difference in the lives of the men and women whose service and sacrifices will never be forgotten.

I slowly turn off the water, knowing I can't stall forever; today is happening whether I'm ready or not. Stepping out of the shower and wrapping myself in one of Graham's thick, white towels, I place my hands on either side of the sink, locking eyes with myself once more.

The person staring back at me has changed.

He's loved by a force of a man—one who speaks honestly and openly about his feelings and needs. He's surer of himself— as a partner, friend, and son. And despite the constant ache in his chest, he's finally feeling free. Free of the hate that had been slowly weighing him down and holding him back all these years.

I have not forgiven my father, nor do I think I will ever be able to. We are all responsible for our actions and their consequences. But for the first time in my life, I feel like I have a better understanding of who he was and what he was going through to at least be able to view him with a more empathetic heart—one that acknowledges the severity and validity of struggles with mental health.

Forcing myself to move more quickly, I finish getting ready, making do with my still-damp hair, and throw on the uncomfortable but sharp suit I'd laid out the night before. Stepping out of the restroom, Graham is sitting at the foot of his bed looking as handsome as ever in his signature deep navy suit.

"Hey you," I say, already feeling lighter being around him. *It's the Graham Effect.* I walk in his direction until I'm standing between his legs as he loops his thumbs into my pockets, pulling me slightly closer.

He looks up at me with the sincerest eyes, eyes that I've fallen head over heels for. "I was going to join you, but I figured you needed a moment alone before the madness of this evening."

As much as I would have loved his company, his intuition is spot on. Every step of the way, Graham has been by my side—holding me, supporting me, and loving me more intensely than I ever thought humanly possible. But he's also given me the space to feel every inch of my grief. To wrap my mind around the magnitude of this loss. He's allowed me to grieve on my own terms, and for that, I couldn't love him more.

"Thank you..." I lean down, planting a soft kiss on his lips. "For knowing me and for loving me. I know these last few months haven't been easy on any of us, but please know how much *you* being there has meant to me."

Graham reaches up, cradling my face in his, his touch soft yet still anchoring me to this world. "I love you in the most profoundly deep way anyone is able to love another, Will. I will *always* be there for you."

I don't think I'll ever get used to Graham telling me he loves me. The way he expresses his love for me makes my heart swell. "I love you, too...more than you could possibly know," I say, bringing my lips to his once more.

"I have something for you," he says against my lips. He stands up and walks over to his closet, retrieving a large, square package tied with a gold ribbon. "Here," he says, placing it on the foot of the bed where he had just been sitting.

"You didn't have to get me anything...you've already done so much."

"Just open it," he says, standing behind me and wrapping his arm around my chest. I undo the thick ribbon and lift the box's lid. After removing the white tissue paper, I stare at the finished cover of our coffee-table book, one I hadn't had the chance to see in person yet. *No Longer Invisible* written in a striking gold font is embossed across the front.

"Graham...I..." The words get lost in my throat.

"Turn to page thirty-three," he whispers against my ear. I slowly open the book, resisting the urge to scour every single page and photograph and turn to the page he indicated.

My heart catches in my throat. In a gorgeous black and white, matte finish, the photograph I took of the Army veteran I had the honor of meeting stares back at me—his eyes telling a story no words could ever do justice. I turn to look back at Graham, unable to string any sort of statement of appreciation together at this moment and instead, just bury my head in his neck.

"What you've done is so important and I am so proud to see it all come together like this. Look at me," he says, gently lifting my chin to meet his gaze. "This book, as well as your father's, will resonate with so many people. But even if it reaches just one person...just one person who is struggling to overcome whatever challenges life has thrown their way, I want you to look back at all you have done and feel the greatest sense of pride. Because I do, Will...I am in awe of you and the strength you have exhibited through all of this."

Taking my face in his hands once more, Graham kisses me, more urgently than before. His lips part, so in sync with mine, and I can feel his breathing pick up. *He's shaking*.

"I know I'm throwing a lot at you right now, but I actually have one more thing for you."

"Are you trying to kill me?" I whisper, pressing my forehead against his.

Reaching into his jacket pocket, he places something small and hard in my hand. *A key*.

"Will, my entire world changed the moment you came into it, and if the last couple of months have taught us anything, it's that life is far too short to spend it wasting whatever time we have by putting off things our hearts know we want." He leans forward, bringing his lips to mine again with a slow tenderness that sets my soul ablaze. "Please move in with me," he says between kisses. "You are the first thing I want to see each morning when I wake up and the last thing I want to see as each day ends."

I'm officially at a loss for words. Is this sudden? Maybe. It's a step I've never taken with someone before, but Graham's right... life *is* short and there isn't anyone I'd want to take that next step with.

Looking into his beautiful eyes and feeling the intensity of this man's love, I so clearly see a future I've always dreamed of— a true partnership filled with passion, laughter, and trust. Someone who challenges me and supports me unconditionally.

A beautiful wedding surrounded by our friends and family. Him with our children.

He's everything I've ever wanted, and everything I never knew was within my reach.

Graham and I pull up to whatever secret location him and Klair have been sneaking off to all week. The two of them, who have become quite inseparable over the last couple of months, have kept me completely in the dark about tonight's event. While I would give everything to be back home, curled up on the couch with Graham instead of here in this uncomfortable suit, I know that between the two of them, tonight is going to be unforgettable.

Klair and Dean are waiting for us at the entrance. She's dressed in a striking black jumpsuit with her hair swept to one side, and Dean looks incredibly sophisticated in his charcoal suit. They ooze Old Hollywood glamor and could not complement one another more if they tried.

"Get over here," she says, pulling me into a long hug. "I love you forever, Will Cowen...never forget that." She's been my rock throughout this entire ordeal. I truly don't know how I would have been able to move forward without her.

"I love you right back, Klair Thompson."

They lead me through a pair of unremarkable doors that blend seamlessly into the windowless building they belong to. Graham takes my hand, giving it a gentle squeeze. "You ready?"

I take a deep inhale to steady myself. "No, but we might as well go in anyway."

We find ourselves in the midst of an intimate gallery exhibit —soft music accompanies the even softer lighting, tables for seating intertwined with those for serving small bites and drinks, and neat stacks of both my father's book and the coffee-table book seem to be everywhere. But what really takes my breath away, literally stopping me in my tracks, are the larger-than-life portraits I've spent months curating and memorizing that adorn every wall.

It's equal parts exquisite and unnerving and I couldn't love it more.

"You guys...this is stunning," I say, turning to see all three of them watching me, anxiously awaiting my reaction to their hard work.

"Yeah?" Graham asks quietly, running a hand through his hair.

The only thing I can do is nod. Being here and seeing it all makes this all finally feel real, and while that realization causes my eyes to sting, my heart overflows with happiness and appreciation for everyone who had a hand in planning this. People have begun mingling and admiring the photographs, their passionate enthusiasm brings the entire venue to life. I see Mitch and Camila across the room, who both give me a warm smile and my parents are deep in conversation with one another in front of a portrait of a female Air Force veteran.

My mother turns for the briefest of moments and I can see the tears brimming in her eyes. Even though she is happily married to my dad and has been for years, my biological father's death has impacted her in a way neither of us imagined. He was her first love, and since he passed, she's been opening up to me more about their early years together. As hard as it was to picture them young and happily in love, it's nice to think about them together in a different light...even if it was short-lived.

Klair is at my side, gently tugging on my elbow. "Let's head over this way...it's about to start."

Without questioning her, I follow as she leads the four of us toward where Graham's parents are standing.

"*Ay cariño*...come here, sweetheart. It's been *too* long," Camila says, wrapping me in her warm embrace. She's elegantly dressed in a cream, off the shoulder dress, with her dark hair carefully styled in a low bun. Mitch pats me on the back as he passes, his classic handsomeness accentuated by the sleek, black suit he's wearing.

"Ladies and gentlemen, I just want to take a quick moment of your time," Mitch says, speaking into a microphone that's appeared out of thin air. His commanding voice fills the room as the murmurs of tonight's attendees die down. "First and foremost, on behalf of the entire Austin Publishing House family, I want to thank you all for attending this truly one-of-a-kind event. When you've hosted as many of these things as I have, you think you'd be used to all of *this* by now." A quiet laughter ripples through the crowd.

"But I have to say that in all my years in this industry...I don't think I've ever been a part of something quite this special." Despite his natural ability to captivate any crowd, Mitch's tone is especially somber this evening. Next to me, Graham reaches for my hand, giving it another squeeze. *Three times.* I steal a glance in his direction, and he gives me a reassuring smile as I mouth, *I love you, too.*

"For those of you who don't know, tonight we are here to celebrate and honor two significant works of art that our team was fortunate to work on. The debut novel *I Should Have Told You Then* by the late Scott Russell and the coffee-table book *No Longer Invisible* curated by the one and only Will Cowen are both officially out in the world today. While they are sold separately, these two masterful contributions to the literary world are deeply intertwined..." Mitch looks directly at me, his expression soft and filled with a gentle kindness. "...and deeply important to all of us here at APH."

His words are a punch to the gut. *Don't cry, Will.* I wanted to make it through this event without shedding any more tears because I think I've cried enough in the last few months to last a lifetime.

"It has been one of the greatest honors of my life to see these two works of art get to where they are today. As you immerse yourself in tonight's exhibit, join me in appreciation for the immeasurable resilience and indomitable force of the human spirit of the service members featured around the room."

Mitch turns to face me once more, taking a step closer as if the two of us were having this conversation alone instead of in front of a room full of strangers and colleagues. "And it is my honor to officially announce that *all* proceeds from both books' sales will be donated to charities and foundations that provide support to service members, veterans, and their families who are suffering from post traumatic stress disorder and other invisible wounds. We will never be able to repay these courageous men and women for their service to our nation, but *this* is a start."

Everyone joins together for a celebratory round of applause, but I am left frozen in place, completely unable to comprehend the magnitude of Mitch's unbelievable gesture. The only thing keeping me rooted in reality is Graham's firm grip on my hand. People have begun milling around and the hum of the event slowly returns as Mitch comes over and places his hand on my shoulder.

"Mitch, I don't know what to say..."

"Take a walk with me? I want to show you something."

I nod my head and silently follow him as he leads me through the crowd toward the far end of the gallery room. Before we get to a quieter corner of the exhibit, he turns, blocking my view of the smaller frames on this side of the room.

"Will, I know your relationship with your father was a complicated one," he says quietly but with strength. "I lost my father when I was about your age, so I know there aren't really any words that can make that loss feel any less heavy." He places both hands firmly on my shoulders now, forcing me to stare directly into the eyes that Graham so clearly inherited.

"But I read your father's book, and while I can't speak to who he was as a man, I can tell you that as a father, he adored you and was so proud of you. And all of this?" he says, waving his arms in the direction of the exhibit. "You did *this*. You turned your grief and your heartache into something that will positively impact countless lives. *That* is something any father would be immensely proud of."

I can feel myself beginning to tremble. Coming from Mitch, a man and father whom I admire so deeply, his words shake me to my core.

Stepping aside, he positions himself so that he's now standing beside me and puts a comforting arm around my shoulder. "Graham said this might be too much, but I thought it was important for him to be here tonight. Take your time, son." He lingers with me for a moment before turning and heading back to his family while the word *son* plays over and over in my head.

Being able to see this side of the exhibit more clearly, my heart catches in my throat as I take in the simple, black frame centered on the far wall...smaller in size but equal in significance to those surrounding it. My father's youthful and charming gaze stares back at me, his military portrait capturing a man not yet haunted by the tragedies of war.

A version of a man I wish I could have known.

"That was taken a few months before I met him," my mother's voice is soft as she loops her arm in mine, resting her head on my shoulder. "Sometimes, your resemblance to that version of him makes me forget how to breathe. He was the most handsome man I'd ever seen."

I put an arm around her small frame as we both stare at the man who altered both of our lives forever. "What do you think he would think of all of this?" I whisper.

"Oh honey, *that* man would be blown away by everything you've accomplished," she says, pointing at his portrait. She pulls me into a hug that, despite our height difference, feels just like it used to when I was a child. "When I first met him, he was so passionate...about being called to serve his country and doing everything he could to help those who couldn't help themselves..." She walks us toward my father's picture, placing her hand gently on his face, one that I know she sees when she looks at me.

"And in some way, when I look around tonight at what you all have done here, I can't help but think that your father may finally be at peace." Tears stream her face as she grabs mine in her hands. "That in his death, he was able to do the one thing he wanted so desperately to do all those years ago—help others."

She places our foreheads together. "Whether you meant to or not, my perfect and sweet boy, you helped bring peace to his heart and added something meaningful to his memory. It won't be easy, sweetie. It may not even be possible for you—but just try to remember that forgiveness is for us...*not* for the person who needs forgiving."

My mother gives me a kiss on the cheek before returning to where I can only imagine my dad is patiently waiting, torn between wanting to give us this private moment and wanting to smother us with his love. I turn to face my father for the last time, knowing in my heart that I have to begin moving forward. It is then that I notice the small, gold name placard beneath his frame.

> In memory of
> U.S. Marine Corps Master Gunnery Sgt. (Ret) Scott Russell
> Veteran - Father - Author.

Graham was right. All of *this* is far too much. *God damn it.* I'll never be able to rewrite the past or even my memory of my father. But maybe, in time, I'll be able to reframe how I remember him. Looking back toward my family, both chosen and blood, an overwhelming sense of unwavering love and belonging rushes over me.

Klair is wrapped in Dean's arms, their love innocent and filled with the promise of everything that comes with new beginnings.

Mitch and Camila, who have both shown me nothing but warmth and kindness, stand holding hands...an unspoken understanding of what this evening means to me flashes across their faces as our eyes meet.

And Graham, who's sandwiched between my parents, his arm around my mom and the other shoved in his pocket as he talks animatedly to my dad. He's become my anchor, my reason for being, and when I think about all the moments in our individual lives that led us to where we are today—together and in love, taking the exhilarating leap into the unknown, hand-in-hand—I am in awe at the stroke of luck that allowed our paths to cross when they did. *When I so desperately needed them to.*

I see her as I'm walking back toward them. Leaning against the doorway, unsure if she wants to step inside or turn back around. Lana and I make eye contact from across the room, causing my blood to run cold. Her face is pinched with pain and loss, and as she wraps her arms around her thin body, the desire to comfort her overpowers every other emotion I have been feeling toward her these last few months.

Raising my hand slowly, I wave in her direction, indicating for her to join me, but just as soon as she appears, Lana turns away from me and the man who loved her like a daughter. *Don't turn your back on her.* My father's words ricochet in my mind. His relationship with Lana is one that I know very little about, and until now, I liked it that way.

Whether it's a selfish need for understanding or closure or because of genuine concern, I know now that the only way to truly move forward is with Lana.

Together.

It had taken her three days to reach out after the book launch.

After the confusion at the hospital and everything that followed, I had texted, emailed, and called Lana every single day, but after days of hearing nothing back, I assumed she wanted nothing to do with me now that her secret was out in the open. So, when she showed up at the event, I knew that a conversation was coming, whether either of us was ready for it or not.

When she reached out asking to meet at the nearby coffee shop, the very place where we met for the first time, I had to remind myself to take it slow, regardless of my excitement and nagging curiosity. I couldn't shake the feeling that whatever *this* was needed to be on her terms, but the truth is, I've genuinely missed her. Getting to know and work with Lana over those many months was the highlight of my career and if I'm being honest, I don't think I'll ever have that again. Which is depressing because now knowing all the facts, none of it was truly real. *At least between her and me.*

She's already seated as I walk through the familiar café door, enveloped in the comforting scent of fresh coffee grounds and baked goods. Two lattes sit untouched in front of her and as I get closer, I can see she's visibly trembling, her hands tapping gently on her lap.

"Hi stranger," I say quietly, fearful of startling her.

She looks collapsed in on herself. As her gaze meets mine, while full of beauty, her expression shows the signs of many sleepless nights. *I can relate.*

I take my seat across from her as she pushes one of the lattes in my direction. "Thank you."

"Of course...I know this should have happened a *long* time ago, but I appreciate you coming." Her voice is filled with tension and sadness, but she still offers me a small smile. *That's a good sign, right?* "Will, I don't even know where to begin," she says, looking down at her hands.

"Why don't we just start with how you're doing?" My question seems to catch her off guard because her sharp eyes shift quickly to meet mine.

"Please don't ask me that," she snaps, tears now brimming in her eyes, which she tries to quickly wipe away.

Leaning forward, I place my elbows on the table. "But I want to know, Lana. Of all the people in the world, I feel like *you* can relate to how I'm feeling. Lost, confused..." I can feel myself start to choke up. "...heartbroken."

"I just...your father meant so..." Her words get caught in her throat, but she reaches across the table, clasping our hands together tightly. "Will, please know that it was *never* my intention to hurt you. I had no idea things would escalate as quickly as they did, but I hope on some level, you can believe me when I say that...especially after getting to know you."

This is where my confusion lies. *And my hurt.* Lana *had* gotten to know me during our time working together and I guess

I could never picture doing this to someone else. Especially someone you claim to care about.

"This whole thing has blindsided me, Lana...you have to see that. My relationship with my father had been nonexistent for years, so all of this has really just reopened old, painful wounds and introduced ones I never even saw coming."

"I know and I..." I put my hand up to stop her.

"Hold on, I just need to say this," I interject. My intent today is not to make her feel worse because it's clear how much pain she's in. I don't want to be the reason she hurts even more. "When you came bursting into the hospital and handed me what turned out to be my father's book and his letter, I was so overwhelmed with confusion, but because of everything that was going on, I had to put that on the back burner. So, when I opened it and finally was looped into the truth, I was angry—an emotion I don't feel often."

Leaning back slightly into my chair, I slowly remove my hands from hers. "I felt so betrayed and like a fool, something my father had made me feel for my entire life, but coming from you? The deceit and the continuous lies crushed me."

Her shoulders sink at my confession. "But over the last several months, I reread my father's letter repeatedly, so many times that I can recite it from memory. He said not to turn my back on you, which I have no intention of doing. I was hurt and confused, but please know that I am not mad at you, and I could *never* hate you."

I watch as the relief washes over her. With tears streaming down her face, she grabs for my hands again and tightens her grip. "Will, you have no idea how much that means to me. Saying how sorry I am feels so meaningless in this situation, but I'm never going to be able to stop apologizing. I am so, *so* sorry."

"I appreciate you saying that...but if we're going to move forward, I don't want to keep making you feel like you have to apologize. I do have some questions if that's okay? Like how you and my father even met in the first place?"

Dropping my hands and leaning back into her chair, she lets out a deep exhale, one she must have been holding onto this entire conversation. "I was a Field Intelligence Officer in the Marine Corps, one of the only women in my unit, and a damn good one. Not that I was doing it intentionally, but I was presented with opportunity after opportunity to outshine my peers and rose through the ranks quickly. The men didn't like that..." Her voice trails off as she looks out the window. I can only assume what happened next and it for sure isn't my place to pry.

Bile rises in my throat and my fists clench. After my time interviewing several female service members and veterans for the coffee-table book, military sexual trauma is far more common than people would like you to believe, and yet it's hardly ever talked about.

"Your father came into my life at one of the lowest lows I'd ever felt. I'd just separated from the Corps after the worst year of my life. I was broken, empty, reliant on booze and drugs and meaningless sex. What I told you about my mother when we first met? Her only daughter joining the military was hard enough—the Marine Corps of all things. When all of this happened, she couldn't handle it. I had nothing and no one, so when he offered me a hand when it felt like my entire world had turned their back on me...that is something that I will be forever grateful for."

She takes a long sip of her latte before wrapping her arms around herself. "He recognized my pain and trauma before I even could, and if your father hadn't been there that day, I promise you we wouldn't be sitting here having this conversation."

"Obviously, I had no idea...I am so sorry, Lana."

"I'm not. From one second to the next, meeting your father was a pivotal moment toward my recovery and he never left my side as I got the help I so desperately needed." She smiles softly and I can't help but wonder what memory of him she's thinking about.

That version of my father isn't one I've ever known and I'm ashamed at how jealous hearing this makes me. "Wait, was he sober?"

"Oh yes...when I met your father, he was at least six or maybe seven years into his sobriety."

Okay, well now that *actually* makes me angry.

"Six or seven *years*? He'd been sober for six or seven years and didn't reach out *once*?" I shout, unable to contain the rage fueled by the abandonment of my father. He'd been sober this entire time and instead of reaching out to his actual kid, he's off playing savior to a complete stranger. I know none of this is Lana's fault, but come on...

Lana stares at me with knowing eyes. "Will, I'm not going to sit here and try to make excuses for your father or speak on his behalf." She places her hand on my forearm. "But I will say that as a recovering addict myself, I had to throw everything I had into my sobriety...every ounce of focus and energy I had, because I knew that if I got relaxed or didn't take it seriously enough, everything I worked so hard for would all come crashing down. I had to put my sobriety ahead of everything else so that someday, the things and the people I loved most in the world could come first. I think your father might have been the same way."

It's a beautiful sentiment and the logical part of me can understand how that makes sense, but it certainly doesn't change how much it hurts. Was I a trigger for him? Did he keep his distance because I reminded him of the worst version of himself? Unfortunately, I'll never know, and if that isn't the saddest realization, I don't know what is.

"And the book?" I ask quietly, unsure of how that fits into all of this.

She's quiet for a moment, absentmindedly tracing the rim of her mug with her finger.

"Actually, the book idea came from a journaling class I forced your father to come to with me at the VA."

Now that's something hard to visualize—my hulking father sitting through a class meant to help you to open up about your feelings.

"During the class, we were prompted to write letters to our loved ones and your father was really struggling to open up about his past and his feelings. I suggested he try to fictionalize the scenario...keep the emotions but switch up the storyline. Once he did that, the words just started flowing."

"So why not just give them to me then? Why the charade and why involve you in all of this?" I do my best to mask the irritation in my voice, but I'm struggling to understand why he didn't just reach out to me. I was right here.

"Answer this honestly for me, Will..." Lana leans forward, her gaze intensifying, piercing my very core. "If you had originally gotten that package and saw it was from *him*, would you have actually read it?"

She's got me there. I know myself enough to know that I probably wouldn't have even opened it. If I saw his name on something, I would have thrown it straight into the trash. The thought racks me with guilt.

"That's what I figured," she says, leaning back into her chair. "I know what he did was wrong, and the fact that I went along with it makes me feel even worse, but Will, he desperately wanted you to hear those words. He had done enough for me that I didn't see the harm in offering to put my name on it. Initially."

Other than just blowing up my entire life? *Sure.* Again, I have to remind myself that my anger is not directed at Lana.

"But when you expressed interest in publishing the book and meeting with me...everything just spiraled out of control." She turns, looking out the window once more. "And then Scott's condition got worse."

After my father passed and the initial shock of everything that went down in the hospital began to wear off, his doctor informed me that he had been suffering from liver failure for quite some time, the effects of years and years of alcohol consumption. Even though he had taken steps toward his sobriety, the damage was already done.

"Even if it was through me, he was so excited to be talking to you and those conversations became the *only thing* that seemed to manage his pain. Trust me, I know just how wrong it was but I couldn't bear to see him like that..." Her broken voice trails off. I don't understand Lana's relationship with my father nor can I barely wrap my head around the intensity of her grief as it is so different from mine. But as we sit together in our shared pain, I want more than anything for her to know that I don't blame her.

"I can't pretend to understand all of this but I need you to know that while I am frustrated and hurting, none of it is geared toward you. I hope you trust me when I say I forgive you."

The café door opens, letting an exhilarating chill from a quiet New York City morning mingle with the warmth we've been cocooned in. My attention is momentarily pulled from Lana as I hear Graham's throaty laugh fill the room, forcing me to turn as he walks in, arm-in-arm with Klair, Dean following closely behind them.

My people. There are no words to describe the light and

happiness these three have brought to my life during some of the darkest moments over the last couple of months.

Lana starts to stand as they get closer, reaching for her coat. "I'll leave you so you can spend time with your friends."

"Please stay," I beg, reaching across the table and grabbing her hand. Truthfully, I hadn't given much thought to what comes next when I came to meet Lana this morning. But the invisible string tied between us feels oddly permanent—a bond forged in heartbreak, loss, and similar but different traumas. My father was Lana's anchor in sobriety, the person she relied on most in this world. He represents something to her that I will never understand, but it's a relationship I feel called to honor. His dying wish was for me to not turn my back on her...and after everything she's shared with me—everything we've now been through together—how could I? Our lives feel irrevocably bound to one another.

"Just please stay...I don't know if and what you believe in or what power you place emphasis on, but there is no doubt in my mind that we came into one another's lives for a reason." For everything to unfold the way it did, every fiber of my being believes that. "And whatever that reason is, I *need* you, Lana. You are the only one who knew my father in a way worth knowing and there are so many questions that are still unanswered...but for right now, just stay."

Despite the heaviness of this conversation and the depth of the grief we share, her entire face lights up into the slyest grin.

"Besides, you're kinda stuck with us," I say, squeezing her hand. Lana laughs quietly as Graham, Klair, and Dean join us, noisily pulling up a few extra chairs to our far too small bistro table.

I glance around at the faces of this chosen family and something warm and hopeful emanates from my chest. The love I feel for Klair and Dean, Graham, and now Lana—whose hand

I'm still holding—overwhelms me. Whatever happens next, sitting here surrounded by all these different versions of love feels exactly like the kind of new beginnings I've always held close to my heart. Ones filled with friendship, community, and a love like no other. Graham wraps his arms around me, nuzzling into my neck and planting a kiss along my jaw. "Everything okay?" he whispers into my ear.

Placing my hand on his cheek, I slowly bring his lips to mine, the love I have for Graham radiating throughout every ounce of our kiss. He smiles when we pull apart, the same smile that still takes my breath away no matter how many times I see it. Leaning my head against Graham's shoulder, he immediately jumps into Klair and Lana's seamless conversation about upcoming book releases and work drama, with Dean playfully interjecting every so often in a way that sends the entire group into the most beautiful and contagious round of laughter.

"Now it is."

ACKNOWLEDGMENTS

This is truly a "pinch me" moment and I doubt I'll ever be able to fully recover from the emotional rollercoaster that was this experience. There are so many people to thank but I want to start with you, the reader - thank you for picking up You & I, Rewritten and for giving a big piece of my heart and soul a chance. For sticking with me and cheering me on as I tried something new...something I never in a million years thought I would be able to do. For believing in me and for inspiring me with your kindness and generosity and beautiful hearts. I have so many stories to tell so hopefully you aren't sick of me yet!

I wrote this book during a time when it seems like a lot of the world was and still is questioning the validity of queer love. When so many don't think we are worthy of love and that our stories don't deserve a happily ever after. But to every member of the LGBTQIA+ community, regardless of where you are on your personal journeys with your identity–whether you are out or still learning to love who you are–know that you are loved and worthy and have a whole community rooting for you to find your happy. More than anything, I hope you know that you deserve to live a life filled with the most beautiful and magical love you could ever hope for.

To my editors, Brooke Crites and Britt Tayler - thank you for pushing me and correcting me and forcing me dig deeper when all I wanted to do was give up. I am forever indebted to your brilliance.

To my insanely talented cover designer, Sam Elias - thank you for bringing Will & Graham to life. Working with you has been the highlight of this entire experience.

Thank you to the incredible authors, who even in the midst of their own writing and deadlines and publishing chaos, took the time to not only read my early drafts, but offer feedback and guidance every step of the way.

Ashley Winstead, you brilliant, ray of sunshine - your mentorship and kindness has been invaluable every step of the way and you truly are one in a million. I cannot thank you enough for just being you.

Sophie Sullivan - thank you doesn't seem to quite cover my sincere appreciation for your guidance and friendship throughout this entire process!

Steven Rowley - thank you for cheering me on and always checking in on me...your friendship was such a bright spot over the last two years and I am honored to know you.

Elena Armas - thank you for reminding me to always follow my dreams and for writing THE STANDARD of book boyfriends. Your writing has inspired me more than you could ever imagine and I've loved watching the world fall more and more in love with you and your work.

Marley Valentine – there are no words to describe how incredibly blessed I am to know you, We are family and this love story could not and would not have happened without you.

Kristie Lewis – we have been talking about THIS since 2017 and you were the first person to read my writing all those years ago. Thank you for guiding me to this moment and always being in my corner. I adore you!

There are so many other phenomenal authors and friends who have helped shaped You & I, Rewritten into what it has become: Alison Cochrun, P.J. Vernon, Taylor Smith, Allison Ashley, Becca Borison, Kristin Mulligan, Sarah Adams, Chloe

Liese, DJ Smyter and the entire Steam and Scream Book Club...
I adore you all and will never be able to say thank you enough!

To Michelle Vasquez, Madison Wolfe, Brady Parkin,
Rachel Eichenblat, Katie Nelson, Bailey Rae, Jordan Haynes,
Nikki Ramirez, Marissa Sanchez and the entire Write It Good
Crew – thank you for humoring me when I said I had written a
little love story and for giving me feedback and enthusiastically
messaging me as you were reading. I could not have written this
story without each and every one of you.

To Phil Dowell – thank you for being the most vocal and
passionate champion of LBGTQIA+ stories, for always saying
and doing the right thing and for loving romance as much as I
do. Thank you for always supporting indie authors and using
your platform to always uplift others...what you say and what
you do matters and I will forever be grateful for your friendship.

To Michelle Wramble, my OG ride or die. You have been to
hell and back with me. Literally. My highest highs and my
lowest lows, you were there. You believed in me in a way no
friend ever has. Do you remember sitting around as co-coun-
selors at a summer camp in 2008 dreaming about writing? Your
friendship changed my life and I will love you forever.

To Katie Sterling – thank you for cheering on this dream.
For being such a trusted sounding board and a safe-space with
each and every idea as they came to life. Thank you for loving
me and this story unconditionally and always believing in it and
me. I am so thankful for you, your friendship and your over-
whelmingly beautiful heart.

To Lianna Cohen – thank you for sharing your passion of
romance with the world, for being a force to be reckoned with
and for championing own voices as loudly as you can. I am so
thankful this book brought us closer and I am so proud of all you
have accomplished.

To Joanna McDonald – I truly believe you and I were fated

to meet one another and I am so glad that we did. Your feedback and support during this entire process has kept me going. Thank you for having the biggest heart of anyone I've ever met and for being there for me in ways that I'll never be able to repay you for.

To Chelsea Holien – thank you for loving and believing in this story as much as I do. For being the fiercest advocate to not only me as an author, but as a person and friend. The way you loved and championed this story will forever be etched upon my heart and I can never say thank you enough for the way you've brightened up my life. Sisters in Arms forever and ever.

To my Klair - I can't thank you enough for allowing readers to fall in love with you the way I have. Your friendship came at a time when I needed it most and I am so blessed to know you. Thank you for being the best friend I've ever known and loving me unconditionally. Tell baby Becks his guncles adore him!

To my Grandma Jenny - what I wouldn't give to be able to share this with you. Thank you for sharing your love of books and storytelling...you've given me a lifetime of passion and the tools to realize this dream.

To my siblings, Ryan, Haley, Lexie and Austin - It has been the honor of my lifetime being your older brother. I am so proud of who each of you have grown to become and wish you nothing but all the happiness and love the world has to offer.

To my mother, Tracy - thank you for raising me to lead with my heart and compassion, always. For instilling in me the importance of love and kindness and that having big, complex emotions isn't a weakness. For being an example of resilience and grace and for always putting me, and everyone else, first. So much of life felt like it was you and I against the world...and if I don't say it often enough or haven't said it lately, I couldn't have asked for a better mother. I love you.

At its core, You & I, Rewritten is about fathers and sons and there are three men who have altered my life in the most permanent of ways.

To my Father in Law, Alex - thank you for loving and protecting me like one of your own. For raising the man of my dreams and always supporting the two of us in all of life's endeavors. For calling me son. Of all the things in my life that I hold dear to my heart, sharing your last name is one that I am most proud of.

To my Dad, Mike - while you had no actual obligation to do so, you chose to be in my life and in doing so, changed everything for me. Some of my happiest memories are shared with you - from road trips with countless food stops and chaotic but memorable camping adventures to training for high school sports and doing everything I can to make you laugh. Thank you for pushing me to be the best version of myself that I can be. For instilling in me the importance of treating everyone around me with dignity and respect. And for giving me the foundation and confidence to make mistakes and learn from them. I love you.

And to my Father, Tom - there is not a day that goes by that I don't think of you and what life and our relationship could have been. I think of the important milestones in my life that you've missed - my military service, career successes and my marriage - and often wonder what you would think of the man I've become. On some level, I think I've always strived to live a life that you'd be proud of and after all these years, I pray that you've finally found peace. I will love and miss you forever.

Lastly, thanks to my husband, Alexx - my better half, the ultimate book boyfriend and the reason I've found any semblance of happiness in this world. Thank you for loving me as fiercely and unconditionally as you do...in a way that is so uniquely and beautifully you. There aren't words big enough to describe just how much of you and our own love story is woven within these pages - you and it has inspired me more than you will ever know. I hope you know that all that I am and all that I have is because you love and believe in me so, from the bottom of my heart, thank you for leaping with me.

I love you endlessly.

ABOUT THE AUTHOR

Chip Pons grew up in a small town in Northern Michigan before eventually traveling the world serving as a photojournalist in the U.S. Air Force, where he met and worked alongside his husband and better half.

He currently lives in Washington, D.C. and works as a Public Affairs professional for the federal government. When he is not writing, he can be found awkwardly dancing to Taylor Swift albums, playing with Margot, his miniature schnauzer, and snacking, like all the time.

This is his first novel.

Find more at www.chippons.com

Photo: Adam Griffin www.adamgriffinphoto.com

twitter.com/chippons

instagram.com/booksovrbros

Printed in Great Britain
by Amazon